D0617169

A GOOD
DOCTOR'S SON

Also by Steven Schwartz

To Leningrad in Winter

Lives of the Fathers

Therapy

A Good Doctor's Son

A NOVEL

STEVEN SCHWARTZ

William Morrow and Company, Inc.
New York

Library of Congress Cataloging-in-Publication Data

Schwartz, Steven, 1950–
   A good doctor's son : a novel / Steven Schwartz. — 1st ed.
     p.   cm.
   ISBN 0-688-15401-8
   I. Title.
PS3569.C5676S57   1998
813'.54—dc21
                                        97-23601
                                          CIP

Printed in the United States of America

First Edition

1 2 3 4 5 6 7 8 9 10

BOOK DESIGN BY RENATO STANISIC

www.williammorrow.com

For Emily, Zach, and Elena

ACKNOWLEDGMENTS

For her steady encouragement and for asking the right questions, I'm grateful to my editor, Claire Wachtel. I'd also like to thank Ya'acov Gabriel, Elise Goodman, Mark LaFramboise, Deanna Ludwin, Terrie Sandelin, Louis Schwartz, Polly Schwartz, and Mike Vogl. I'm especially indebted to my wife, Emily Hammond, who glimpsed this novel before I did.

A GOOD
DOCTOR'S SON

1

O N E

I grew up in Garden City, a small Pennsylvania community where my brother, Adrian, and I were the only Jews in our elementary school. I got along better with the kids than Adrian, played sports and made friends more easily, but still I had my troubles.

One day I went into Mrs. Nick's—short for Nicodemus—a corner grocery store and fountain down the street from us. I sat at the counter with Warren Banks, my best friend. We didn't sit next to each other. You always had a seat between you, even when you went to the movies. It hinted of homosexuality to sit next to each other, to wish to be that close to another boy, and also maybe there was just the thing of wanting to spread out, establish your territory. I don't know, but I do remember that day in Mrs. Nick's store when Warren and I sat there spinning the stool between us, its silver sides whistling as we slapped the green vinyl top to make it go faster.

"Cut it out," said Mrs. Nick. We stopped. "What do you want?" she asked Warren.

"Root beer float," Warren said. Mrs. Nick nodded at him, looked at me. She had her hair up in blue curlers. She lived in the back with her husband, who worked at the shipyards in nearby Chester. My father was a doctor in the town.

"What about you, moneybags?"

I heard laughter from down the counter, where the teenagers hung out.

"Black and white," I said inaudibly.

"What?"

"Milk shake. Black and white." I was burning up with shame. Warren looked straight ahead. The three teenagers at the other end snickered. They were just out of high school and worked the night shift at Scott Paper in Chester.

Mrs. Nick went over to the fountain and mixed up ice cream and root beer and filled it with soda water. She brought the frosted ribbed glass over to Warren and set it down in front of him. Then she disappeared into the back of the store.

I sat there with my head down. I could hear Warren sucking gently on his straw. We came here every day after school to have drinks at the counter. Why had she said that? *Moneybags*.

Five minutes passed. Mrs. Nick didn't come out. I slid off the stool and glanced at Warren. He was trying to go slow on his drink but was already down to the dregs. I went over to the magazine rack and looked at the cover of the new *Superman* comic. Jimmy Olsen had superpowers. His freckled face and red hair were still there, but his arms and shoulders rippled with muscles. Superman, meanwhile, had changed places with him and looked puny and frightened. Lois Lane was in the background glancing desirably at Jimmy. It was all turned around and all temporary, of course. I knew Superman would be restored to his powers, Jimmy would return to being a cub reporter, and Lois would get straight her hopeless crush on the man of steel.

I reached in my pants pocket for a quarter left over from lunch. It was 1960, and *Superman* comics had just gone up from ten to twelve cents.

Warren came over and stood next to me at the cash register. He was from the project where many of the kids I went to school with lived. The project consisted of squat brown stucco buildings constructed during the Second World War. They had tiny yards tied together by a maze of chain-link fences. A metal pole webbed with clothesline stood in the corner of each yard, taking the place of a shade tree. The driveways were concrete runners with weeds growing between them. Fights broke out regularly, dogs choked on their chains, and mothers screamed openly at their kids. I wasn't allowed to go in there, except to Warren's house, which was on the edge closest to our home.

"Hey, Mrs. Nick," said Corky Innes, shooting a thumb my way, "you got a customer." Corky "Kong" Innes lived with his brother, Richie, down the street from us. Everybody called him Kong because of his car, a souped-up black Dodge so shiny "you can see your pimples in it," Corky would say. With a 426 hemi, dual quads, a Detroit locker, and Hooker headers, the car was rumored to need a parachute to stop. Under its dash, the Kongmobile had a record player installed that played forty fives. Warren and I would sit in it at Mrs. Nick's, listen to "Sea of Love," "Mr. Blue," and "Kansas City," stick our elbows out the windows, and pretend to peel out.

Mrs. Nick stayed at the other end of the counter washing a glass by hand.

"Hey, Mrs. Nick," said Corky, and I wished he would shut up. "You got a paying customer here."

"That's all right," I said quietly.

"I can buy it for you," said Warren.

I shook my head. I just wanted to get out of here. My face had turned red, and I was afraid if I stayed around, I'd start crying.

But Corky, whose father owned a tavern in Chester, and who I was beginning to see was a true lunkhead when it came to social matters that I instinctively understood, wouldn't drop the subject. He grabbed the quarter from my hand and swaggered over to Mrs. Nick.

"Here you go," he said, and slapped the coin onto the counter. The quarter wobbled in front of her, then stopped dead with a dull tink. Mrs. Nick let it lie there, as I knew she would. Corky, dimwit, confidant to his gonads, palmed the quarter, tossed it in his mouth, and swallowed it with an audible gulp. It was one of his tricks. Years later he would develop cancer of the larynx, an irony that was lost on us now. We weren't thinking about cancer or what would become of us, including Mrs. Nick, whose store would close up in five years after she had a fatal heart attack, her store eventually becoming a beauty parlor, then a funeral home, and there would be no sign of that day when I was refused service and Corky ate my quarter and then pretended to barf it up and hand it back to me, a true idiot, who had forgotten why he was even holding it.

I walked out of the store, Warren following. We didn't talk about what happened on the way home. But we did pass the Olans' house. Broken bottles and trash were in their front yard, and freshly painted since the last time they'd erased it was GO HOME NIGGERS, on the side of their white clapboard house with blue shutters. Two weeks ago they'd moved into the house on Rynard Road, the only black family in Garden City, including the all-white project. Their house had been stoned, their car's windshield smashed, their two children taunted when they'd tried to attend the local elementary school.

"Hi, Officer Dennis," Warren said as we walked past the Olans' house. He was patrolling back and forth on the sidewalk in front. His uniform said: "Garden City Police."

"Howdy," he said. "You boys just getting home from school?"

"We went to Mrs. Nick's," said Warren.

"Where's my hoagie then?" said Officer Dennis. He was Gloria Dennis's father. Gloria was two grades ahead of us, in fifth, and "developed."

"We ate it," said Warren.

"You ate it, did you?" Officer Dennis joked. "Well, that's not going to help me now, is it?"

I wanted to keep walking, but Warren had stopped and was staring at the Olans' home. You couldn't see any movement inside. They kept their curtains drawn even in daytime. Their father, I'd heard, was escorted in and out of the house to work at his accounting office. Groceries were brought to them through the back door. Officer Dennis said, "So what's new at school?" Officer Dennis seemed to want company. "Your father doing all right now, David?" he asked me.

I nodded. After the Olans had moved in, their baby needed a doctor. My father had gone over, and on the way into the house a brick had hit him in the back. It had knocked him down, but he'd gotten up and gone inside anyway.

That was two weeks ago, and I knew that my father's going there, his speaking out against the attacks, his telling reporters that he was ashamed of the community, all this had to do with why Mrs. Nick had called me moneybags and not served me.

"Well, you tell him hello for me," Officer Dennis said, and I nodded again. He was being so kind to me that I wanted to drag him back to Mrs. Nick's and have him make her sell me a milk shake and my comic book.

I saw the curtains part and a little girl peek out the window; then they were closed again, quickly. The house still had the name Stewart on the wood plaque that hung from the porch. The papers had said that the Stewarts, who had moved to Kennett Square, had been threatened for selling the house to Negroes. My father pored over the newspaper every day, shook his head, and mumbled angrily. "Like hostages, they're kept inside like hostages," he said one night at dinner, a comment he told the reporters too. My mother sat in silence, not disagreeing but not sharing his fury. She had never wanted to move into this neighborhood anyway.

At my house, Warren and I scuffed our sneakers against the flagstone steps.

"Want to come in?" I said to Warren. He shook his head no; he had to go home and help with dinner. His dad worked the graveyard shift at Sun Ship, and his mom worked late in the cafeteria at Chester-Crozer Hospital. His sister and he fixed dinner for themselves at night. I looked up at the bedrooms of our house. My brother would be in his, my mother in hers. I didn't want to go in.

"Maybe I could go home with you," I said.

"Yeah," said Warren, "you could stay for dinner. Ask."

But I knew my mother wouldn't let me. She'd be too afraid for me to be alone at Warren's in the project at night, and I didn't want to make her any more anxious than she was already. Or unhappy. She'd been "sad," she told me, which meant she spent a lot of time alone in her room.

We lived across the street from a park, in the biggest, most conspicuously affluent house in Garden City, a three-story fieldstone colonial with white shutters, a tall, peaked roof, and a large picture window that looked out on the park. My father had wanted to live here, a working-class section outside Chester, a pocket among the more prosperous communities of Swarthmore, Rose Valley, and Wallingford, because he'd found a piece of property across the street from the park and fallen in love with the location and the unpretentious neighborhood. But there were no Jews besides us, no one my mother socialized with, and my brother was regularly beaten up at school. I had done better, making friends, "passing," and fitting in, except now for Mrs. Nick.

I punched Warren in the arm and he punched me back, and then I went inside. There were no sounds in the house, just the ticking of the grandfather clock in the foyer. The living room, which we hardly used, caught the last of the winter light coming into it through the picture window. My mother collected glass bottles, which she displayed along the wide ledge under the window. My favorite was a translucent blue bottle about four feet high with a gently fluted opening and spired top. I couldn't explain it exactly, but the bottle looked desirable to me, I suppose I mean sexual, and I had sensations of excitement whenever I gazed at it. It was graceful and slender, an ice-blue color that shimmered in the morning light. The other bottles rose in height from either side toward the blue one in the middle, like the pipes of an organ. I went over and touched its tip, a frozen tear on top.

I heard a toilet flush upstairs, my parents' bathroom.

My brother, who was two years older than I, lay on his bed reading. His teacher, Mrs. Fitzsimmons, had sent home a note recommending that he not read so much. Adrian was spending his time at recess reading rather than playing kickball or baseball or getting fresh air. Mrs. Fitzsimmons believed he should involve himself more in physical activity and the company of his classmates.

"Hi," I said, standing in his doorway, not wanting to go all the way into his room. He didn't like to build model airplanes and aircraft carriers. He didn't have baseball pennants on his walls as I did, or pictures of wild animals. Adrian had movie posters: Charlie Chaplin in *Modern Times,* Marlene Dietrich in *Blue Angel,* Humphrey Bogart and Walter Huston in *The Treasure of the Sierra Madre.* It was the other thing he did besides read: watch movies and pretend to make them. He spent a lot of time looking at me with his thumb up to his right eye. "Tracking shot," he'd say as I came out of the bathroom. Or he'd cup his hands to his face: "Close-up." It was annoying. I'd lie in bed at night and wish Warren were my brother, or somebody like him. Adrian was heavyset—the term I'd been told to use by my father—and kids at school called him swivel hips, because of the way he walked. He had one friend, Perry, who lived across town and, like Adrian, had "introverted" interests, the other term I'd learned to describe Adrian's unpopularity. I held my breath during every recess that Adrian wouldn't get picked on and beaten up (no doubt why he stayed inside and read). Unlike me, he didn't fight back, or even try to, nor did he have a protector like Warren. Adrian just lay there and covered his face with his arms and let them wallop him. He didn't cry or make a fuss afterward, and for that reason maybe nobody really tried to hurt him. It was just to humiliate him, pound on the fat boy, like a stop along an obstacle course. They'd thump him awhile and then go back to what they were doing, playing softball or using the swings or pitching pennies, and Adrian would stand up, brush himself off, and go find a book somewhere.

"Where's Mom?" I said.

"In her room," said Adrian. "You just get home?"

"Yes." I thought of telling him about Mrs. Nick, but I knew there was nothing he'd say to help. What could you say when you were a whipping boy for the whole class?

"Look at this," he said, and pulled a long wooden box out from under his bed.

He opened the latches. It was a skeleton.

"Where'd you get that?" I said, impressed.

"Dad loaned it to me. It's a teaching skeleton."

"What do you mean?"

"They use it in medical school. *This is a child,*" he said, conspiratorially.

"A child?"

"About six years old."

I reached out and touched the small skull.

"I'm going to make a film with it," said Adrian. He was squatting down, as was I, next to the skeleton, and I could see the rolls of fat under his T-shirt. His forehead had broken out in perspiration, his fair cheeks reddened. I wondered what he'd been doing in here before I came in, and then I realized it was just excitement, excitement about an idea. Nobody I knew at school got excited about ideas. Just Adrian.

"What kind of movie?" I asked.

"A horror film," said Adrian. "I'm writing the script," and he nodded at the Royal typewriter on his desk. He'd gotten it for his last birthday. "*Buried Coccyx,*" he said.

"What?"

"That's the title."

"What's it mean?"

Adrian shifted his hips with irritation. He was sitting on the bed holding the skeleton in his lap. "It's a mystery, stupid. The victims lose their coccyx."

"Their what?"

"Their tailbones. The murderer cuts them off. He collects them like arrowheads."

I looked at the small skeleton. It was frail and delicate. "He does this to children?"

Adrian hesitated. "Well, I haven't decided that part yet. I can make the skeleton look bigger on camera."

"Do you have a camera?"

"Dad's going to help me rent one. A sixteen millimeter." Adrian tilted his head back and hooded his eyes. "I vill be zee greatest director of zee century! I'll find a part for you," he added.

"All right," I said, and got up to go.

"Where you going?"

"To see Mom."

Adrian shook his head. "She's resting." Resting. It could mean anything, but it probably meant she was "sad."

"I'll check on her anyway," I said.

"Fade out," called Adrian as I exited through his doorway.

I went down the hall to my mother's room. She was sitting by the window staring out. She was still in her nightgown, at four-thirty in the afternoon. "David," she said, as if surprised to see me. I had the feeling she'd been sitting here for hours.

"Hi," I said, not going into her room too far either. It smelled of sleep and unwashed sheets. My parents' bed was still rumpled, the room unstraightened, clothes on the floor. Several bottles of pills that my father prescribed for her were on the nightstand. A round tray with a coffee cup and a plate with an uneaten roll rested like a still life at the small table for two.

"Do you want your lunch?" she asked.

"Lunch?"

My mother stared at me, as if trying to remember. She closed her eyes and swallowed. "I mean, dinner. *Dinner,* David."

"Are you all right?" I asked.

"I'm fine," she said. "You go play now. I'll be down in a minute to fix dinner." She turned away, and I felt my chest tighten, my eyes start to water. I thought of the child skeleton in the box under Adrian's bed.

An hour later my father returned from his office, and the house came to life. He'd been tied up with patients all day. He made us grilled cheese sandwiches and milk shakes. Mother joined us. She'd gotten dressed, a blue sweater and a tan skirt, and she sat at the table with her cheek resting on one hand, smiling pleasantly. Everything would be all right. Everything was fine. We were a family. Dad was home.

Adrian ate one helping of chocolate cream pie for dessert, and when he asked for another, my mother gently turned him down. She picked up our plates and began to wash the dishes at the sink. Except for her having been upstairs all day, she was fine. Maybe she had just been resting after all. Tired. And I started to feel better. I didn't even mind after dinner when Adrian stood in our old Radio Flyer wagon and asked me to pull him along the wall of the dining room while he shouted, "Dolly shot! Quiet on the set!"

Not long after I went to bed, I heard raised voices in my parents' bedroom. I could make out my father saying something about keeping the house clean, and my mother answering she hated it here and she missed her sisters in New York and why had she ever agreed to move, and then my mother crying and my father saying, "Oh, for God's sake," and leaving the bedroom. I got up to use the bathroom and saw that Adrian's light was still on. He was typing. I thought about going in, but either he had been listening or he hadn't been listening. Either way, like Warren and me with Mrs. Nick, we wouldn't talk about what was right in front of us.

Downstairs the phone rang, and I heard my father answer it and say, "Yes," then a long pause. "How high is it?" he asked, and then he said, "All right, I'll be right over." He came upstairs and saw me standing in the hallway. "Why are you still up, David?"

"I—"

"Go to bed. Right now." I glanced at Adrian's door, as if to excuse my behavior by my brother's, but my father didn't care. They never bothered Adrian. He stayed up all night, read and wrote and went to school and got straight As, and that was Adrian. But me, I was going to be normal, sleep regular hours, have decent friends, make average grades, not be a budding, precious genius. Live a boy's life. I hurried back into my room.

I couldn't sleep, especially when I heard my parents raising their voices again. It was like a storm that never went away entirely, the thunder becoming distant enough that you forgot about it, but not for long. "Take your pill," my father said, "just take it," and I heard the bathroom water running and then silence. I imagined my mother's mouth opening submissively, my father placing the pill on her tongue and tipping her water glass up to her lips. Her swallowing mechanically. I don't know for sure if that's what happened or if she even took a pill that night, but I know, sitting alone on my bed, I felt her complete helplessness.

My father came out from their bedroom. He closed their door and stepped quietly down the stairs. The hall closet opened, then the front door. I heard him leave.

I ran to the window. He'd parked the Buick on the street. We had only one car. Some families, some of the kids I knew from Hebrew school, the wealthier doctors, had two cars, but nobody in Garden City had a second car.

The headlights flickered on and off as he tried to start the car.

Mother had been complaining about the battery for weeks now. I saw him get out and angrily slam the door and start walking down the street.

There was something instinctive, if crazy, about what I did next. I pulled on my clothes and ran after him. I followed him down Media Parkway onto Walnut Road. I knew by this time where he was going. He stepped so purposefully, with long, determined strides, that it couldn't be a regular housecall. I ran across the winter lawns, trying to keep up. Once he stopped and looked around when he heard me, but I had already ducked down behind the McClearys' wheelbarrow, which always stayed in their cluttered front yard. When he turned from Walnut onto Rynard Road, I saw the Olans' house.

I was surprised to see no policeman patrolling out front, but then I'd never been here this late.

Still, there were floodlights on the lawn, and the house was lit up like a stage. My father went up the front walk, the same walk where a brick two weeks earlier had knocked him to the ground. A policeman opened the front door, and my father disappeared inside.

What to do? I could go home. Wearing just a flannel shirt, I was starting to freeze. But I hadn't come all this way only to fade back into my own home. Well, I didn't want to escape. My nature was too curious to let me turn away. My mother's "sadness" terrified me, as if I might catch it, or some form of it, which perhaps Adrian, sitting at his typewriter, had already contracted. I wanted to follow my father into his world.

I was standing in the yard adjacent to the Olans', the Wileys'. Mrs. Wiley worked at the school as a dietitian, and her husband was in maintenance. My father had read us Mrs. Wiley's comment to the Philadelphia *Evening Bulletin*: "Nothing yet has convinced us they won't make good neighbors." It was less forceful than my father's comment that the neighborhood was holding this family hostage, and perhaps the reason he'd gotten a brick in the back and why Mrs. Nick wouldn't serve me. In some way I'd wished he hadn't spoken out.

I'd worked so hard to be like the other kids in my school. My hair I kept as much as possible in a ducktail. I wore lavender hi-boy shirts and stuck a black comb in my back pocket and said, "That's boss," as often as I could work it into a sentence. Meanwhile, the kids with whom I went to Hebrew school and who lived across the township line looked and dressed like the young lawyers most of them would eventually become. They wore Arrow shirts and khaki slacks, navy turtlenecks, and corduroy sport coats with green suede patches on the elbows. Their hair, wavy and dark and Semitic like mine, was parted down the left side in a clean white scalp line. At Hebrew school I studied about everybody from Theodor Herzl to Hank Greenberg, and when I went back to Garden City Elementary in the morning, these people and my heritage didn't—and never had—existed.

I was fascinated by the Olans because they'd tried to break into the new neighborhood, as we had, and because they were having an even harder time than we were. When I stood on a milk crate under their back window, I had only wanted a glimpse of ourselves in the extreme. Their kitchen, tidy, clean, had the same Formica breakfast table as ours, a light blue oval with a large toaster on it. Right below my nose, under the window, was a wash sink filled with soaking clothes. I was amazed, given everything that was happening to them, that the Olans could carry on with life inside. Suddenly my shoulders were grabbed from behind and I was yanked backwards. Two seconds later I was flat on my back on the cold grass with a flashlight shining in my eyes.

I could see through the glare that it was a policeman and that he was from Garden City. "What are you doing here?" He was young, or young compared with Officer Dennis, who would have understood why I was here and to whom I could have explained my curiosity.

"I'm just looking," I said.

"You're just looking for trouble," he said. "Now get out of here."

But at that moment the back door opened, and Officer Dennis, who was indeed inside and had come out to see what all the commotion was about, saw me and said, "David?"

"Yes, sir," I said.

"Bring him inside, Tim," he told the officer.

And I wound up at the Olans' kitchen table. Mrs. Olan had just made a pot of coffee. She was a tall, thin woman with glistening black hair and long, lanky arms that seemed to be in every place at one time. She brought me milk and cookies and put her hand warmly on the back of my head, and I missed my own mother doing that. My mother hadn't touched me or held me much in the last year, and it seemed she was always wringing her hands or looking at me too anxiously for me to want her to touch me.

Mrs. Olan, though, had been crying. Her eyes were red, and against her dark skin they looked fiery. Mr. Olan came into the kitchen with his head down, saw me, and blinked hard. "He's Dr. Pete's boy," explained Mrs. Olan.

Mr. Olan nodded at me, and I said, "Hello, sir," as I'd been trained to do.

Officer Dennis leaned back against the kitchen counter, sipping the coffee Mrs. Olan had made. Everyone was quiet in the kitchen, and after Mrs. Olan sat down at the blue Formica table, Mr. Olan came over and patted her shoulder, and she took his hand and pressed her face against his palm. "She's sleeping now," Mr. Olan said. Officer Dennis looked down at his coffee cup. Something was wrong, terribly wrong, I realized, beyond the neighbors hating these people. Something at the center of their lives that mattered more and was less comprehensible than any forces outside their home.

I put down the chocolate chip cookie. It was homemade and tasted delicious, but I thought it was insensitive to be gobbling cookies and gulping milk right now.

I heard footsteps down the stairs, and my father came into the kitchen with his black doctor's bag. His face was pale, the shadows

16

deep around his eyes. He had sharp, strong features and dark curls, and people had said he reminded them of Tony Curtis, but he looked worn down, sunken and deflated like my old basketball in the garage. When he saw me, it startled him, but only momentarily. So thick was his distress that even my inexplicable presence here couldn't jar him from his heaviness. He turned to the Olans. "The ambulance will be here soon," he told them, and Mrs. Olan put her hands up to her face.

My father and I walked home. I carried his doctor's bag. I felt immensely important to be at his side. He didn't ask me what I was doing at the Olans' house. If anything, he seemed glad for the company on the long walk back, much longer than it had taken either of us to get here. He said that he wished the baby hadn't been allergic to penicillin, and he should have made the decision earlier to put the child in the hospital, but he hadn't wanted to split up the family. "Under the circumstances, David," he told me, although it was as if he were talking to himself.

Two hours later I heard sirens going by our house, then more sirens. I heard my father run downstairs, followed by my mother. My father woke up our next-door neighbor Mr. Phillips for a ride to the Olans'. The fire that had been set destroyed the Olans' garage and most of their kitchen. The only good thing—and it wasn't good, as it turned out—was that the Olans hadn't been at home. They'd gone with their baby to the hospital, bringing along the two younger children asleep in their pajamas.

But the Olans' baby passed away during the night. I couldn't bring myself to say "died" for a long while because it was just the same as with my mother's "sadness," a soft phrase that let everybody, including me, off the hook. They had lost their baby and they'd lost their house in the same night. Smoke damage would make the place uninhabitable, and they'd soon leave, surrender and move to Darby. The neighborhood, which did not become integrated for another twenty-one years, would never quite recover from it, as I would never

17

recover from the day Mrs. Nick didn't serve me and I allowed myself to slink away. The next year was 1961, and Warren and his family would move away, my mother would be hospitalized for depression, Adrian would break his shoulder trying to take an aerial shot of the park from our garage roof with his rented sixteen-millimeter camera, and I would decide I was going to be a doctor, a good doctor like my father, part of the great chain of cause and effect.

T W O

After the Olans' baby died, my father threw himself into his work even more. Whether out of anger at himself for not saving the child or rage at the community, he began to see many destitute patients. His waiting room soon filled to bursting with poor Negro families, who called him Dr. Pete and blessed him heartily.

I visited him as often as I could. His office was in a purple-brick building, wine-colored (indeed a few of his patients called him Dr. Wine for that building) with a white cupola on the roof and an arched red door like the entrance to a gingerbread house. My father's building stood on Ninth Street in the middle of Chester's "Doctors' Row." It felt like a real community, that I became somebody of significance by being there.

I kept the magazines stacked and the toys neat in the waiting room, and although my mother was mostly horrified that I spent so much time there, as often as I could after school and all day on Saturdays, I actually loved the atmosphere. The smell of sickness didn't bother me, and I got to know the patients, the older Negro women and men, who pumped my hand and called me Dr. Pete's boy and told me what a good man my pop was and that I was going to be just like him. I'd drop off blood samples at the hospital or pick up X rays from the lab on Edgemont Avenue. I'd run to Mr. Lew's delicatessen to get pastrami or corned beef sandwiches for the nurses, or I'd walk Mrs. Candelloti under an umbrella to the bus stop. I was doing well in school and even in Hebrew school, bringing home honor roll certificates and winning the Arnold M. Rubin Award for studies in Judaic history.

All that changed one day when I walked in on my father and one of his nurses, Josie, and saw them embracing. I was twelve and knew what I had seen. Later my father told me that he had only been comforting Josie, but then he added, "Mom doesn't have to know anything about this," and tousled my hair. I understood that we had struck a kind of deal, my silence for his affection, a deal I did not, as it turned out, take without consequence to myself and others.

What did I actually see that Saturday afternoon in my father's office? I saw Josie's blouse unbuttoned, my father's lips on her throat. I saw both her shoulders bare, white as ash, cool as milk, her slender fingers fanned like shells behind his head, then tangling in his dark curls. But these are my fantasies of Josie. The Josie there was a young nurse with thick chestnut hair who soon left his practice to move to San Francisco, and all they were doing was embracing, and neither Josie's shoulders nor her breasts, the stuff of romance covers, could have been exposed in her buttoned-up nurse's uniform. I saw nothing. I saw they were in love.

Josie had baby-sat for us once when I was eight years old. I remember she had shampooed my hair at the kitchen sink. She had handled my mother's sacred bottle collection, showing Adrian and me how with the right "very tender touch" she could play "Oh, What a Beautiful Mornin' " on these bottles, transforming the collection into a shimmering xylophone. She seemed to know exactly where to strike each bottle for the measured sound. When she got to the stately blue one, my favorite, I gasped. She chimed it with a tiny cocktail fork, singing in a startlingly clear voice:

> *Oh, what a beautiful mornin'*
> *Oh, what a beautiful day*

Later that evening she let Adrian read one of his Hardy Boys books in bed, and for me, who didn't like to read, she sat on the edge of my mattress and held my hand to foretell my future. "I see a stadium."

"Connie Mack?" I said, knowing we were conspiring.

"Yes, and somebody's stepped up to the plate, and he has long, luscious curls hanging out the back of his batter's helmet." And she reached up and ran her slim fingers, ringless, over the back of my neck, scratching lightly at the nape, those same fingers that so gently had massaged my scalp earlier during a shampoo, and at eight years old I'd felt the stirrings of something that I couldn't identify but that I didn't want to stop. She kissed me good night on the forehead. Four years later I'd see my father and her embracing, she twenty-six, he forty-five. I would be struck by how *familiar* they were with each other, that this wasn't new. Whatever I saw, it wasn't new at all.

When I was fifteen, my parents decided to separate. But by then I had already descended into behavior that would culminate finally in tragedy. At the time, though, we were temporarily distracted by what was happening with Adrian. He was on the Scott's Hi-Q team, the local high school version of the *GE College Bowl,* the well-known television show where college kids answered questions such as "The secretions bufotoxin, bufotenine, and adrenaline are concentrated in the parotid glands of which venomous creature?" and huddled together for the answer.

Scott's Hi-Q was sponsored by Scott Paper, which had loads of money and practically owned Chester at the time and where many of the citizens of Garden City worked. Three other kids along with Adrian made up the school's Scott's Hi-Q panel: Margie Commodore, Bill Ferris, and Jane Fugate. Adrian had only joined the group when he was a senior, and in the beginning, during the matches, the other three, who had been on the team since they were sophomores, would consult when they were asked a question and leave him out of the proceedings.

Then Adrian started to act independently, answering before they'd finished putting their heads together. "Is that the answer for your team?" the moderator asked during one match. The question had been "Water boils at one hundred degrees Celsius. At what temperature does mercury boil?" Adrian knew immediately that the answer was 356.58 degrees Celsius. Don't ask me how he knew. He hardly ever appeared to study, yet he never lacked answers. Margie Commodore, Bill Ferris, and Jane Fugate looked at one another.

They nodded subtly, glancing down at the end of the table where Adrian sat. He'd never been a team player and didn't want to be included any more than they wanted to include him. Adrian, who'd tried out for the team when a fourth member had transferred from the school, had yawningly answered the five pages of test questions, getting the highest score. The first day of "practice," when the coach, Mrs. Lutrell, fired ten questions at them like pitches, Adrian had said, "Could we speed up the pace a little? We're never going to win if the questions are this slow and this facile." Which hadn't endeared him to Mrs. Lutrell, who had coached the team for ten years, or the rest of the group, but he was right. Scott's Hi-Q had never placed higher than fifth (out of eight public school teams), and they needed to do better. It took Adrian, with his extremely low tolerance for intellectual torpidity, to point this out.

With his contribution the team started to win matches, and it wasn't long before Adrian was sitting in the center position with CAP- TAIN written on his placard. People started coming too. The home contests were held in the school auditorium, which was where the detention students stayed after school. In the past these detention students, ironically the only audience, had snickered viciously at the questions and thrown paper airplanes and erasers at the panel when- ever Mr. Chong, the detention monitor, stepped out of the room. But then, after Scott's Hi-Q won its first five matches, other people started to drop in, and soon the front three rows, then half, then most of the auditorium filled up. By the last two matches of the season the Chester *Times* had sent a reporter to do an article on the team and a feature on Adrian.

He was getting tremendous attention for being the star of Scott's Hi-Q, and I meanwhile, having just gotten my learner's permit, was hanging out with the new generation of greasers at a store that had replaced Mrs. Nick's. My father was too involved with his office to pay much attention, Adrian was lost in the world of Scott's Hi-Q, his first real fame, and my mother was on her third visit to a hospital, a new private one. I spent every day playing poker with Crow Randazzo and Vic Quint in Chuckie Halbert's basement. Our pots sometimes grew to fifty dollars or more, an astronomical sum for fifteen- and sixteen-year-olds in 1967, and I had to keep "borrowing" money to make up the debt I owed because I lost frequently.

"I'll raise you ten," Crow said one afternoon. He meant ten dol- lars, not ten cents. Initially we had played for nickels and dimes, but that amount quickly escalated into dollars.

"I'll see you ten and raise you ten," I said, holding four kings. They'd been dealt to me outright, no discards necessary. All I ever seemed able to draw was a pair, or three of a kind maybe. I never drew a straight or a full house, like Crow did.

I pulled the last twenty out of my pocket. It had come from my father's wallet, as had the rest of the money I used to play poker. He either didn't know or didn't care. Well, he cared, of course, but he was preoccupied with my mother's failing mental health and with his office, and in his free time he liked to see Adrian win at Scott's Hi-Q. I thought of it as a kind of payment for being ignored by him and neglected by my mother, though I didn't think of it in those terms at the time. I didn't reason out that I wasn't getting any love, panicking that my mother would never leave the hospital and would abandon me, and that if anybody were going to be noticed, it would be Adrian, whose fortunes rose as mine fell and who had made himself a beloved star. I just took the money. At school I thought constantly about these poker games. I had it in my blood to get to Chuckie Halbert's dank basement (his parents both worked) to hunch under that dim sixty-watt bulb at the table with burn marks from our cigarettes and bottle rings from the beer that Vic and Crow drank, young alcoholics that they were, while I waited for the deal, the crisp flick of those cards sliding facedown in front of me, then everything quieting for a raptured moment.

The sensations went through me all the way to my stomach and into my groin. My leg jiggled, and Crow would snap, "Stop moving your fucking leg," and I would, for a moment, but then it would start up again, and I'd pick up my cards, my hands sweaty, peeking at each one so that Ks came up slow and nice and I said, "Four kings."

I was sure, finally, I had won a big pot. There must have been a hundred twenty-five dollars in there, fifty at least of my money. Chuckie threw down his cards disgusted, Vic followed, but Crow said, "Straight flush, ten high," and for a moment I just stared, unable to believe it, that luck had dealt me this amazing hand and I couldn't win.

"Four kings beats a ten-high straight flush."

Crow didn't stop raking in the money. "Not in my book," he said.

"You cheated," I said, because even then I knew, and that was the strange thing: I knew, and I kept playing, because at some level I wanted to lose, wanted to be beaten by the game, as do all gamblers, as do all those addicted, and who said you couldn't be fifteen and be addicted? I was.

"You cheated," I said again. Crow, who looked like his name, with raven black hair that he was rumored to use airplane glue on, and whose trunklike arms and squat legs—he was only five-six— made him a master specimen of brute force, wrestled varsity. But it wasn't wrestling season, and even if it were, Crow would have found a way to be here too. I would one day have to investigate why I was attracted to bad boys, as a girl might be, or as someone else might be attracted to tough, slutty girls, but they had a hopeless allure for me, not sexually but in their ruthless lack of compunction about hurting others. Something in me knew to get away from them, but something else in me stuck around riveted to see if I would be taken advantage of again. "You cheated," I said for a third time, demanding a response, a conflagration perhaps. Crow pulled back the right quadrant of his upper lip. Like Elvis Presley, he was possessed of a sneer, something else gentile that I with my small red mouth could never hope to attain.

"Yeah, David," he said, and I was amazed that he could say my name so softly, so sweetly, yet so threateningly. "Yeah, I cheated. Didn't I, Vic?"

Vic smiled, noncommittal. Tall and stiff and seemingly amoral, a junior hatchet man in the making, with an orangy complexion and an irregular mouth wide as a sweet potato that stayed open dumbly no matter how many times people told him to shut it, he was Crow's protégé, a sidekick, a chargé d'affaires, and although he never exactly had assigned duties, he always seemed to be there to execute Crow's wants. "Slip me a fin," Crow would say, and Vic would produce the five-spot from his own wallet without question. "Give me a beer," and Vic would hand him a Bud. "Not that nigger piss," Crow would

25

say, and Vic would dig deeper into the stash of cold beer bottles in the cooler we kept in Chuckie Halbert's basement (his parents never ventured down here) and find a Schlitz. I would wince at "nigger piss" and keep staring at my cards, hoping they would get better. I was, after all, trying to pass, not having learned my lesson yet from the Olans' fire that I couldn't.

Chuckie Halbert was reshuffling the cards, his head down. Did he know too? Chuckie, a large doughboy of a kid, who wore a croupier's cap and whose size should have compelled him to play football, liked to mix foaming beakers of vinegar and baking soda in his basement, build tunnels for his HO gauge trains, observe the graveyard progress of his ant farm, and involve himself in all other subterranean activities. Chuckie was like a big neutral country. He never took sides. But didn't he see that Crow and Vic pulled cards from the bottom of the deck? Or was he in on this too—the pot split with him afterward? Were they *all* duping me?

I got up and pushed open the storm cellar doors and stepped out into the fresh air. My hair, which I had greased back with Brylcreem, as I did every morning and evening, was already popping out of place. Unlike Crow, Vic, and Chuckie, who had sharp, straight follicles and locks of hair that dive-bombed down their foreheads, I had hair that was curly like my father's, "Jew kinky," as Corky Innes had dubbed it years before. For my fifteenth birthday I'd tried to have it straightened at a Philadelphia "salon," with disastrous results. It had turned chemically yellow overnight and clung terrified to the side of my head like a beaver pelt.

I sat in the sunshine now at the top of the slope of the steel storm cellar doors, hearing the boys clatter around below, Crow raking in the pot, I suppose. I would have to get away from these guys, have to turn over a new leaf, as my teachers had told my father. Yesterday he'd met with the guidance counselor, who was worried about my slipping grades, my obvious potential versus my lack of achievement.

"As I told David," Mr. Shelley had said, glancing with therapeutic

26

pause at me to drive the point home, "he has more of a future than wearing tight sharkskin pants and blowing smoke out his nostrils." And Mr. Shelley, a corpulent man with a wee, if jolly, head, pushed my file toward my father so he could see that I'd been busted lately for smoking in the parking lot, being in the hallway without an authorized pass, and wearing T-shirts to school. Mr. Shelley didn't ask why my mother wasn't here or where she might be. I had the feeling he already knew, although I wasn't sure exactly how. I'd simply gotten in the habit of saying that she was "away" or "off" or "gone" or offering some other unspecified, if painfully blunt, explanation.

After our meeting with Mr. Shelley, I walked around the perimeter of the school with my father. Adrian and his teammates were in the process of winning their tenth Hi-Q match and would soon go on to the state championship in Harrisburg. We were all (which may or may not have included my mother, "all" in our family was getting harder and harder to define) supposed to go up together and watch.

My father and I stopped at the beginning of the track. It was mid-May and had already turned warm. Crow, Vic, Chuckie, and I had come out here and raced one day after school. We'd torn around the track in our ankle-high, black-glazed Italian shoes with brass buckles ("wop sculpture," Crow called them) and our black leather jackets with their sleeve zippers open to the wind, our white neckerchiefs knotted tight around our throats. Technically Crow'd won, but we'd all collapsed after one lap, coughing up old cigarette smoke. Vic, orangy sweet potato grin as always, had run with a ciggie in his hand, spitting and hawking up phlegm, and now here I was with Dr. Nachman, physician to the poor.

We sat on the bleachers. My father put his hand on my shoulder. "You doing okay?" he asked.

I felt like sobbing when he did that, but practiced in the art of meaningless hood babble, I said, "I'm golden."

My father looked at me for a long moment. Inside my head I was Muhammad Ali, bobbing and weaving, dancing around the ring—

pop! pop! pop!—nailing Sonny Liston. But in his gaze I could see myself sitting there, a valueless lump of leather, buckles, and dripping Brylcreem.

"Do you ever think about wanting to be a doctor anymore?" my father asked. "I miss having you around the office." His voice was so concerned that I couldn't clear the lump in my throat to answer. I hated how easily he got through to me, how any tenderness did. I'd worked hard at crusting that part of me over. I found it disturbing that in seconds the whole baked shell could be busted through as easily as cellophane.

"Not no more I don't," I said, working as many double negatives into a sentence as possible, because this, after all, was the indigenous language of Crow and the guys.

My father took out a cigarette, lit it, smoked a puff, and then stubbed it out on the track's cinders. He'd been trying to quit. "David, I have to tell you something. Your mother and I are going to separate."

I was stunned. Completely and utterly stunned, and enraged, and I suddenly realized that my behavior was all about rage, my rage, and that I would never, never stop, stop whatever it was I was doing because I hated him, or hated Josie, I wasn't sure, somebody, I hated somebody with all my might.

"Yeah," I said coolly, and ran my fingers through my Brylcreemed hair, sniffing them a little afterward the way Crow and the guys did. "Well, it goes, you know, it goes."

"What?" my father said, his color rising. "What do you mean, it *goes?*"

"It goes," I mumbled, "down. It goes down."

He looked at me with complete scorn. It wasn't what I wanted to tell him. "David, don't you have anything else to say?"

I shook my head.

"I'm very sorry about it. So is your mother."

"Deuce," I said, sucking air loudly and fakely and looking out over the baseball field where practice was beginning.

"It's no one's fault."

"Yeah?" I said. "Nobody?" He looked at me sharply. His dark Tony Curtis curls had gone gray, and he'd gained weight, his once-square, handsome face sagging. "It's somebody's," I said, and added, "Fault."

"You think so." I couldn't tell if it was a question or not. I decided it wasn't. "You don't understand everything, David. You think you do, but you don't."

"I understand what I saw." I kicked at the cinders with one of my rat-stabber shoes.

"All right, David," my father said very quietly, and I knew the subject was over. We waited in silence, watching the baseball players warm up, and then he said, "We have to think about now. This is very hard. Your mother and I have talked about it extensively, that's the important thing. Nobody is blaming anybody. We want you to know it's just a separation. Nothing has happened permanently. Mom wants to have her own place for a while."

"Yeah," I went back to saying. "Yeah."

We stood up, my father first. He put his hand on my back and pushed me along. I hated myself too, for my inability to resist his touch even after what he'd said. I wanted to run, to scream at him, to beg him to stay or make Mom give us another chance, to do something. *He was a doctor after all.* He was supposed to prevent stuff, heal people, not cause them pain. Couldn't he help his own family?

"Let's see if your brother is through yet," he said instead, and we went into the auditorium, where Adrian was still surrounded by admirers. Adrian had lost all the baby fat around his florid cheeks, which, along with his long, curled lashes, had once made him look puffy and delicate. Those long lashes now blinked with an alluring, self-satisfied tolerance of all who patted his back and shook his hand as he slouched coolly in the auditorium doorway. It was as though he had been secretly training and waiting to make his surprising leap into popularity during his senior year, timed for its last-minute dark horse surprise.

I saw that Margie Commodore was hanging by his side, staring up at him with adoration. Margie, his teammate on Scott's Hi-Q, whose strained, squinted gaze made it appear as if a large polynomial had wrapped itself around her head and was squeezing all the fun out of her life, now beamed openly at Adrian, her features soft and yielding. She was in love. With Adrian. That was the way girls, people, looked when they were in love, and watching my father watch Adrian, his relaxed pride, even now in the midst of his marital troubles, I saw that he loved Adrian too and that I was being left behind, out of the race for love.

So when Crow and the guys tried to come up from the poker game I'd lost in Chuckie Halbert's cellar, I wouldn't let them. I latched the metal bolt. They banged and rattled the doors from down below and then gave up and exited the front door.

"Why'd you do that?" Chuckie said.

"Felt like it," I said. "Inconvenient?"

"Fuck you, Nachman," said Crow. "Here," he said, and threw a wad of bills at my feet. "I don't want to take money from a crybaby."

I stared at the crumpled bills on the ground. It wasn't even my money. It was my father's, and I'd handed it over to Crow. I picked it up.

"Yeah, better take it," he said. "One of your father's Jew lawyer friends might come after me."

"What?" I said. Despite all, despite every foul word possible coming out of Crow's mouth, he'd never said this one, and for the longest time now I'd thought no one noticed or cared. "What did you say?"

"Give me a ciggie," he said to Vic.

Crow blew smoke out his nostrils. He narrowed his eyes and looked at me. He was supposed to be part Apache, but then everybody from the project supposedly was part Indian.

"You cheated," I said.

"You know," said Crow, whose hair really did look as if it were glued in place, "I'm getting tired of being called a cheater. Keep it up."

He started to walk away, with Vic and Chuckie in tow. I went over to my car. Since I had just a learner's permit, I was allowed to drive only with adult supervision. But with my mother in the hospital and my father at work, I took the car out on my own. We'd finally gotten a second car, an F-85 Oldsmobile station wagon. My father drove the old Buick to work. Crow, meanwhile, had a '61 Chevy Impala that he'd dropped a 409-cubic-inch engine into. When we weren't playing poker, we were usually cruising around town, driving back and forth to HoJo's, up to the high school, down to the park (although I mostly stayed away from there because it was too close to my house). I had to have the car home before my father got back. But I wasn't about to sit home by myself. I thought about my mother too much when I was there, wondered about her. Over the weekend, before I'd known about the separation, we'd visited her at the hospital, and she'd shown us where she ate and watched TV and played cards and did crafts—occupational therapy, she'd said. She had seemed fine to me, so well, in fact, that I'd made the mistake of asking when she was coming home. "Soon, David," she said, but then added, "I need to stay here awhile longer," and I'd forced back the tears, because I realized how we couldn't help her, I couldn't, and that she wanted or needed to be at this place more than with us.

After my father had told me about their separation, I'd pushed it out of my mind. I had poker after all. I had these guys, and I had my stolen trips in the car.

Vic and Chuckie got into Crow's Chevy, and I got into the

F–85 Oldsmobile. Despite the fancy letter-number designation that made it sound like a fighter plane, the F–85 was slow, a family car, and no matter how much I tried, I couldn't pretend it had power. It was no more a car that was boss than my hair was straight or I looked good in shiny black Italian shoes. But I tried. We'd taken the cars down to Todmorden, a new development that was still under construction, and we'd raced them there, Crow beating me by a good five lengths. Now I followed, out of habit, out of need—where else was I going to go? For better or worse, much worse perhaps, I followed Vic, Chuckie, and Crow up Rynard Road, past the Olans' old house, where a white family had moved in shortly after the fire and lived for the last seven years. I thought of these guys as my family, glue-haired Crow Randazzo, sweet-potato-grin Vic Quint, and croupier Chuckie Halbert.

We pulled onto Providence Road, doing the loop around HoJo's, then passing the Tastee Freeze and cruising through the parking lot there, stopping to talk to some girls from our class, and then pulling out again, our two-car caravan. We finally wound up at Todmorden. Paul Vale lived here. He was someone I'd gone to elementary school with, a nice boy my parents always wanted me to play with, who was on the track and cross-country team and in the band. When we were thirteen, we'd gone once to a Phillies game. Recently he'd called and asked if I wanted to see the Sixers with him at the Spectrum; I'd always had the feeling his parents had pushed him to call. I'd made up an excuse not to go.

The trouble was that I just didn't know what to do with that kind of person. He didn't put glue in his hair, he didn't turn his eyelids inside out and make choking sounds in the back of Spanish class, he didn't steal money from his father's wallet to gamble in some dank basement, and he didn't have a crazy mother, a father who worked twelve to fifteen hours a day, and a genius brother. I wondered what somebody like Paul was doing now, maybe off practicing in the band or training for cross-country or, God forbid, studying (he had skipped geometry and was already in calculus). Paul wanted to be a medical researcher. He was in the biology club. His parents, who owned a diner in Media, worked hard to provide for Paul, his younger brother, and his baby sister. No doubt they would help him realize his dream of medical school, while I would still be here drag racing in front of his house. In some skewed way I could see myself being buddies with Crow, Chuckie, and Vic for the rest of my life, all of us working at the shipyards in Chester and hanging out at Wally's Frog Pond, a tavern Crow frequented because he could pass for twenty-one and, as he told us, "nobody gives a shit at Wally's anyway."

We sat in our cars for a while, parked along the gutter. Paul Vale's house was up ahead at the bend, the first and as yet only house in the new development. Kids came down here to park and make out. None of us had a girlfriend, although Crow was fond of telling us he'd done it a number of times with a girl from the project, sixteen-year-old Lorraine Novis, who had teased hair and thighs that "she wraps around your face like earmuffs." I was shy and awkward around girls, especially terrified of someone aggressive like Lorraine Novis, who winked at me on occasion. The more modest and discreet Jewish girls, whom I knew from Hebrew school, had told their mothers I was "a hood," which secretly pleased me. The project girls, the Lorraine Novises, who wore black leather jackets like us, thought of me as cute but not really of their ilk. First of all, I was on the small side, and to be frank, if maturing females could sense such a thing in some pheromonelike way, I hadn't actually reached puberty yet. It was a great, dark, brooding, miserable secret of mine, which only compounded my already substantial inferiority. Nightly I searched my groin for the smallest trace of manhood but found only the same bare pubic bone and Grecian genitalia, miniature and bald as a nude parakeet. I was almost sixteen, in tenth grade, and probably the last kid in my class to reach the threshold of adolescence. It had something to do with why I didn't play sports (I wanted to avoid the locker room) and why I hung out with three other losers who didn't date.

There would be no tense situations in the back seat of a car, with me undressing her and her undressing me and she exclaiming, "Why, you're just like my *little* brother!" Or worse: "Are you handicapped? I mean, like a dwarf—down there?" or "Will you always have a little parakeet?" or some other dreadful scenario that I lay awake at night tormenting myself about: her putting a hand up to her mouth in a little O of surprise after she got a hot grip on the bald parakeet and then fell out of the car giggling.

I suppose it was the rough equivalent of a girl's being flat-chested, but actually worse, because at least if you were flat-chested, there was still a good chance you'd already started menstruating and probably had sexual feelings, whereas I was just straight faking it—once again— only in a different form, sitting in the back seat of Crow's Impala talking about eating hair pie and the beaver Sue Jefferson shot us up on the assembly stage and French fucking Lorraine Novis between the tits and shooting your wad into her throat. *French?* Why not Polish or Austrian or Pango Pango fucking? What did it matter to me? I understood but experienced—could *feel*—none of it, and would laugh extra-hard, if hollowly, at a string of jism jokes that made as much sense to me as a planarian splitting itself in two and having sex.

Vic got out of the car and came back to my door. I was just sitting there, behind the wheel, if a little small, with my elbow on the window, listening to the radio and WIBG's Hy Lit say, "This is Hyski O'Ronney McVaddio Zoot! Uptown, downtown, crosstown! See you later, alligator jive!"

"Crow wants to know if you want to drag."

"Why?" I said, irritated by the idea, irritated by my spineless presence here. "He'll just beat me."

"He says he'll race you backwards."

"What?"

"He says," said Vic, scratching his nose, "he'll race you backwards to make it even."

I thought about this a moment. Yeah, that could make it fair, and maybe I could even win. It was more a matter of steering straight than speed. What else were we going to do anyway? Just get back on Providence Road and cruise some more? We'd go to HoJo's again, try to talk to some girls, a prospect that secretly terrified me because one of these days they might actually get into the car like we always asked and want to do something, and then Crow, Vic, and Chuckie would be there for the big (little) parakeet moment. "Sure," I said, "I'll drag him." It would keep us off the streets at least, so to speak.

In a few seconds Crow turned his car around and skidded backwards, laying rubber, his tires smoking, wide slicks. He pulled into position next to me, his gleaming dual carbs popping up from his car's hood like silver fists. Vic and Chuckie got out, and Chuckie sat down on the curb. Vic walked around behind our cars, standing between the back fenders, his arms raised. Crow leaned over and rolled down his window and shouted over his deafening engine with its glass pack, *"Drag to the bend!"* I nodded at him and revved up the F-85's engine, making it scream, though it didn't really scream so much as whine. No matter how hard I tried, it was a family station wagon, not meant for this kind of abuse. It wanted a nice owner, a law-abiding family with a puppy for meandering Sunday afternoon drives after church into the countryside, now and then braking gently for an apple cider stand.

Vic's arms flapped, like a stupid bird or clumsy angel. I jammed the automatic gearshift into reverse (Crow had a three on the tree) and off we went, backwards.

Crow's Chevy shot behind straight as a dart. But my ability to maneuver the station wagon and control its reverse trajectory was not nearly as easy as I had imagined, and when I approached the bend in the road and tried to turn, the F-85 fishtailed left, then right. As I frantically tried to adjust the wobble and bring the rear into line, my palm slipped too far down the steering wheel, and the car jumped the curb of the Vales' front yard and hit Paul Vale's three-year-old sister. Only moments before, she'd pushed open the aluminum screen door and come skipping outside to play. Her mother, home for the afternoon from their diner, was in the basement doing the wash.

The car struck Sarah Vale with a small, sickening thump before it ran into a coach-light post in the yard. I see myself desperately trying to steer the car away from her while she, as three-year-olds will do, stands rooted to her spot, frozen in fear, yet unable to conceive that the car, that I or anyone, would harm her.

I have gone over and over and over the moment, and even now in my forties I continue to wake from nightmares, unable or, in some perverse versions, unwilling—the worst of the worst nightmares—to turn the wheel enough to avoid Sarah standing there in her pink bathing suit. Perhaps these versions, when I willfully won't turn the wheel, are my unconscious expression of the monster in me built from my shame and guilt. I only know that I've prayed and begged and pleaded not to have this memory for just a single moment, but it is this memory, this action, this life that I do have, and much of what happened to me came out of this confluence of me and that irrevocable instant, the worst and the best of myself.

THREE

Everything snapped silent: the revving of our engines, Crow's vibrating exhaust pipes, the radios, the high whine of the F-85's transmission. I got out of the car and saw Chuckie's face, the cavern of his mouth, then Sarah. Behind me, Crow said, "Jesus Christ. Nachman, you—" and did not complete his sentence. Now it was all part of an endless loop that would play forever.

Vic and Chuckie ran inside to get Mrs. Vale. I have a hard time remembering this part because I seem not to be there but outside it all, listening dimly to Crow say, "We weren't racing. You backed up and gunned it too hard, and your car jumped the curb by mistake."

Sarah was lying on the ground. The car's impact had thrown her about ten feet to the left side of the front walk. She'd hit the ground and lay limp, blood coming from her nose, her lips dusky. She was whimpering, and I remember bending over her body to check her pulse and Crow shouting at me not to move her.

In the next moment Mrs. Vale came running across the lawn with Vic and Chuckie, her arms fully extended as if she were reaching across an impossibly wide river. She knelt down, her body arched protectively over Sarah. Vic and Chuckie stood behind her with Crow. "Did you call the ambulance?" I asked, and they looked at one another stupidly, then ran back inside.

I knelt beside Mrs. Vale and listened to Sarah's low whimpering, a sleepy, distant sound. Her eyes were closed, and under her shallow breathing I could hear a light rasping. Her shoulders were twisted one way and her legs the other, as though she hadn't fully unwound herself from an airplane spin.

"It's Mommy, honey," said Mrs. Vale. "Can you hear Mommy?" she said. Sarah lay there whimpering, her eyelids shut but fluttering. I knew the blood coming out of her nose wasn't a good sign, and I dabbed at it with my sleeve as if this might superficially help. Mrs. Vale spoke, more a murmured thought: "I was downstairs washing. I thought I locked the screen door." I realized she wasn't blaming anyone but herself yet, and she didn't understand what had taken place or why or who was responsible.

Behind me I could hear Crow whispering with Chuckie and Vic, who had come back outside after calling the operator. The ambulance would be here in a few minutes. They stood away from us—Mrs. Vale, Sarah, and me—in a semicircle at our backs.

"What happened, David?" asked Mrs. Vale, looking up, noticing for the first time my car on her lawn. It was the last time she'd say my name with such trusting inquiry.

The ambulance crew arrived and checked Sarah's vital signs and looked for broken bones. They had tensed up when they saw the victim was a child. Nobody had told them, or maybe they did know and were shocked anyway. My father had once said to me, after he'd come home from treating a little boy who'd been in an automobile accident, "When it's a child who's hurt, there's an urgency and concern that's different than with an adult. You can't help it, no matter how experienced you are, no matter what you've seen."

The police stayed behind to talk with us. A neighbor who lived across Brookhaven Road had driven Mrs. Vale to the hospital behind the ambulance. Mr. Vale would meet her there.

Up and down Todmorden Drive the police walked. They found where Crow had turned his Chevy around and come to a stop next to me to line up our cars, a hundred feet from the bend. They stood there and studied the skid marks for quite some time, talking back and forth, and while they did, Crow said to me, "You backed up wrong. That's what you tell them." He'd looked at me, the first time I'd seen this combination of fear and meanness in his face so his brow appeared to thicken and drop over his eyes like a fat log. "You could get us all cooked."

The police asked to see my license and discovered it was a learner's permit. That's when they called my father. They spent a long time bent down on one knee studying the tire tracks in the grass. They searched for skid marks at the curb too, but there were none. I'd jumped the curb before I even had the awareness or ability to hit the brakes, the car completely out of control.

"So you didn't see her?" one of the policemen asked. He had red hair, a mustache that looked like a small furry badge itself, hundreds of freckles on his arms. His partner was younger, wiry, and watched us carefully as if to prove he was closer in age to us and not to be taken in by anything we said.

"I did see her," I said, "but I couldn't stop." I could feel Crow's eyes on me.

"Where did you hit her?"

I walked over to the spot where I thought it had happened.

The one policeman with freckles squatted down and brushed the matted grass with the palm of his hand. "This is where you put on the brakes?"

Crow coughed, then spit.

"I don't know," I said. They studied me a moment, then went over to my car and looked at the bumper. They rubbed their fingers against a small dent—on the wrong side. My mother had backed against the garage getting out. Sarah's body had not dented the bumper. She'd been knocked away from the car, pushed up and out by its full impact. It's a terrible and disbelieving sight to see a child tossed in the air, and I found it incomprehensible enough to think at first I'd hit a doll, so weightlessly did she take flight before bouncing to a stop.

My father came shortly after. He walked over to me and put his hand on my shoulder; I tried then to keep myself from crying, and I succeeded.

Sarah Vale lapsed into a coma shortly after arriving at the hospital. A burr hole had been drilled into her skull to relieve the pressure and evacuate the blood between her skull and brain. That's all my father knew or would tell me. When I'd asked him how much danger she was in, he'd said, "She has a subdural hematoma. The first forty-eight hours are crucial, David. We'll just have to wait." I hadn't been able to think of anything other than when the phone would ring, and when it didn't, I just sat and stared at it, my mind blank. I had this idea that if I didn't move, I wouldn't be caught off guard and no further bad news could happen.

Adrian stayed with me while my father drove to pick up my mother from her hospital near Chadds Ford. He'd been summoned out of a Scott's Hi-Q match at Eddystone and brought home by one of the teachers.

Everybody was coming back.

"You need anything?" asked Adrian. He was supposed to remain at home with me until our parents returned. My mother had to be checked out, and a part of me, in some disproportionate way, felt as guilty about that as about the enormity of what I'd done. I was making her leave before she was well. She'd be angry. It was easier to focus on this, something in my own family.

"Want me to make you a snack?"

I hadn't eaten anything since lunch. It was now almost eight o'clock, four hours after the accident, and I no longer was hungry. I shook my head.

"You'll feel better if you eat," said Adrian, sounding like our mother.

"I can't," I said.

He sat down across from me at the kitchen table. I wondered if he'd resented being called away from a Scott's Hi-Q match. Of course he did.

"They'll be home soon," he said, meaning our parents. I could tell he didn't know what to say to me. Even the policeman who had taken our statements at the scene had a hard time looking at me.

Adrian put a piece of apple pie in front of me, à la mode. It looked sickening. "Thanks," I said, and took a sliver of vanilla ice cream on my spoon.

"I'm sure things will be fine," he said. "Remember when I fell and smacked my eye on a rock? Everybody thought I'd have to wear a patch. And Howard Lesser burned half his body with that stupid rocket fuel he used to make. He recovered, right? And what about Bill Welmer's concussion after he got hit in the head with a baseball bat—"

"No more, okay?"

"I'm just trying to make the point that kids are more resilient than you think."

"I get the point."

Adrian looked at my fast-melting ice cream. He went to get a spoon, then began taking larger and larger bites. After it was almost gone, he said, "Do you want to tell me what happened?"

We'd avoided any talk about the accident itself.

"Not really," I said.

"It would be good to tell somebody."

"I backed up."

"That's all?"

"Not really," I said, "but I don't want to talk about it now."

My mother came home that night around ten. "David," she said, and hugged me hard.

"Have you heard anything?" I asked my father.

He shook his head.

"Can you make a call?" I asked him.

"I did, David. I stopped and called on the way here. She's still in a coma."

"But she was whimpering. She was all right before the ambulance came."

"She wasn't all right, David," said my father firmly. His impatience stung me. "She was in shock, and she could cry, but that doesn't mean it was a strong vital sign."

I shook my head. I wanted to believe that she hadn't gotten the proper care, that someone else's error might be cause for fault. "She didn't seem that bad," I said.

"She's deteriorated, David. There's a possibility"—he glanced at my mother, whom I could tell he'd discussed this with already—"there's a possibility of damage to her spinal cord too."

I felt myself sink further into a gaping hole that I'd been stepping over with a combination of hope and belief in her initial signs, her whimpering.

"Is she going to be paralyzed?" I asked.

"David," said my father, nervous himself, I could see, though I was helpless to stop asking him these questions. *He knew more, why wasn't he telling me?* "We just don't know the extent of the injuries. It's wait and watch at this point."

"Come with me," said my mother. I had hardly noticed that she'd been standing right next to me. Her sunglasses were on, and I realized she must have been crying on the way here. She reached out for my hand. "I'll put you to bed. Everything will be better in the morning," she said, and I chose to believe this, anything.

The police called the next morning and wanted to speak with me. I'd heard the phone ring and then my father's muffled voice from their bedroom. (He'd gotten up and closed the door.) My mother and he talked together afterward, and I could tell it was about me, not themselves, their softly joined and worried voices. Everything else apparently had been put on hold, including their separation, which suddenly wasn't an issue.

"David," my father said, coming into my room. I'd been lying in bed awake for the last five hours. I couldn't make myself get up, nor did I dare go back to sleep and have more dreams. "The police would like to speak with you this morning. They say it's just a routine talk."

"Have you called about Sarah?"

"The same. No change."

Detective Aronson met us at the sergeant's desk. He shook hands with my father first, then with me. "Come on back," he said easily.

I sat with my father in the two chairs placed in front of the detective's messy desk. Pictures of his wife and two daughters stood next to a stack of wanted photos, and I looked away.

He wore a yellow tie and forest green sport jacket. Clean white wheels of skin rounded his ears where he'd just gotten a fresh haircut. Under his blue eyes he had deep hollows, and a birth stain peeked up from his white collar. I wondered how far down it went.

"David, I just want to go over a few things with you," he said, finding my file on his desk. He held it at a distance to read it, then located his glasses and said, "That's better. You were backing up?"

I nodded.

"You didn't see the girl."

"Pardon?"

"You didn't see her, David. She's small." To the side of his desk, he held his hand at the level of an unseen child. "You couldn't see her behind the station wagon, right? Or could you?"

"I'm not sure," I said, though I was. I saw her standing on the lawn as I tried to make the bend. Then I lost her right before the impact.

"What speed were you going?"

"Speed?" I said. I thought of Crow saying, *We weren't racing.* "I was just backing up."

"Those are awfully long tracks in the grass for just backing up, David." Detective Aronson turned a page in the file. "We couldn't find any place in the grass where you put on the brakes. You can tell the spot where that happens. Any reason you didn't put on your brakes?"

"It happened fast. I don't remember it well."

"We found some skid marks from the other boy's car. Randazzo. Any idea how those got there?"

I shook my head.

"They were up the road a hundred and twenty feet from the Vale's house."

I said I didn't know why.

Detective Aronson clicked his pen a few times and stared at me, as if sizing me up again. I tried not to look at my father. As far as he knew, I had just been backing up.

"We found another set from Randazzo's car just about the place where your vehicle backed onto the Vales' front yard. Looks like he stopped suddenly. What do you make of that?"

"I don't know," I said.

"By the way, what were you doing down in Todmorden?"

"Driving around. We'd stopped there."

"Any reason why?"

I shrugged.

My father spoke up. "I thought this was a routine talk."

"It is, Dr. Nachman," said Detective Aronson. "We're just trying to put together a picture of what happened." He smiled imperceptibly at my father. His blue eyes had gone dim. "This little girl's parents want to know exactly what occurred. You can understand that as a parent and a doctor, right?"

"Are you going to bring charges?" asked my father.

Detective Aronson laid his large palms across the open file. "We haven't decided on that yet."

"I think we'd better wait to answer any more questions," my father said.

"It would be advisable if David cooperated with our investigation."

"I'd like to talk with an attorney first," said my father.

"That's your right," said Detective Aronson, and took off his glasses to rub the bridge of his nose.

On the ride home my father abruptly turned from Providence Road onto Single Lane, an aptly named street so narrow our car scraped against the hedges on either side. A sturdy three-story colonial house with a bank of eight green-shuttered windows across its top floor and a rooster weather vane on its roof rose behind the lane's tall hedges, which dwarfed our car. My father shut off the engine and twisted toward me. "What happened, David?"

I didn't hesitate. "We were racing."

"My God," he said.

I told him everything.

I woke my father up in the middle of the night. He sat up immediately, as he always did when the phone rang for him at this hour. He'd write down all the information on a yellow pad he kept on his nightstand, advise the parents what to do about the child's fever or vomiting or croup, and then promptly go back to sleep until the morning, when having forgotten everything, he'd look at his pad and remember.

He planted his feet on the floor. I saw that my mother wasn't in bed. The light in the living room was on, and I guessed she'd fallen asleep reading, as she liked to do. I'd been lying in bed since ten o'clock—it was now two A.M.—unable to let go into sleep. Patterns of squiggly gray lines had started to appear in front of my eyes as I stared straight up at the ceiling, and I'd forced myself to get up.

"What's wrong, David?" my father asked.

"Can you take me to the hospital?"

"To the hospital?"

I realized, exhausted from lack of sleep, that I wasn't making sense. "I want to see her."

"Now?" said my father.

I nodded. "Please," I said. "Please, Dad."

He rubbed his eyes, "David—"

"You've got to," I said. "Please do this for me."

He blinked at me. He got up heavily and pulled on his clothes.

My father had called ahead to prepare the nurses at ICU for our visit. The hospital corridors were empty, though well lit at three A.M., orderlies going up and down mopping the floors. One of them, Joseph

Jackson was his name, greeted my father. "How you doin' tonight, Dr. Nachman?"

"Fine, Joseph," he said. Joseph glanced at me, smiled encouragement, then leaned a moment respectfully on his mop as we went past. He had four children, the youngest, I knew from seeing her at my father's office, about Sarah Vale's age. I hadn't been anywhere except to the police station and here. It was strange to come out in the middle of the night, under darkness, and sneak into the hospital, but I knew I couldn't have come here during the day.

A nurse met us at the desk across from ICU. The sign on the double doors with their darkened panes of glass said IMMEDIATE FAMILY ONLY. Visits were limited to ten minutes between the hours of seven A.M. and ten P.M. "Thanks, Susan," said my father to the head nurse, and he pushed open the doors. I took a deep breath and followed him inside. When I saw her, I felt a thick, dull blow against my stomach, the sensation of hitting her, the sickening thud, except it was inside me now, and I thought for a moment I would have to leave, but then I gained control of myself by watching my father.

Sarah's bed was almost directly to our right as we walked in. I hadn't seen her at first because her head was shaved and bandaged in a white turban from the craniotomy—the burr hole. She looked small and still in the bed. All around her I could hear the other patients in the unit: the rasping of augmented breathing, the swishing in and out of the ventilators, like milking machines. She looked too little for the island of her white hospital bed with its tubes and wires running everywhere. My father pulled the curtain around us.

He bent down and shined a flashlight on her eyes, which had bruised circles—raccoon eyes.

"What's that mean?" I said.

"It's common with head injuries. The bleeding tends to run along certain lines, around the eyes, for instance." He looked at the base of her skull, shined his flashlight there.

47

"Is she getting better?"

"I don't know, David. We'll just have to see." She had a ventilator in her mouth, the tube taped to her face. Wires from the cardiac monitor ran to pads under her gown, a pink one with teddy bears they gave to the children. A gathering of stuffed animals was next to her head, in poses of vigilance. Her right arm had an IV running to it and was strapped to a padded board.

A nurse came in and stood a moment stroking Sarah's hand and smiling down at her.

"Any change in her breathing?" my father asked.

The nurse shook her head. "We keep talking to her, though."

I'd watched my father's nurses around children. They were always gentle, sweet, respectful, but when a child was seriously ill—leukemia, cancer, polio—they treated the child with a reverence and piercing kindness.

The nurse lifted Sarah's arm to take her pressure, wrapped the cuff lightly around, then unfastened it. When she finished, she laid the limp arm down again as though trying to attach a leaf back to a branch. She changed the IV and checked the catheter bag fastened to the bed, then took a washcloth off her cart and started to wipe Sarah's face.

"Can I do that?" I asked.

The nurse looked at my father. He'd squeezed his lips together, studying Sarah, trying to determine her prognosis. He didn't like to feel helpless. He didn't believe in it, the way other people didn't believe in God.

He nodded.

"Just dab at her face," the nurse said, and her eyes met mine, not unsympathetically, and then she left the room.

I needed to hold the washcloth with both hands at first to control my shaking. I touched the damp cloth to her face—all the open, unbruised spots—trying to speak to her through my fingers. I remembered the time I'd gone to Paul's house on our way to the Phillies game. The Vales had lived in Garden City then, and I'd ridden my bike to Paul's. Mrs. Vale had been at the sink, washing dishes. "Paul's upstairs finishing his shower. He'll be down in a second. Come in the kitchen and sit with us." Sarah lay on her stomach on top of a peach-colored blanket in a cone of sunshine. The sun had come out strong that June day and warmed up the kitchen early. I hadn't seen Sarah before, just heard that Paul, at the age of thirteen, had a new baby sister. Mrs. Vale was wearing pink rubber gloves to wash the dishes, and Sarah had begun crying. "Oh, you," she said to her affectionately, and started to peel off her gloves.

"I can hold her," I said, and Mrs. Vale tilted her head, as if amused by my offer.

"If you'd like, David."

I picked Sarah up and put her against my shoulder, felt her light presence in my arms, and bounced her a little, walking across the linoleum with my hand on the back of her tuft of blond hair, a whiter color than Paul's.

Mrs. Vale watched me and then said, "David, where did you learn to do that?"

"My father's office," I said, which was true. I'd held babies for their checkups. Then Paul had come downstairs, his hair combed wet and parted with sharp accuracy to the side, his letter jacket on, and we were ready to take the train to Philly.

I had this idea now that if I kept dabbing at her face, she'd wake up and speak to me. I'd cure her, some special touch I had both to hurt, then to save her. I concentrated hard.

"It's time to leave," said my father, and I laid the washcloth on the side of the metal table. The nurse had come back in, and she asked my father to help turn Sarah on her side. I listened again to her breathing, the swishing through the ventilator, and tried to take comfort in the sound.

When we went out the door, I heard the nurses say, ". . . a couple of hours' sleep," and I thought at first they were talking about me, because they looked up at us and abruptly stopped. Then I realized the two nurses must have been speaking about Sarah's parents; they'd been sent home to try to get a little rest.

⁓

I slept for ten hours. When I woke up, I was disoriented, having no idea what time of day it was. My mother had let me sleep. They weren't going to make me go back to school. Nobody had said a word about it. I had the feeling they'd already spoken with the principal and my teachers, and everybody had agreed it was best to keep me out for the rest of the term, which was only a week more until summer.

My mother was downstairs making dinner, chopping vegetables, with an apron on. It was as if she'd never left, standing by a sinkful of potato peels. She had on her glasses, and when I walked in and said hi, I could tell I'd caught her thinking about me, as if she'd been arguing with herself in private. "David, you startled me. How do you feel?"

"Better," I said. I did. I'd slept deeply, some long, merciful, dreamless bridge from ten hours ago to this moment. I'd felt as if I hadn't even moved during all that time, as if I were trying in some empathetic way to lie down and be as still as Sarah Vale.

"You slept so long. I was beginning to worry about you."

I could tell there wasn't any news; my mother was too matter-of-fact.

"Have you heard anything?" I asked anyway.

"Nothing, David. Your father's been calling to check."

"Is he coming home soon?"

"I hope so," said my mother without any hint of irritation.

"Is Adrian here?"

My mother pushed the pile of potato peels to the side of the sink. "He said he needed to stay at school today." I thought that Adrian must be trying to separate himself from me—or maybe us. Maybe too he was trying to show our mother that he didn't need her. "Why don't you take a walk before dinner?" my mother said. "It will do you good."

The thought had never occurred to me that I might walk freely outside the house. "All right," I said. I had started—standing there talking to her as if she'd always been here and never left—to feel hopeful.

I lost track of time walking in the park behind our house. A small arboretum formed part of the park, and I wandered through it, the place all to myself on this May afternoon. I studied the tags of the trees—*Acer rubrum* (red maple), *Gleditsia triacanthos inermis* (thornless honey locust), *Crataegus oxyacantha* (English hawthorn)—spending a long time mouthing their syllables, trying to figure out the Latin pronunciations. I examined the leaves, noting their edges and shapes, how translucent or opaque they were in the last of the day's sunlight. Some of the trees were just starting to leaf out, and I rubbed my fingers against their tight rolls, like tiny green cigars, or felt the fuzzy, hard buds of the late bloomers. Ironically, on the day of the accident I'd found the first hairs on my groin, proof of a hideously delayed puberty, their appearance something to celebrate that I could only note with curiosity.

By the time I was ready to leave, I'd gotten closed in the arboretum; it shut after dark, and I had to climb the chain-link fence to get out. I walked up Ridley Drive, the steep hill heading from the arboretum toward our house. I passed by Mrs. Shavinsky's house, and her dog, Bert, barked at me through the pickets of a peeling gray fence. I put my hand out for him to sniff. He was rumored to bite, but he was friendly now, and I tickled his nose and said, "Good dog. Nice Bert. You're a sweet boy, aren't you?" I stayed there a moment petting his head through the fence while he licked my hand and whimpered to be let out.

51

When I got home, I could see all the lights were on. My father had left his car in the driveway instead of putting it in the garage as he usually did.

They were sitting on the couch in the living room we rarely used.

"Hi," I said.

"Hello," said my father quietly.

"Is Adrian home?"

"He's at a friend's. David, sit down," he said. His leg was touching my mother's on the couch, and I took some pleasure in this. Unintentionally I'd brought them back together.

"Sarah Vale died at six o'clock," my father said. My mother put her hand up to her eyes, wiped the tears that appeared. I looked at my watch, a strange gesture, I realized, but it was as if I had to know exactly what I'd been doing at the moment, what leaf I'd been looking at, what Latin name I'd been trying to pronounce.

I dropped my wrist. My voice sounded low, flat, unrecognizable to me, as if it were underwater, sunk in confusion, disbelief. "How do you know?"

"How do I know?" asked my father.

"I mean, how—who told you?"

"Ben Hersch called me from the hospital."

Ben was an ENT man, my father's closest friend. They'd gone to school together at the University of Pennsylvania.

"David, this changes everything. You know that."

I nodded. "Can I come over there?" I said.

"What's that?" asked my father.

"Can I—can I come sit between you two?"

My vision was blurred by the wetness. I wiped my eyes with the back of my arm, smelled Bert's cold nose and wet tongue on my fingers.

My mother patted the seat next to her. I walked over and sat down narrowly between them, tucking my hands between my knees, my shoulders concave. She put her arm around me. I collapsed against her, and when my father patted my back tentatively, I wept harder.

F O U R

I moved into Adrian's room—for some reason it was easier to endure his room than my own—and I lost myself in reading, perhaps the first time I had in earnest ever read, other than for the required homework assignments.

I found an old book with a water-stained cover that had belonged to my mother before Adrian appropriated it. Its title was *Ten Rungs: Hasidic Sayings* by Martin Buber, and my eye went directly to a sentence that said: "This is the secret of the unity of God: no matter where I take hold of a shred of it, I hold the whole of it."

I read it over and over, couldn't stop reading. Each time I read it I heard the word *murderer* a little less in my head, though it would not go away completely. I had to read the passage almost constantly and recite it to myself like the men davening at temple, the ones who were always there for the minyan and went to the funerals and spoke with dry, crusted lips the words of God and never stopped praying. I had to speak the words in order to hold the idea, and by holding the idea, I too had a shred of God and a measure of forgiveness. At dinner

I ate quickly (and little) and hurried back to Adrian's room, and I spoke again the words and hoped that if I spoke them well enough, I could find some small place, some remnant, some loose thread from God's garment to grab and hold on to and keep myself from being destroyed or destroying myself.

One by one my family came to me to discuss my future. First was Adrian.

"It's an exciting place, Manhattan," said Adrian, plopping down on the oversize green velvet easy chair in his room. He was home for the day from Young Judea camp, where he was a counselor this summer. He'd decided to go to New York University. Columbia had offered less aid. And he liked NYU because of its film program. If that didn't work out, he could always be a doctor, he had said with a blitheness that disheartened me.

"It will be nice to have my own apartment there eventually, around Washington Square," said Adrian. He'd visited the White Horse bar, the place Dylan Thomas had resided, and had a beer, all legally, since the drinking age in New York was eighteen, not twenty-one, as in Pennsylvania. New York was heavenly, even in the heat of summer. "Tons of stuff going on, museums, music, poetry, dance, restaurants, cabbies, subways—the Village! It's quite the human carnival."

"Uh-huh," I said, turning a page. I was reading *A Tale of Two Cities,* having finally put down the Buber book.

"Be nice if you could come up there sometime and stay with me. Look around yourself at schools. NYU would be a good choice for you too."

I read about Charles Darnay pleading not guilty to being a traitor.

"Phenomenal bookstores," continued Adrian. "You wouldn't believe the Strand, thousands of review copies for sale." He gestured at the books I'd been reading, stacked like colorful chimneys by the bedside. "I see you finally like to read."

I glanced up. Adrian didn't even look like himself—that is, the person who had once lain on this bed as I was doing now. He no longer had brown pearl frame glasses with special kidskin ear stems because the backs of his ears broke out in rashes from plastic. Now, in readiness for his new life as a college freshman, a life he was promising me too, if only I'd enter the right plea, he wore contacts, sported a goatee, and had sideburns shaped in skinny columns.

I was reminded of years ago when I'd tentatively come into Adrian's room—an inhospitable odor about the place, a sedentary sweetish smell like cut flowers just before they wane—and I would watch him lie on his bed and read, his head supported by his left arm cocked at the elbow, his right index finger deftly flipping a page every ten seconds—a natural speed reader—this position held for hours on end as he read one to two books in an afternoon. In the midst of reading one day, he had called out to me in my room and beckoned me to come see him. "I think I'll call you Ennui from now on," he announced. It was before he had any friends, and certainly before he was lionized for Scott's Hi-Q. He had only me—Ennui—to talk with and annoy. "Ennui, would you kill that fly over there please? It's disturbing my concentration," he said as he reclined (he didn't lie, but reclined, like a male nude) on the bed and read one of the books from his library, surely the biggest twelve-year-old boy's library in Garden City and perhaps of any boy his age in all Pennsylvania, if not the country.

Underneath the bed, I was always aware, rested the skeleton. I had checked recently to see if it was still there. It was, and it seemed appropriate that I'd inherited a position above it as the keeper of its crypt and this library.

"I guess I'm just saying it would be nice for you to graduate on time and go to college." Adrian stroked, with two fingers, his new goatee, an annoying tic he'd developed during his short, if revelatory, stay in New York when he'd gone for freshman preview at NYU. "We'll talk later," he said.

I shrugged and kept my eyes on the page, but I was sorry he was giving up so easily on me, his old Ennui, and leaving.

"Are you going to be around?" I said when he was almost out the door.

He stepped back into the room. "Sure."

"Maybe we could play chess tonight."

"I can't tonight," said Adrian. "The Scott's Hi-Q team is having a get-together before we all leave for college." His team—the word had been that Adrian was "off"—had lost the state championship in Harrisburg. I wondered if he blamed me for this too. "You want to see a movie tomorrow?" asked Adrian.

"I can't"

"You can't?"

"I'm under house arrest."

"Oh," said Adrian. "I forgot." The police, since Sarah Vale's death, had been coming by twice a day to check that I was remaining at home. And my parents, as if afraid I would harm myself, didn't let me out of their sight.

Adrian gestured toward the chessboard set up at his desk. In between books, I'd been playing by myself. "Well, maybe we can have a match tomorrow," he said. "I'm not going back to camp until Monday." But he had already left in a sense anyway—that is, left home, taken his first big step out the door with the trip to New York. I was angry at him for leaving me. He could go off to his new life and expect I'd want or be able to join him, while I remained here—or was sent away.

"Sure," I said, and went back to reading my book.

My adjudication hearing was in four weeks. My lawyer had advised me that I could plead guilty and try for a lesser charge. Under a plea agreement I might be sent to St. Gabriel's, a residential home and a less punitive option than the reform school at Glen Mills, or I might get lucky and be put on probation; it was at the judge's discretion.

On the other hand, if we went ahead with a not guilty plea it would be a full-blown trial, prosecuted intensively by the district attorney's office. Because open beer bottles had been found in Crow's car, because I'd been driving on a learner's permit without adult supervision, and because a death had occurred, the case was being treated as a criminal one in juvenile court rather than a vehicular offense in traffic court.

"One other thing," the lawyer had told us over the phone, speaking with my father while I listened on the extension. "If the district attorney believes he has the evidence, he could charge David with murder instead of manslaughter. The case would be directly transferred to adult court at that point."

"Does that mean we should plead guilty so he won't do this?" asked my father.

"Not necessarily," said the lawyer, whose name was Lance Schnabel. "It just means he'll be collecting evidence during this time, and we have to be sure he doesn't turn up anything that will make him want to prosecute more aggressively. The three other boys have given statements saying they were not driving recklessly and that David's car jumped the curb and went out of control when he backed up. Of course, under oath and cross-examination, they might produce a different story. David," Lance said, jolting me into the conversation, "you're sure these three other kids"—I could hear papers being shuffled—"Randazzo, Quint, and Halbert, will corroborate your story?"

I cleared my throat. I felt small and distant, removed from the conversation, certainly not its focus. "Yes," I said, and didn't elaborate. I had let my father explain to Lance Schnabel what had happened. He had omitted the racing.

The police knew we'd been doing something in Todmorden, but they didn't know what exactly. There were no skid marks from my car, no sign of the course I'd laid out. As far as anyone could say, without opposing testimony, I'd just lost control backing up, and I couldn't tell whether Lance Schnabel believed this or not himself.

"All right then," Lance said. "I think we should go with a not guilty plea and let them stumble around without a witness, trying to make this anything more than a very tragic and unfortunate accident, but with no intent. David," said Lance, and I sat up at the kitchen table where I was listening, "you'll want to express your remorse to the family. I suggest you write them a letter and keep a copy of it for me to show the judge." There was a pause while everyone waited for me to answer. "David? Are you up to doing that?"

"He is," said my father.

I wanted to plead guilty and tell what happened. What I'd been trying to say, what I'd been trying to tell my parents was that if they didn't let me plead guilty and tell my story and be held account- able for what I'd done, I'd punish myself worse than any justice system could. I needed them to understand how it felt inside—fault, blame, *none of it mattered* except that I'd done this thing: I'd killed a child.

—

"Can I speak with you a minute?" asked my father. It was nine A.M. Normally he would be at the office by now, until nine tonight. It had been years since I'd hung around his office, straightening the magazines, unfazed by the toy chest with its mucus-encrusted stuffed bears, their pilled gray fur and hollow consumptive eyes (missing their brown buttons). I would gather them—they were a family of three— to my breast, place them back in their home, smile, and show the world how invincible and dedicated I was, as a doctor had to be.

"All right," I said.

"David, do you think you could find some other penance?" My father nodded at my book. I had just started reading *Lives of the Saints*.

"What do you mean?"

"Rather than plead guilty, could you find some other way to make this up to Sarah Vale and her family?"

"She's dead," I said. "How can I make it up to her?"

"There are ways to honor her memory. Constructive, positive means that make a contribution. You could get a job and donate to a charity in Sarah's name. You could work as a volunteer in the pediatric ward of the hospital. You're old enough to serve as a Big Brother. Countless ways exist for you to do good. But being locked away won't help accomplish any of these."

This all sounded reasonable. But I wasn't being reasonable lately. I thought myself beyond reasonable—and beyond redemption.

"David, I want you to think about what I'm saying, and I want you to think very seriously about how you testify. What you decide can affect your getting into college, your choice of career, even who your friends and family are."

"Family?" I said, hearing a key word.

"Your own family. Whom you marry. We're not talking about a misdemeanor here, David. We're talking about a felony. That's not going to be something passed over lightly. It will follow you for the rest of your life." My father's tone softened, as if he realized, which was true, that this aggressive approach wasn't working. "We have an excellent lawyer who can present your case, perhaps without your having to say a word. You had an accident. That's what he'll get across."

"But I'm guilty."

My father crossed his arms and stared at me. I could understand what a woman would see in him. His posture radiated competence, authority, trust, and the promise of care. "Not if it's not true."

What did he mean? *Not if it's not true.* Not true that you're not guilty? Or not true that you're guilty? When I took the sentence apart in my head, the two parts negated each other and rendered the words meaningless. It denied blame while avoiding a positively phrased plea of either guilt or innocence. Such a thing as I had done fractured truth and precluded the ability to talk about it in direct statements.

"You can't bring Sarah Vale back to life, David, if that's what you're trying to do. You can't be perfect"—he nodded at my book—"or saintly enough to redeem her death. I know what it's like, believe me."

I sat up in bed. "What?"

"I said, I know what it's like. I've had the same feelings. I know what it's like to bear the burden of someone's death."

I thought about the Olans' baby.

"It's different," I said. "You were trying to *save* people."

He sat with his hands on his knees, and I could smell the Old Spice after-shave lotion he used, and I did something odd. I reached up and touched his cheek. I hadn't touched his face in years, and I wanted to feel the stubble of his beard, feel what was starting to happen to my own face. He jumped at the surprise of my touch, then took my hand, my fingers, and gave them an affectionate tug. His eyes damp, he left the room.

—

When my mother came in, it was almost bedtime. She sat across from me, still on Adrian's bed, in the straight-backed desk chair. She had changed into her pajamas and a powder blue robe with silver satin lapels. I remembered she'd gotten the robe before she'd gone to the hospital her first time, years ago.

"How are you feeling?" she asked.

"Fine," I said. "How are you feeling?" It was something I would never think so reflexively to ask my father, who we assumed always felt fine, since he was a doctor and took care of other people. But something was changing for my mother too. "I think I'll move those bottles to the basement," she'd said yesterday. "I'm tired of looking at them." What had struck me was how she'd turned against them suddenly, as if she were turning against her own fragility, sick of it too.

"I'm happy to be home," said my mother. She'd been leaving the house three afternoons a week to attend a pottery class in Swarthmore. While at the hospital this last visit, she'd learned to throw pots in occupational therapy, and her doctor had recommended she continue at home. When she would come back from class, her hands would be caked with dry clay, her jeans dusty with white powder. Wearing a discarded white dress shirt of my father's, its tails hanging over her jeans, she'd plop down on the silk couch—an unthinkable act!—and sigh heavily. "God, I'm beat," she'd say. The activity exhausted her, took all her concentration; I'd never seen her so involved in anything outside housework and felt elated for her and apprehensive at the sudden changes. Dishes stayed in the sink overnight; laundry piled up, unless we all did our own. As for my father and her, they appeared to be marking out new territory—that is, my father appeared to be stepping back in deference to her newly drawn territorial line: pottery, rejected housework, no makeup, and sloppy clothes pushing out her previous borders.

"I suppose you're here to ask too that I go along with an innocent plea," I said.

"I'm here to apologize," said my mother. "If I had been home, this wouldn't have happened." She pulled her robe closed and tucked her arms into her stomach, leaning slightly forward on them.

"It's nobody's fault but my own," I said. I couldn't stand to hurt my mother or have her blame herself. She was doing so well now, and I wanted to protect her.

"What is it, David?" she said, so softly it made me shiver.

"Nothing," I said. "Nothing." Meaning nothing mattered, but I couldn't get the words past the stone in my throat. "I'm horrible," I said. "I don't want to go anywhere. I can't face anyone. I can't imagine facing anyone again." And maybe because of the way I said it, or could barely say it, from some deep, wordless place in my stomach, my mother saw for the first time what I was talking about, how scared I was of myself. She had tears in her eyes too.

She came over and sat beside me on the bed. "David, we're going to stand behind you. Your family. You don't have to go through this alone. Does that make sense to you?"

"Yes," I said.

"Do you mind me going to my class in the afternoons? Is it all right to leave you alone then?"

"It's fine," I said. "I want you to go. It makes you happy, doesn't it?"

She took my hand. I could feel the dry caked clay in the grooves of the skin. This clay was to be part of my mother's hands now. "Stay for a minute," I said, and she let me hold her hand for a long time.

One afternoon, a week before the trial, I was left alone in the house. Adrian was at camp, my mother was out at her pottery class, and my father at work. Theoretically, if I had dared, I could have left the house. Even the police came by less often, every other day now, or just called to speak with me on the phone to make sure I wasn't driving around. It had been two months since the accident. Yet I couldn't imagine walking out the front door any more than I could jumping onto an electrical fence, which is what it would have felt like to face anyone. I'd go from Adrian's room and the stack of books surrounding the bed to the living room, where I sat at the picture window (my mother had indeed removed the bottle collection to the basement, in preparation for her pottery, which had begun to appear) and watched the baseball players across the street, the family picnickers, the lovers on the grass. And I'd go to the kitchen. I was starved all the time. I'd take Jell-O and oranges and leftover pot roast back to my room and eat voraciously, and privately. I didn't like to eat downstairs, with the curtains open. I worried that people were driving by, pointing out our house, glancing in the windows.

I took off my clothes and looked at myself in my parents' dressing room mirror: I could see my ribs. My hipbones jutted out like saddle horns. My calves, under the cover of a light blanket of dark hair, were slender cones. My pectoral muscles finally had lost their boyish in-distinguishable smoothness, but what definition there was looked drawn on with chalk. On the other hand, the dark hair around my groin had sprouted thick and spongy as if from heavy hormonal rains, virgin growth in long-barren fields. My penis, after years of a sec-ondary existence, a small plug as inconspicuous as a valve on a child's swimming pool float, was now quite impressive, especially from a side view, my testicles a weighty sack beneath the sloped, trunklike organ that was a good deal more plump and sturdy and thick and glinting with purple-veined engorgement than I could have imagined two months ago. Although I had forbidden myself to touch it for pleasure, just standing in my parents' dressing room closet watching myself in the full-length mirror, letting the air tickle my skin, had produced an erection that unfurled vigorously before my eyes. I marveled that my body flourished with complete disregard for all that was happening, under its own laws of evolutionary will.

The doorbell rang. I had brought up last night's leftover spaghetti and set it on the floor while I looked in the mirror. When I heard the bell and started for it, I accidentally kicked the plate, and the tomato sauce oozed onto my parents' carpet. I didn't know what to do. If I stopped to clean it up, the police, who I assumed it to be, might leave. I threw a towel over the spot, pulled my clothes on, and ran downstairs.

It wasn't Officers Chavez and Merle. It was Dana Asher, a six-teen-year-old classmate, her copper hair parted down the precise cen-ter of her head and hanging loose on her smooth shoulders, small, rounded golden mounds, which also applied to her breasts, visible inside the brilliant, yellow-marigold bathing suit top that she wore along with cutoff jeans.

I was hungry, famished, ravenous, and I backed away from the door, aware in the instant of her appearance, seeing in her health and vigor, how lonely and disgusting I was, *devouring food in my room*, and what the hell was she *doing* here?

"Hi, David," she said, and lifted one of her caramel shoulders in a shy, awkward greeting.

I stood there, my hand on the doorknob. "Hi, Dana."

"Aren't you going to ask me in?"

"Why?" I said.

She laughed. *"Why?"*

"I mean, did you come by to—" I wanted to say "sell something." Dana was a cheerleader and Pep Squad captain, and they were always selling candy or seeds or magazines to raise money for the teams. "Pick something up?"

"I came by to see you, silly," she said.

"Oh." I moved back from the door. "Come on in," I said. The only other person who had come to visit me was the rabbi. We'd spoken about Martin Buber when he saw what I'd been reading. I'd been disappointed when he couldn't stay longer, though I acted fine. He'd gone downstairs and talked in soft tones with my parents before he left.

"Thanks," Dana said after she stepped inside. She smiled. Dana had perfect teeth, without need of braces, a stunning wide grin that was her trademark as captain of the cheerleaders' squad. She would climb to the top of a pyramid, thrust her pompoms into the air, and without removing her blazing smile, stretched tight as a drumskin, ventriloquially manage to scream, *"Go, Bulldogs!"* at which point she'd swan-dive to the thrilled oohs and ahs of the crowd into the waiting arms of the two male cheerleaders below.

We stood in the foyer. "Can we talk somewhere?" Dana asked.

"Sure," I said, and went with her into the living room. I sat down at one end of the couch. Dana sat at the other. She pulled her legs up under her on the sofa. I was aware that I was staring at her feet, as much because my mother never allowed us to put our feet on the couch as because her toenails were painted a pale shade of pink, something that was probably called Passion Shell, or whatever toenail polish was named. I also simply could not look her in the eye.

"How are you doing, David?"

"All right," I said. "I wasn't expecting visitors."

"I know," she said. "I heard you were . . . you know, required to stay home."

"House arrest," I said.

Dana nodded and smiled at me, but it wasn't, I thought, a warm smile, nor was it the cheerleading one she used to work the stands, her come-on-everybody-let's-hear-it! smile. I imagined a girl like Dana, as pretty as she was, as tan and sexy and popular and fortunate never to have run anybody over, had a million smiles. But this smile, a little too tight, even for a social smile, a little too forced, made me uncomfortable and alert to something. Some little voice said, watch it, watch it.

"Is it hard being stuck here all day?"

"No," I said. "I prefer it actually." I saw Dana look at me, maybe for the first time, at my arms, which were bare because I was wearing a T-shirt.

"You look different, David," she said.

"I've grown a little bit," I said, and crossed my arms so they would seem more muscular, meaty.

"Yeah," she said, "you have. Stand up," she demanded.

"What?"

"Stand up."

"All right," I said, and slowly got off the couch.

"Turn around."

"Why?"

"Oh, you," she said, and put her hands on my hips and twisted me around until my back was to her. "There," she said, and then pressed her back up to mine. She shifted her buttocks against me. "Let's stand closer," she said, and pressed herself into me even tighter. That I would have imagined even ten minutes ago I would be standing butt to butt with Dana Asher, head of the Bulldogs' cheerleading squad, would have been laughable. But here she was passing her hand across the tops of our heads, trying to determine how much taller I was than she now.

She broke apart and said, "Geez, I remember when I was taller than you."

"Well," I said, "I've nothing else to do around here except grow." A comment that Dana laughed at, generously, I thought, extending it—her laughter—until I became uncomfortable. "Can I get you something to drink?" I asked.

"What do you have?"

"Soda, lemonade, ice water—"

"Beer?"

"I think so." My father liked to drink beer when he came home from work.

"Well?"

"All right," I said, and got her a Budweiser from the extra refrigerator in the basement, rushing back up with it.

Dana was looking at my mother's pottery. "Who did this?" she asked.

"My mother," I said.

"Your mother? Is she home?"

"Now?"

"No, I mean, is she—"

"Yes," I said, realizing what she meant. It was a small community, and of course everybody knew each other's business. I don't know why it should have surprised me that Dana and everyone else would talk about us, would know my mother had breakdowns and went for treatment to a private hospital, and I suddenly understood why Dana was here. Her mother worked as a volunteer for the Ladies Auxiliary at Chester-Crozer Hospital and had no doubt encouraged Dana, help-mate like herself to the less fortunate, to pay me a visit. Her mother knew my father, as she did all the doctors, and respected him, and yes, I could imagine the exact conversation about what a shame, it was, how heartbroken "that boy's parents must be," why don't you pay him a visit sometime, it would be a real act of kindness. . . .

"Hey," said Dana, mimicking opening the bottle with her teeth.

"I'll get a bottle opener."

"What about you?" she called after me as I went toward the kitchen. "Don't you want one?"

"I don't think so," I said.

I came back with the bottle opener. "So you don't take even a little sip once in a while?" asked Dana. "That's not what I heard, David."

"What do you mean?"

"I heard you and your buddies drink quite a bit."

I cocked my head, hearing the note of . . . what? Teasing? Or was it something else? Anger. Perhaps seeing the confusion on my face made Dana walk up to me and tap the neck of the bottle against my chest. "Come on, loosen up. Aren't your parents gone?"

"My mother will be back later."

"How later?" she said.

She brushed her breasts against me.

I felt as if I were in some kind of stage production: *The Fantasies of David Nachman.* As if a producer had come by and said, "Okay, kid, give me whatever you got, come on, let me see." I couldn't imagine *any* reason in the world why Dana Asher, the most alluring siren in our whole school, had come here to fulfill my sexual desires, but here she was rubbing her body up against mine and coaxing me sweetly to take a sip of the beer that rose up cold and stiff between our throats.

"All right," I said, and opened the bottle, taking a sip.

Dana pulled away from me, twisting her hips. I imagined that underneath her jean shorts was the bottom of her two-piece marigold bathing suit. Meanwhile, I was in a day-old T-shirt and baggy corduroy pants. Shoeless, my toenails were unclipped.

"I've never seen your house," said Dana. "Where's your room? This way?" She grabbed the large beach bag she'd come in with and headed for the upstairs. I followed, as if in a trance. A month or so ago I hadn't been much interested in girls; they'd had no power over me, and now they had nothing but power, and if Dana had asked me to walk off the roof with her, I would have done so. I didn't care that she was here because her mother made her visit or because she felt sorry for me. Out of pity, out of charity, what did it matter? Something in me was dazzled enough not to care, to forget what I had done, to bury it in desire.

Dana walked down the hall, brushing her hand lightly over the wall. She glanced in my parents' bedroom, and we wandered in there. "Can I use the bathroom?"

"Sure," I said, and she went into my parents' bathroom, something else, like sitting on the couch, we never did. When she came out, I was still standing in the same spot. Dana sat down on the edge of my parents' bed, two twin mattresses pushed together. My mother wasn't sleeping here now; she was staying in the guest room. I suppose that meant they were separated but living together. As it was, with my father at work and my mother at her pottery class—she sometimes stayed into the evening for extra time on the wheel—they rarely saw each other, and I was often, as today, the only person home. The house, large as it was, felt lonely and deserted, as if the family members who once resided here only visited now.

"So," Dana said, "you want to talk about what happened?"

"What happened?"

"Your accident." She crossed her legs, and I saw the muscle in her thigh raise, from all that leaping and jumping, those high scissors kicks and exuberant splits. Dana was also a swimmer and a gymnast, always at the lunch table with the jocks. Once again I wondered what she was doing here. Her mother, yes, but suddenly that didn't seem right.

"Is that why you came by?"

"I guess I'm just curious what really happened," she said. "Everybody is. Were you actually racing like people say?"

"Is that what people say?"

"That's the rumor," said Dana, and she turned her knees toward me. "Wouldn't it be good to get it off your chest? You can tell me."

Then we both heard it, and there wasn't need anymore to pretend. A small click, then a whirring, then a screeching. Dana shot a look my way and said, "Um, I'd better go. I have to be home early," and she grabbed her big beach bag, which I'm sure did have her suntan lotion and a colorful towel for the Wallingford Swim Club, but also a tape recorder, a small reel-to-reel one like the kind I had that frequently malfunctioned, as hers obviously had, and that she no doubt had intended to play for the kids at the swim club, my taped confession. "Bye," she said, and flew down the stairs.

I walked into my parents' dressing room and lifted the towel from the rug. The blood-red spot had spread and congealed into their carpet. I sat down next to it and looked at it and imagined Dana laughing and telling her story with embarrassment and glee to everybody at the pool. All the lifeguards would crowd around to hear what had happened. Dana would put a hand to her mouth as she got to the part about the tape getting eaten. It would mean nothing to them that I was sitting here looking at this stained carpet, nothing to anybody.

I wandered into my parents' bedroom and then into their bathroom. I opened my mother's medicine cabinet and found the Valium I knew she used for her spells. I took one, then another, then three more, then the whole bottle, and what I remember was going back to the carpet and trying to clean up the mess I'd made before I fell down and blacked out.

Thirty-six hours later I woke up in Chester-Crozer Hospital. I came to nauseated, opening my eyes and seeing the creamy yellow moon outside the window. I had a crushing sense of failure at not being dead. My mother and father were at my bedside, my mother's eyes puffy and red from crying. My mother had been the one to find me when she came home from class.

I said, "I'm sorry," and then fell back asleep until morning.

I was discharged from the hospital in the care of my parents and two weeks later stood in the courtroom next to Lance Schnabel to enter a revised plea. I'd gotten a haircut the day before so my hair was bristle short, shorn of springy curls, devoid of creams or gels.

The judge asked if my counsel was satisfactory to me. "It is your right as a juvenile to be informed that an attorney hired by your parents could represent their interests over yours. Is this clear?"

I nodded.

"What is your plea then?" the judge asked.

"Guilty," I said quietly.

"Is this admission of your own free will, David, and not under the influence of alcohol or narcotics?"

"Yes," I said.

"Have you discussed this matter thoroughly with your parents?"

"I have."

"You understand by admitting to the charge, you're waiving your right to a trial by a judge and to call witnesses?"

"I understand."

"Have you spoken with your attorney about all the rights you are waiving with this plea?"

"I have."

He turned to Lance Schnabel. "Your client is not presently under mental duress or suffering from mental instability?" the judge asked him.

There was a pause. "He is not," said Lance Schnabel. My parents sat in the first row directly behind me. I could hear my mother breathing hard. The Vales had been advised to stay home since there was no testimony to be given.

"You are satisfied then your client is entering this plea knowingly and of his own free will?"

"I am," said Lance Schnabel.

"Disposition will take place on August eleventh, at ten A.M."

I was released back to the custody of my parents.

In return for my pleading guilty, the charge of vehicular homicide had been reduced to reckless driving resulting in death. Whether on August 11 the judge would sentence me to reform school or put me on probation remained uncertain, Lance Schnabel had told us. I lay awake much of the night before August 11. When I came downstairs in the morning, my mother was in the wing-back chair, dozing. My father had canceled all his appointments, the first time I ever remembered him doing that.

The Vales came into the hearing room. I knew it was them, without even looking around. Lance Schnabel sat next to me and patted my shoulder once or twice while we waited for the judge to finish readying his papers, the longest few minutes of my life, it seemed. A probation officer made notes at the table across from me. She'd given me a battery of psychological tests and interviewed my parents and teachers, without giving us a hint of her findings. Her recommendations would be a strong factor in the judge's ruling.

He finally looked up and past me to the Vales. "I have the deepest sympathy for your loss, a tremendous burden that no parent should have to bear. As a father myself I cannot convey how difficult it is for me to conduct a proceeding like this."

The judge turned his gaze toward me. "Mr. and Mrs. Vale have lost someone more dear to them than their own lives, and your parents have lost their son as they knew him. These are harsh words, David. But there is no way I or anyone can soften the result of your carelessness."

He looked down a moment, then folded his hands together in front of him. "I am, however, cognizant of your remorse, which the court has considered strongly in its determination. It is the decision of this court, after reviewing the submitted psychological, school, and home evaluations, that you be allowed to remain in a familiar environment that can support and care for you. Additionally, as you have no previous record and do not appear to be at risk for further criminal violations, I am suspending a sentence of three years to Glen Mills School for Boys and placing you on probation." I heard two gasps simultaneously, one of relief from my mother, the other an expulsion of air from the Vales. "As part of your probation you will see a social worker once a week until you graduate or the probation department determines such treatment is no longer necessary. One more thing, David. To begin your grown-up existence under these circumstances will be near to impossible, but you have parents who love you. I urge you to find hopeful ways to face your life in the shadow of this tragedy."

The judge pounded his gavel. I felt relief and dread, a dim awareness that I wouldn't have to leave my parents, a fearful freedom to be suddenly part of the world, a hundred conflicting emotions.

I turned around and walked over to my parents. I let them move me between them soundlessly down the aisle. I was being careful not to look at the Vales, but some part of me—perhaps the part that wanted to be hopeful—did look up and saw in an instant their fixed grief, the corners of both their mouths pulled down in frozen silence, their stunned looks that it was over, this was all. They had agreed reluctantly to the plea bargain. They had wanted to hear me testify in court about exactly what had happened, and they had wanted greater restitution, personally from me, and from my parents, a matter that was proceeding on its own with the insurance company.

I did owe them more—and more and more. How much more they could never imagine. No one could except me. I, in short, owed them my life. That was why I had wound up in the hospital in the first place and why I have tried for so many years afterward to get back what I so willingly threw away.

2

F I V E

I went back to school in the fall. I spent my time studying and ig-
noring the whispers in the hall. "That's the guy who ran over the
little girl," I heard every day of my first week. I spoke to no one,
didn't raise my hand in class, jogged around the track by myself during
gym, and sat in the first seat of the bus looking blankly out the window on the way home. I was prepared for something to happen, and
when nothing did, I wasn't disappointed, just lonely. It's a strange
thing to be lonely for contact, even threatening contact, but that's
better than none at all. After a while I was so good at moving in a
narrow space, my own airless corridor, that people stopped staring at
me in the halls.

At the difficult times, such as lunch, I would sit at a table in back
near the milk machine. The kids who ate here were irregulars—that
is, they changed from day to day, unlike most of the other tables that
had been claimed by various groups and cliques, one of which, however ratty with its leather jackets and greasy hair, I had formerly belonged to. This one, the milk machine table, as it was called, was for

leftovers and mostly the kids who sat there did so in order to study throughout lunch for a test. I sat at the far end watching the wall. At two minutes to one I folded my aluminum foil up into a tight square and deposited it in the trash can on the south end of the cafeteria. That left me exactly thirty-eight seconds to make it upstairs, enough time not to have to linger in the stairwell or do anything but take my seat in world history. I knew, after a while, how many minutes and seconds it took between each class and what direction I could go to make it from one class to another without time left over. I didn't use the bathroom because the one time I'd done this, somebody—I didn't know who because they'd come up behind me while I was standing at the urinal, two of them, I think—had smacked the back of my head with a heavy textbook; my nose rammed against the tile, spouting blood. I stopped it up with tissues, told no one about the incident, and it never happened again.

Then too, I avoided the bathroom after that and would simply hold it, impossible as that was sometimes, until I got home.

Life the rest of the time was more promising because I spent what remained of my day at my father's office, helping him. Alice, my father's receptionist, had cut down her hours because she was having back problems, and rather than my father's hiring anybody additional, I'd persuaded him to let me fill in for two hours every afternoon. I'd answer the phones, schedule appointments, track X rays, and do as much as I could with the mound of paperwork on the desk.

One afternoon my father said he wanted to speak with me about something. I expected it would be about school. I'd lately been called in by the same guidance counselor, Mr. Shelley, who had spoken with my father and me the year before. He'd asked how I was doing since "all this happened," not able to bring himself to say what it was exactly but referring, I supposed, to Sarah Vale as well as to my suicide attempt.

I said I was doing just fine and waited. "Your teachers tell me you're very quiet in class, David," he said.

"I don't have much to say," I said.

He glanced down at my file, which was on his desk. "Doing any sports this semester?"

"No," I said. I'd never done any sports, at least not since seventh grade, when I'd played on the hundred-pound football team, before puberty had separated the boys from the men, the jocks from the rest of us.

"You're not still seeing Mr. Randazzo and Mr. Quint, are you, David?" The less Mr. Shelley liked somebody the more likely he was to call him by his last name. I hadn't seen Crow and Vic since my suicide attempt. They'd left me alone, as if aware of how dangerous I was, to myself, if to no one else. They hadn't tried to visit, and they hadn't come back to school this year. Chuckie had, but he was in Business Education, a track that had its own wing, as did the academic program that I was in. I'd passed him a few times in the hall; we'd made eye contact and gone on, he more embarrassed than I.

"I don't see them anymore."

"That's terrific," Mr. Shelley said. "That's really terrific you can make that a reality." Things were going to be extraordinary for me, in his opinion. His phone rang. He put his hand over the mouthpiece. "Could we continue this later, David?" he asked.

"Sure," I said, more than glad to leave, although a little disappointed too. I went through whole days at school without speaking a word to anyone. In small groups, which our English teacher put us in frequently, I simply sat mute and took notes, the secretary.

"We'll talk more," he said, giving me the okay sign. As I left, I heard him speaking about insurance premiums for his car, a sporty new apple-red Mustang all the kids had gathered around one day in the parking lot when he first drove it to school.

Now my father took me into his office and sat behind his desk. At ten after six he had finally finished up with his last patient, a thirteen-year-old boy with asthma whose attacks were severe enough to land him in the hospital. Hysterical that her son couldn't breathe, the boy's mother had called our house at two that morning. My father had met her at Chester-Crozer Hospital, and the boy had been stabilized on a prescription of aqueous epinephrine. After the boy had been discharged two hours later, my father had gone home, gotten an hour more of sleep, then arrived at the office by eight. The boy had slept all day and come in for the last appointment, although my father would have seen him regardless.

"David," he said, "do you remember the Olans?"

"Yes," I said, having not thought about them in years. They were no longer patients of my father since they'd moved out of the area, and I associated them with catastrophe and perhaps a turning point in our family, my mother going into the hospital, my father burrowing even further into his practice, and, perhaps, my spinning out of control.

And Josie, his young nurse.

But then too I was always trying to find the thread of it all.

"I was remembering the family today, and I thought of something I wanted to tell you that happened to me when I was a boy." My father paused a moment, glanced down at his hands. He had replaced his black horn-rimmed frames with light brown ones that made him look younger. My mother and he still slept in separate rooms, but they were respectful to each other and didn't fight; they'd become quieter together, more tempered, watchful. Of me, I suppose. Then too my mother went six days a week for classes to the pottery center in Swarthmore. She had a friend, Mr. Richardson, whom she had met through her classes, an older man, a bachelor. One day I would understand he was gay, but at the time he was just a kindly gentleman, with silver hair and a mustache neat as a puzzle piece, who picked my mother up for class and spent time with her.

"My sister, Bea, was in the hospital with influenza. She was four years older than I and played piano very well. My parents had gone without, as my mother used to say, so they could afford a piano for her. Bea watched me, hovered over me, babied me, and although I

80

complained about her, I was quite attached to her and upset that she had suddenly gone from our house in Wilmington, where we lived at the time. My father worked as a presser there, and my mother took in people's laundry that I would deliver.

"Around midnight one evening there's a knock on the door. I'm only nine years old, the same age as you were that night you followed me to the Olans' house. I'm not supposed to be up. My mother has given me strict orders to stay in bed and sleep, for fear I'll wind up sick and in the hospital like my sister. But I've left my room and gone to the top of the stairs. Both my father and mother go downstairs to open the front door. It's a policeman. I hear him whispering to my parents, and then my mother puts a hand over her mouth and makes a sharp, painful noise, like an animal yelping.

"The policeman leaves, and my mother and father walk up the stairs. My father is holding my mother around the shoulders; she is weeping so hard her whole body shakes. I am frozen at the top of the stairs, even though I know I will get in trouble. When they see me, they look down, only barely noting that I am there. 'Go to your room,' says my father. 'Is it about Bea?' I ask. 'Everything is fine,' he says. But I know it isn't. I know he has lied to me. I know that my sister has died and that the policeman has been sent by the hospital to tell my parents and that from this point on everything will be different for me.''

My father sat a moment with his head in his hands. "That's when I decided to be a doctor. I thought the night when you followed me to the Olans that's what you had decided too. I see how unfair this was for me to assume."

I had a lump in my throat, whether for me or my father I didn't know. I didn't like to think about his family, or lack of it. Unlike my mother with her two sisters and brother, my father had no other siblings, and though I'd known about Bea, I'd never known exactly what had happened to her.

In the outer office I could hear the phone ringing and ringing.

Someone should get it, I thought. My feet wanted to run for it. But my father sat in his high-backed brown leather chair and just waited for my answer.

"I don't think I will be a doctor," I said. My father fixed his eyes on me. He was understandably surprised. I'd been coming here every day after school and throwing myself into work, everything from refilling paper towel dispensers to keeping the drug reps company while they waited for my father to have a spare minute. How could I not be considering this? What was I doing here then?

"I'm sorry to hear you say that, David. I was hoping you'd even want to join me."

When I said nothing, my father removed his glasses and rubbed the bridge of his nose a moment. "You have to start thinking about colleges in any case," he said. "Have you any in mind? Do you want to be in New York with Adrian?"

"I want to stay around here." I had the thought that I would continue working for my father while I went to school. I told him this.

"You just said you didn't want to be a doctor."

"I don't. But I still want to work here."

He started to take a cigarette out from his desk drawer, then thought better of it and closed the drawer with both hands, keeping his fingers against the front, as if to hold back his impulse and temptation. He carried packets of Chiclets in his lab coat pocket and chewed them by the handful. "Where are you thinking you'd like to go then?"

"Temple," I said. "I could commute there at night and work here during the day."

"You don't need to work here, David," he said. "You're a great help, and the patients and their families are fond of you, but you need to concentrate on school full-time."

"I want to continue helping," I said. "It's important to me."

"Maybe you'll change your mind about medicine once you're in

82

school. We have a long way before you need to decide." He took out a pack of Chiclets, tilted the box toward his mouth.

"I won't change my mind," I said.

The moment I answered I felt an enormous relief: My life, in a small way, was back to being mine. Though he'd been trying to let me know that out of tragedy—his sister dying—could come some good and that I was like him in this way, I was in fact not like him. I didn't think an equation of my healing others in return for what I'd done would be the answer to my pain, as it had been for him. It was not that simple. It had been simple to follow him to the Olans' house and to carry his doctor's bag on the way home, but all that had come after was not simple.

Only a week before, I had been riveted by *Oedipus Rex* in English class. We'd avoided all the symbolic Freudian issues of Oedipus sleeping with his mother, although there had been a few titters when Mr. Lincoln said that Oedipus had served in a "husbandly capacity to his mother" after murdering his father unknowingly at a crossroads.

Our discussion had focused almost entirely on whether Oedipus could be blamed for what had been predicted for him by the gods since birth.

I spoke from the back. "I think the point is that Oedipus had choices all along the way to avoid his fate, but he didn't see them as choices."

Mr. Lincoln, who was in his twenties, wore jeans and had shaggy hair that lapped at his ears, flouting the dress code we thought existed for teachers too. Startled by my voice, he looked at me. I'd broken my silence for the first time in six months. "Would you elaborate, David?"

The entire class had turned around to watch me. "Oedipus didn't have to kill his father, King Laius. It wasn't his only choice. His rage got the best of him. He overreacted."

"But, David," said Mr. Lincoln, seeing an opportunity to draw me out, "Oedipus was under attack. Certainly he can't be blamed for striking out in self-defense. He had no idea the man was his father."

" 'Swiftly I hit him with my staff; he rolled out of his carriage, flat upon his back. I killed them all.' It's that 'I killed them all' that shows his zeal," I said. "That's his doing alone. That's the step beyond his fate—that satisfaction and arrogance."

"Still, David, that just suggests the excitement of the moment. His adrenaline, if you will. It doesn't mean he had any choice, does it?"

"He bears the responsibility for what he did."

I could feel the class shift uncomfortably, as if all of them were aware that we—I—were talking about this on a personal level. I was impatient for swift justice, intolerant of anyone, like Oedipus, whose behavior had twisted the idea of murder into the realm of grotesque misfortune.

"I believe the issue of responsibility cannot be answered so easily in the view of Sophocles," said Mr. Lincoln. "Unless we decide he is just telling us the gods are toying with Oedipus. Notice that the intersection where Oedipus slays King Laius has three roads. Fate may be one road, free will another. Irony is perhaps the third road that we all go down, but for whom is this irony played out in our own lives?"

Mr. Lincoln had lost the class. He'd made that fatal error of being too pleased by his own analysis and words. He'd looked up flushed from his speech, and we all were mute. He apologized immediately for going on, but by that time I was already thinking about the end of the play, how Oedipus shows no mercy toward himself, no compassion, striking out his eyes and exiling himself, as willful in his self-punishment as he is in his violence against the king. And I understood that I'd come to the same sort of decision: that what I had once wanted most, to be a doctor, to follow my father, to be a part of a family of doctors, was not to happen. I would forbid myself that future. I would be the son of a doctor, the brother of a doctor perhaps, but not a doctor myself. I would poke out my eyes, in my own way.

I was sitting one afternoon at the top of the parking lot steps, waiting for the bus home, when Paul Vale came up to me.

"Hi, David," he said. I'd been looking up, an unusual position for me. I tried to keep my head buried in a book, or my eyes on some distant point in the landscape while I waited for the bus, a time when people were likely to be talking, these social interludes between the business of classes. But lately, because it was April, and spring was here and the trees had leafed out and the lilacs had budded promising their dizzying fragrance and the earth was moist from the early rains, I couldn't keep to my strict regimen of focusing only on my books or my teachers' faces. My feet made soft impressions on the field that I crossed after the bus left me off. Nature was cracking through the carapace I'd built of my shame, and I frequently got stuck daydreaming, wondering what I'd do this summer, whether I should go for a walk or a swim or throw a ball in the air or even just talk to someone. Or go for a drive. I could drive now. Two weeks ago my mother had said, "I've got a surprise for you," and taken me to the motor vehicles department to pass my test, get my license finally.

Afterward she'd handed me the keys to the car; we no longer had the F-85, which my father had traded in for the benefit of everyone after the accident. I'd driven slowly, very slowly. We'd stopped at Howard Johnson's in Media and had a Coke, and my mother said I could borrow her car if I wanted to go to a movie or down the shore. Was there a friend I'd like to go with?

There wasn't, but I didn't want to disappoint her, so I said I was sure I could find someone. I don't think my parents had any idea how lonely I was at school, how much I kept to myself. On Saturdays I worked all day at my father's office; on Sundays I'd read in my room or take walks in the park, sit by the creek and read some more. My mother had looked pained, hopeful, and nervous when she'd asked me if I had a friend. Her hair was tied in back, and she wore a summer dress, light green with bright yellow daisies. Her fingers wrapped around her Coke tightly. I tried to gauge how tightly. I'd noted for so long every twist of her fingers, every tremor of her small shoulders. She was little, light. I was always surprised to see her in a bathing suit—how large her breasts were actually. Of her two sisters and her brother, she was the only one who had gone to college. And unlike them, who were talkers, she listened—maybe too hard. When I had so little to say, and spent so much energy holding back every feeling I had, pretending that a solitary routine was pleasing, it was almost unbearable to sit in front of her at a table and have her gentle attention upon me. "I want to drive some more," I'd said abruptly at Howard Johnson's, and I'd popped up from the table.

"Hi, Paul," I said now. It wasn't that I hadn't seen Paul around school. He'd been there. He'd seen me. I'd catch him looking at me, not with malice or bitterness, more with curiosity, at least that's what I supposed it was. Curiosity about how I felt seeing him. I wasn't prepared for that reaction, for that scrutiny; I expected anger, simple hostility or glaring resentment, coolness even, not this open wonder about me, this concern for how I was doing. Such generosity chased me away faster than any rebuke.

"Your bus is late," he said.

"It will come soon. It's always a little late." What was he doing here? He practiced track and cross-country and was in the band. Why wasn't he at one of his many extracurricular activities?

"You want a ride?" he said.

"A ride where?" I couldn't think.

"I don't know," said Paul. "I can give you a ride home if that's what you want. I thought we could just talk."

86

I looked at Paul's letter jacket. Varsity track, swimming, and golf—the school's newest sport. He had his blond hair cut short, freckles on his nose, and I'd have had to be blind—Oedipus—not to notice the resemblance to his sister. He had a brother, Russell, in eighth grade, and then there had been Sarah, a mistake, Paul had told me on our outing to the Phillies game, our brief attempt at friendship, our love for baseball not enough to bind us together as we sat between innings eating hot dogs and I searched my brain for something to talk about with him: his family. Why his sister was so much younger than he. A mistake, he'd said, joking, intending for me to understand that of course she wasn't a mistake now, they loved her, he could call her a mistake only because she'd been born and loved and cherished and his parents hadn't used birth control, and we were two thirteen-year-olds giggling about sex, trying to sound knowledgeable.

"Okay, thanks," I said, and lifted myself stiffly, carefully, from the steps, a breeze blowing my shirt open at the neck. I thought of last year when I'd worn only half-buttoned-up white shirts (minus any chest hair) under my leather jacket with its jangling slew of zippers. I wore chinos now, nondescript Arrow shirts with stays in the collars, and a thin maroon belt like my father. In fact, I looked like him, except for his white lab coat.

I followed Paul down the steps to his car. "You're not going to practice?" I asked. Which practice I didn't know. I just assumed he had some practice.

"The teachers have a meeting," he said.

"That's right," I said, remembering this.

We got into his car, his parents' car actually, a Buick Riviera. I hadn't counted on this. I'd thought Paul would be driving his beat-up Rambler. He'd worked over the summers to save up for it. "Where's your car?"

"It died," he said, and I nodded, but thought that the word hung in the air too long.

I sat in the front, on the white leather bucket seat. I couldn't imagine what his parents would think of this. And I wondered for a moment if I were being set up again, as with Dana Asher. A ruse to make me confess or take me somewhere and drop me off with cement shoes in the Schuylkill. I decided it didn't matter; if that's what Paul Vale (and unseen others) had in mind, fine. I'd let it happen. I was tired of avoiding this, of my own self-imposed solitary confinement. I'd get it over with and I'd either survive or I wouldn't, but I couldn't live with such aloneness anymore.

"How are your classes?" asked Paul. "You have Mr. McPhillips for math?"

"Yes," I said, and tried to think of something neutral to add. "Mr. McPhillips fell asleep while we were doing problems, and Jackie Dimateo managed to stick an apple in his mouth for a couple of seconds."

Paul laughed. "So where do you want me to take you?" I looked out the window. We were driving down Providence Road.

"You can just drop me off at my house. I have to drive into Chester."

"I'll take you. You going to your father's office?"

"You don't have to," I said.

"No, I'll take you."

I thought a moment about whether to be suspicious of his insistence, then decided it was all right. "Okay, if you don't mind."

"It's fine." He merged onto Route 320, the way into Chester. "My parents are both at the diner with my brother. I don't have to be there until five."

I nodded, though I listened for any hint about myself, what his parents thought, what Paul thought *they* might think of him driving me around. Once again I imagined some brutality or at the least a humiliation waiting at the end of the ride.

We pulled up to a light on Twenty-fourth Street, the beginning of Chester. The town had started changing: stores going out of business and being boarded up rather than being filled by new tenants.

The whites were leaving, fleeing to the suburbs. The synagogue where I'd gone until I was thirteen had moved to Sproul Estates, and most of the town's Jews with it. Many of the doctors were already gone, practices relocated in Media, Swarthmore, Springfield, Drexel Hill, and along Baltimore Pike—U.S. 1—a road that ran into Philadelphia one way and out to Concordville the other. I heard Paul say, "You know I'm not mad at you."

When you wait for something for so long, you don't actually hear it crisply. It's a disappointment, and your response is a disappointment. I'd thought I would say something back that showed how sorry I was or burst into tears or try to indicate one tenth of what I'd been feeling. Instead, hearing something I wasn't quite sure about, I said, "What do you mean?"

"I mean," said Paul, "that I don't blame *you*."

Which is what I thought I'd heard.

"I think if those greasers hadn't been there, none of this would have happened."

I saw Paul in ten years. He'd have a family. He'd be a coach for Little League. He'd have kids, more than one, less than five. He'd have a job somewhere, in the sciences. He'd have expectations for himself and his family, and those expectations would be met. I didn't want to think I had contributed to this rigidity in Paul, but I saw it forming before my eyes. He'd come to terms with what had happened, and his verdict was favorable to me, and I'd be fooling myself if I didn't admit that at the moment I felt enormous relief, near glee, at the thought we could blame this all on Crow, conspire together, Paul and I. A person whose opinion mattered was letting me off the hook. I could take this and go, the way was open, and whether I chose to sit in my cell or walk through the door was up to me, for Paul had unlocked it. I could envision our becoming friends; out of this tremendous misfortune we'd become like brothers. I had, in one version of my fantasies, imagined this, knowing that those looks Paul gave me in the hall were sympathetic, solicitous ones, his hand extended. I could see this, yet now I understood what it meant, what was the payment: I give up Crow, Vic, and Chuckie. But much as they deserved to be sold out, lowlifes that they were, I couldn't do it.

"It was my fault," I said.

"You were forced off the road."

"Pardon?"

"You got cut off, didn't you? That's what I heard. Crow tried to scare you and made you swerve."

I thought about this a moment. It was possible certainly, not beyond Crow; maybe my hand hadn't slipped; maybe I had reacted to some slight but aggressive nudge of the back of his car, like a brontosaurus swishing its tail; maybe it had happened that way, despite my memory, which played the incident over and over.

"I don't remember it that way," I said. "We were racing, but Crow didn't cause me to lose control."

Silence. I wanted to fill it with something. Paul had pulled up in front of my father's office on Ninth Street, the purple-brick building. Long ago Paul had once gone here too, as had many of my friends, who now saw doctors in the suburbs. My father's patients were almost all black now.

"Okay," said Paul, and then: "Still, you wouldn't have done that if it hadn't been for their egging you on, right?"

"I don't know," I said, then decided I could be fair to myself too. "It wasn't my idea, if that's what you mean. I didn't suggest it." I could allow this much. His face relaxed, his hands loosened around the wheel. I could see how much anguish he suffered too, trying to put it in order, get it right. We had something in common in this way. Crow wasn't wrestling with all this now; I knew that. "Thanks," I said, and put my hand on the door handle to leave. "I'm sorry," I added. I meant, I was sorry that I couldn't make it all the fault of Crow, a ready villain, but it came out that I was sorry about Sarah. I hadn't wanted to say that, because I knew I could never explain in those two words how really sorry I was and had pledged never to say as much until I found some way to make it clear. But Paul nodded, and he put his hand on my shoulder, a gesture he could have made to many people; he was always the one in gym class who was patting kids on the back when they missed a basketball pass or overthrew first base. He had a kind heart, and I wondered what I'd done to it.

"Where are you going to apply for college?" he asked.

"Temple, I think. How about you?"

"Williams, Dartmouth, Villanova. Penn State is my safe."

I nodded. It sounded thought out, a plan—one filled with possibilities. I looked at my father's office.

"Why are you staying around here?" said Paul.

"I thought I'd help my father."

"Oh," he said, and he gave me a curious look. "I'd have guessed you'd want to get away."

This was probably as close as Paul Vale would ever come to a snide remark, suggesting I leave town. Though it wasn't snide. Just surprised. Why *would* I want to stay? It was, I realized, the obvious question, what my father had wanted to know also. Didn't I want to go where no one would know me? Give myself all the advantages of a fresh start at an out-of-state college?

No, I didn't. I didn't have the confidence to leave. I knew myself here, despite all that had happened. "I suppose it's just easier," by which I meant, familiar. "You want to come in and say hello?" I asked. Why I'd offered this, I didn't know. Maybe I wanted to show my father that I was making progress; he and my mother no longer needed to worry: I wasn't a danger to myself. I was even with Paul Vale.

"I'd better go," said Paul, and our talk was over, as was our semblance of a friendship. If I expected him to invite me along with his group of buddies to a game at the Spectrum . . . well, I didn't. We'd had the conversation I'd been dreading since I knew I would be returning to school. It had gone better than I could have expected. What more did I want?

"See you," I said, leaning through the window. "Thanks for the ride."

"Good luck, David," he said. "At school and all," as if it were the last time we would talk before either of us went to college, and as it turned out, it was.

S I X

Things changed after my conversation with Paul Vale. Whether word
got around or I just let myself relax a little more, people treated me
differently. I can't say I became instantly popular and showered with
attention. Far from it. But small signs showed a change: Janet Buyers
smiled when she passed a paper back to me in biology. A senior, Frank
Taylor, saw me fumbling to find the right change for the milk machine and slipped a quarter in for me, saying, "There you go, David."
I didn't know him personally, but like most people in the school, he
knew me, or knew of me.

I had trouble accepting these small kindnesses. Part of me didn't
think I deserved them, or deserved them yet; it wasn't even a year
since the accident. But they kept happening until even I couldn't
deny that people were generally trying to be understanding. I still
kept in the back of my mind that somebody might come up behind
me and smack me in the head with a book, but that didn't stop me
now from using the bathrooms.

I even got invited to the Old Mill. The Old Mill was exactly what it sounded like, an old flour mill dating back to the 1700s. It had been restored into a gathering hall by the Borough of Rose Valley, and once or twice a year a few wealthy Rose Valley families gave a social there for the junior and senior classes. Everybody was invited, so it wasn't a big deal that I'd received an invitation. What mattered was that I was actually considering going. It was one thing to be at school, where every minute was—or could be, the way I'd arranged it—filled in. It was another to be at some party for the sole purpose of socializing, to have nothing but time on my hands and empty air in front of me.

Nevertheless, I sent back the RSVP that I would be attending. I told my mother I was going out on Saturday night to the Old Mill for a party, and her eyes brightened.

"That's wonderful, David. Can I help you?"

"Help me?"

"Do you want me to shop with you for a new suit?"

"I can wear what I have," I said. It was the one I'd worn to my hearing. "I guess I just wanted to ask if it was okay." I was hoping she'd say no.

"Okay to go?"

"Yes."

"Of course it is, David. Absolutely."

I shrugged. Somehow I'd decided to leave it up to my mother, make it her decision. "I need to borrow the car."

"Yes, by all means. Who are you taking?"

"I'm not taking anyone."

"Oh," said my mother. I could see her disappointment, what she'd imagined. A prom, buying a corsage for my date, photographs.

"I'm not planning to stay long," I said.

"However long you want is fine, David. It will be fun for you."

She said "fun" a little too confidently, too hopefully. It sure didn't feel as if it were going to be fun.

"Come say hello to Mr. Richardson," said my mother, and beckoned me to follow her out to the patio. She'd just returned from her pottery class, and brought Mr. Richardson with her. He sat out back on the patio reading the newspaper. I didn't know what they did all day long, but she'd found a companion, and my father didn't mind. I'd hear my mother and Mr. Richardson's voices. She'd ask his opinion about some fabric choices for curtains. He'd mention a book he was reading. They'd discuss which new bulbs to put in the tulip bed. They passed hours in the comfort of idle talk, which my father never allowed himself or wasn't interested enough to participate in with her.

I shook hands with Mr. Richardson, who rose in a courtly manner. Mr. Richardson stuttered a bit. He blinked rapidly when he asked me questions about school and what was my favorite subject and did I follow baseball. You could see he hadn't had much experience around kids.

"It's good to see you, D–David."

"Good to see you again," I said.

"You're doing well?"

"Fine," I said.

"Your mother says you've been working hard for your f-father."

"I do a little," I said.

I suppose I thought if I kept my answers short, that would prevent him from stuttering. I don't think it bothered him as much as it did me. It certainly didn't bother my mother. She'd gone inside to get something to drink from the kitchen. When she came back, Mr. Richardson and I were just standing there scraping our toes on the grout between the flagstones. It was unbearable.

"Don, you want a drink?" she said, carrying a pitcher of martinis out to him.

"Splendid," said Mr. Richardson.

"I'll see you later," I said.

"Stop in and say hello when you're d-downtown sometime," said Mr. Richardson. Semiretired, he worked part-time as a furniture

salesman at Freed's on Market Street. He'd been in the business all
his life, he'd told me on another occasion when he'd had a few drinks
and his stutter had subsided. He'd worked at Tollin's, Stanley's,
Stern's, and now Freed's. I didn't ask him why he'd worked at so
many different furniture stores in Chester—he'd said it almost
proudly—wondering if it had something to do with his drinking.

"I'm so happy you're going," said my mother. She put her arms
out for me and gave me a hug, which I accepted shyly in front of
Mr. Richardson, who beamed. He was sipping his first martini of the
day and, like my mother, wasn't alone.

Rose Valley was tucked into a section of the township between
Wallingford and Media and had, among its other attributes, the
Hedgerow Theater, famous for giving a start to actors on their way
to New York. My parents had taken us to see a production of *Under
Milk Wood* here, between my mother's visits to the hospital. I had sat
next to them, Adrian on my right, and we'd all said what a wonderful
small and intimate theater it was and how we had to come back. That
had been two years ago, and so much had happened in the meantime.

Now I parked in the Hedgerow lot—no production was going
on tonight—and walked across the street to the Old Mill, which was
at least fifty yards back from the road down a twisty driveway. I
thought about how different my life might have been if my parents
had moved here, how protected these homes were by their iron gates
in front of cobblestone drives, their high hedges and lush gardens,
their leafy oak and sycamore trees, some of the oldest trees in the area,
and how many doctors lived in these colonial houses with their many
stone chimneys and rolling front lawns. We could have lived here. It
would have been possible, I suppose, if my father had been a different
kind of doctor and he'd wanted a different life for us.

I almost had to talk myself into such a possibility in order to make
my legs move along the narrow gravel driveway. I occasionally

stepped off to the side against an overgrown wisteria bush to let a car go by. I could have driven down the lane—the Old Mill had a parking lot—but I wanted time to think and prepare myself and imagine I was like anyone else walking in here.

The mothers of the three girls giving the party greeted people at the door. Wearing long dresses and white gloves, they shook everyone's hand as kids passed through the tall double brown doors with their iron hinges into the Old Mill. I stood in line behind a couple I didn't know and shuffled slowly along to the front. "Grace Longstreet," said the first mother, her blue eyes bright, her smile warm and enthusiastic, eager to hear my name. I hesitated. "David Nachman," I said, and she showed no surprise, didn't drop my hand, didn't give her companions a knowing look ("We've been waiting for him"), didn't make a gesture to indicate I was different from any other person moving through the reception line. She was already on to the next guest, while I stepped ahead and shook Mrs. Tennemore's white-gloved hand, speaking my name with a little more confidence.

What was left of the original Old Mill, besides its fieldstone walls, was a paddle wheel. It sat among weeds at the back of the building, guarded by a rusty chain to keep people away. The actual grindstone was gone, but the building was still handsome and sturdy, wedged between Ridley Creek on one side and a steep wooded hillside on the other. When I walked in, people were standing about sipping sodas and eating hors d'oeuvres, the boys in suits like me, mine a little short in the sleeves—I'd grown a few inches since last summer—and the girls in party dresses, their hair pinned up or loose and full on their shoulders, strands of their mother's white pearls around their necks.

I went over to the punch table and debated. Red or green? At school I'd stretch this decision out, but here I didn't want to be caught moseying, so I grabbed the green punch. I walked to the back entrance of the Old Mill and touched its cool walls, fingering some moss and picking at some quartz with my nail. I was aware of my heart pounding and that my neck was turning red and that I couldn't possibly keep this up for a whole evening. I checked my watch. Four minutes had gone by, a whole four minutes. The invitation had said from seven to eleven P.M., three hours and fifty-six minutes to go, more or less.

It was then that I caught Dana Asher's eye. I became horrified to realize that she was on her way to see me.

"Can I talk to you, David?" she said, making it over to me in three leggy strides.

"I guess," I said.

"You don't sound sure."

"I'm not."

"Let's go outside."

I followed her through the crowd. Even after all she'd done, I still felt something akin to pride, some stupid satisfaction at being towed by Dana Asher, at people thinking we were together. While my brain loathed her, my body plumed itself, puffed out its chest, strode ahead, no memory, no consciousness other than that it was following a pretty girl who had spoken to it. *It* had gotten a whiff of her perfume. *It* had glanced at the slit up her Chinese jade gown. *It* had admired her shapely muscular legs. *It* had melted when she smiled. *It* had decided it had no past, only a present, and it would follow her—hey, why not? anything goes! count me in! I'm game!—stumbling after her on these and other mindless platitudes.

Meanwhile, I hung back, thinking about how, even more than Paul Vale, I'd gone out of my way to avoid Dana Asher at school. I knew all her classes, all her activities, and I detoured around them. On the few occasions when I'd unexpectedly run into her, I'd kept my head down and dashed away, not giving us a chance to face each other. I associated her with the lowest, most debased and hopeless moment of my life, and it was my greatest desire that I'd never have to speak to her again.

"Is this okay? To talk here?"

"Sure," I said. We'd stopped near a foot bridge that led over a stream and onto private property, blocked off by an iron chain between two stone pillars. Dana leaned against one stone pillar, and I the other, and we both watched the rushing water of Ridley Creek, its wet black rocks reflecting the moonlight. I looked over at the Old Mill, lighted up from inside: the faces through the stone windows, snatches of diaphanous gowns and tailored suits. Shouts and laughter and high-pealed greetings. The three mothers in their white gloves had abandoned their posts to move inside.

"I just wanted to tell you I'm sorry, David. I didn't intend for all that to happen."

"Of course you didn't," I said. I didn't mean it to sound sarcastic, just perfunctory. I'm not sure she even heard it. She had a speech she'd been readying.

"I'm not a bad person. You don't believe that, I'm sure, after what I've done. But I'm really not. I had no idea you would . . . it was just sort of a joke at the time. I don't even think it would have been legal, you know what I mean? It was more that I had to do something. Everybody felt so *frus*trated. I just didn't know what to do after what happened. Paul was a pretty close friend, and he wouldn't have ever okayed what I did, but I felt *I* had—"

"Fine," I said, not wanting to get into a discussion about Dana Asher's concern for Paul Vale. I wasn't willing to play confessor for her about what a mean, terrible thing she'd done. I didn't really care. I also didn't feel like explaining to her that it didn't make a difference. If it hadn't been her with her little reel-to-reel tape recorder and her beguiling Delilah ways, somebody or something else would have made me try to take my life. Or maybe not. It didn't matter now, in any case. I was alive; somebody else wasn't. That was my problem. It had always been my problem, and she, Dana, would have to wrestle with hers, without my help.

"I can tell you're mad," said Dana. "That's the way my father gets when he's mad—quiet."

"Let's just forget about it," I said. "It's over."

"Everybody's been saying it really wasn't your fault. Technically."

"It was my fault. Everybody is wrong." I suddenly felt deeply lonely talking to her, deeply lonely for someone else to talk with.

"So you *are* still mad at me," said Dana, and I looked at her directly now, seeing that she was used to getting her way, to wearing people down with her slightly husky, sexy voice and having them want to please her and that she would never be pleased, or pleasing enough; she had a long road ahead of her; that was why she'd come over in the first place, to make it clear she could never be pleased.

"I wasn't ever mad," I said, and walked away, wanting to join the party for the first time since I'd arrived.

Something happened. I walked up to Ronnie Horowitz and Calvin Thompson and said hello. This took us all by surprise, but I'd gotten a boost from speaking with Dana. It hadn't been the same disappointment as with Paul: wanting to believe we were young enough to make a mistake and have another chance, but knowing after we'd talked we couldn't change anything. I'd killed his sister, and he didn't want to blame me, and we didn't even have that between us anymore to screen us from the fact.

Ronnie had looked at me a second, then said, "What's happening, Nachman?" and Calvin had quickly added, "Hi, David." I suppose this would have been a simple act for most people, but considering I hadn't approached a single person in almost a year, it felt momentous, and my heart, now that I'd done it, pounded wildly in the aftermath of my bravery. I don't know what I would have done if they'd moved away, laughed at me, or made some hostile remark; at another time I might have been prepared for it, but I wasn't then. I wanted them to do just what they were doing, stand there a moment and let me talk with them. I suppose I gambled that they would.

"You come by yourself?" asked Ronnie.

I said I had. It wasn't cool to go anywhere by yourself, but there was no sense lying.

"I hate these things," he said. "Bunch of jocks standing around eyeing the meat."

Calvin nodded, which was odd. Calvin was black, a jock himself, or a former one until he'd quit basketball, football, and track this year to be political. That was the thing about Ronnie and Calvin: They were the sixties as far as the high school went. While everyone else in 1968 was still wearing chinos and listening to the Temptations, they wore beads around their necks, grew their hair long, and tried to drum up interest against the war with an underground newspaper, which had been confiscated by the phys ed director, Chester "Chet" O'Connor. He'd sent out his "goon squad," as it unofficially was called, the rec assistants who hung around his office instead of going to study hall, jocks who patrolled the halls. They'd ripped to shreds every single mimeographed copy of *The Bluehead,* Calvin and Ronnie's underground newsletter that protested everything from the lack of choice in our cafeteria food to discrimination against Chester's blacks.

It hadn't been just coincidence that I'd walked up to them. I knew they'd be the most sympathetic.

"Want to go out back?" asked Calvin.

"Sure," I said, though I was starting to enjoy myself now, watching people dance. One young girl with silky blond hair and skinny arms twirled on the dance floor. The band, the Earwigs they were called, from an old *Twilight Zone* episode about earwigs that burrow into a man's head and leave their babies behind to eat his brain, knew only about six songs, most notably "Gloria."

"G–L–O–R–I–A!" screamed the lead singer through the static of bad amps. The girl I watched, her name was Kristy Ward, swirled around the dance floor, her hair whipping behind her. Guys were cutting in to dance with her, and for a crazy moment, until Calvin and Ronnie invited me to go outside, I had the thought that I would too.

We walked out back and sat on the stone wall. A good portion of the crowd seemed to be out here too, and I soon understood why. Up the hill to the bushes kids periodically drifted for a swig from the bottles they'd hidden. Calvin had more class than that, he informed us, and pulled out a silver flask from his back pocket. He passed it to me.

"I'd better not," I said, and they both nodded, understandingly. Perhaps they thought I was on probation, but I wasn't anymore. The social worker, whose caseload covered more urgent matters in Chester, had stopped coming by to see me. "You're doing fine, David," she said. "I think we can assume you have all the right elements in place for recovery." My parents and I had met with her once a week in our living room. She'd had a checklist of items that included school attendance, activities inside the home (music lessons were on it, as well as baking), and an inventory of emotional states: feelings of hopelessness, impulses toward violence, thoughts of suicidal ideation, which she explained meant exactly what it sounded like—ideas of suicide. Did I ever have thoughts like that? Did I find myself planning how I might do it? I shook my head no. I could feel my parents breathe with relief. We went down the checklist, and she politely marked off in the positive column all the right answers.

"You still working for your dad?" asked Ronnie. Ronnie's father had died when he was ten. His mother and he ran the Chester Towers Pharmacy across from the post office. Ronnie worked there every afternoon with her, and most of my father's patients had their prescriptions filled at the drugstore.

"Every day," I said.

"He's all right, your dad. He's the only Chester businessman I know who supported the marches. I remember him out front marching down Market Street."

He was talking about the marches back in 1963 and '64 by Chester blacks for better jobs, improved schools, and an end to the graft of the Republican machine in Chester, which regularly took kickbacks, neglected the schools, hired incompetent people, and generally had a lock on the city. Just about every white businessman I knew supported the machine, except for my father, who really wasn't a businessman anyway.

"We're thinking about doing something like that," said Ronnie. He passed the flask back to Calvin.

"Marching on Chester?" I said.

Calvin laughed. "Not Chester, Media."

Calvin lived in South Media, the only place in our township you'd find blacks. An enclave of about fifty families, South Media had compact houses with brown and green shingled sides and boxy front porches. It was right up the street from the mansions of Rose Valley.

"The Acme supermarket," said Calvin. "We're gonna picket it."

I looked at Calvin. He was over six feet. He'd stopped playing sports in the middle of this year's basketball season and shocked everybody, the coach most of all, since Calvin had been the star forward, scoring thirty to forty points a game. Until Calvin left, the team had gone undefeated and was headed for the play-offs and state championship in Pittsburgh. It was almost as big a deal as what I had done, and indeed, when he quit, everybody talked about nothing else. He'd written a letter to the school paper explaining his decision. He lived in a shabby house; his parents worked at menial jobs; he could caddie at the Springmore Country Club but never golf there, even if he had the money; he had little hope of going anywhere besides Cheyney College or some other Negro school because teachers took little interest in him as a student and automatically pushed him toward vocational courses. It was the same for his fellow blacks, the small band of thirty or so lucky enough to attend prosperous Nether Providence

High. Only they were too cowardly to do anything about it, he'd written.

It had been an angry, impassioned letter, and somebody had clipped a bunch of copies and pasted them up in the bathrooms and written "Fuck you, uppity nigger" at the top, before they were all torn down.

"What's wrong with the Acme?" I asked.

"They won't hire blacks," snapped Ronnie. "They try for the jobs and never get past an application. The only blacks working there are janitors. No clerks. God forbid, no managers. They sell to them. *Oy,* can they sell to them. You know how much blacks spend there every week?"

I didn't.

"A lot. *Capish'*?" Ronnie said, who liked to mix Italian and Yiddish for effect. "A lot more than whites. A woman we know went in there with a business degree from West Chester College and five years' accounting experience, and she was told she was underqualified for a bookkeeping position. They hired a white girl, no experience. The produce manager's cousin. She had a high school diploma."

I took the flask. I can't say why, except that I suddenly wanted to be part of things, and part of things meant drinking. "Go ahead," said Ronnie, and encouraged me to tip it back. I coughed, spit up liquor.

"What is it?"

"Vodka," said Calvin. "Goes down smooth, don't it?"

"Not exactly," I said, and tried again, more prepared this time.

"So you with us or not?"

"Sure," I said, and took another swig of vodka.

I went back inside. The Earwigs were playing "Heat Wave" by Martha and the Vandellas and not doing a bad job of it. Everybody was up dancing. Calvin and Ronnie had decided to climb to the top of the hill in back of the Old Mill and take a piss up there. I could feel the vodka soaking my insides, burning down there in a good way now that I'd gotten by the initial fire of swallowing it. My resistance was melting away too, and I felt my hips shift to the music.

I walked out a little farther from the wall and saw Kristy Ward, still dancing. She'd tied her hair up in a knot on top of her head. Her chest was sweaty. She was dancing with a stiff-shouldered senior who moved his feet in tiny bird steps, his arms frozen at his sides. Kristy looked bored. I could do better than that, I thought. No reason existed to believe this, since I'd never danced, but the vodka had given me a pleasant confidence that I could do anything. *It* was making its wishes known again. *It* wasn't worried about making a fool out of me or the music stopping or the band walking off in protest or the collective voice of the three white-gloved chaperones coming through the microphone and saying, "Shame on you, David Nachman. After what you've done! Dancing!" *It* had burned away such terrorizing inhibitions, like film burns, that slow spreading out of a hole, leaving a blank white screen behind it.

But I stood frozen, watching the clumsy senior wrap his arms around Kristy Ward, all ninety-five pounds of her, I guessed, embracing her skinny, exuberant body. They danced, hug danced, to "You've Lost That Lovin' Feeling." Kristy closed her eyes, pressed her head against his chest, and they moved in a slow, shuffling, graceless circle around the room with all the other couples. The Earwigs' lead singer boomed out the Righteous Brothers, overcoming with sheer enthusiasm what the amps lacked in quality, and several girls lined up in front of the stage to watch him. He was transformed by the melody, his pimpled chin and gawky limbs and droopy mouth suddenly changed into assets of sexual defiance, charged negatives.

The vodka, the sweet cloud that had dropped over my mind and made pleasing, vague outlines of everyone and everything around me, evaporated. I was left with the sharp, stringent awareness that no one could ever touch me without revulsion.

105

Ronnie Horowitz came up next to me. "We're going out for a little nosh. Want to come?"

"I don't know," I said, feeling sick.

"Come on, it's still early, Nachman."

"Okay," I said. "I have my car here, though."

"Where you parked?"

I told him.

"We're along the road right next to you."

We walked out to the road, Ronnie and Calvin talking about our teacher, Mr. Corvan, who taught civics and American history and whose idea of a guest speaker was a visit from a representative of the local Daughters of the American Revolution. When we reached my car, Ronnie said, "Follow us."

I drove out of the parking lot, feeling better. I hadn't even thought to ask them where they were going, and we headed up Rose Valley Road into Media. Two minutes later they were pulling into the parking lot of the Media Diner, Paul Vale's parents' restaurant.

I thought it must be a joke at first or not a joke exactly but a setup. After thinking I was friends with them, they had brought me here, but then I realized it was neither. They just wanted to eat. They weren't making the connection. They wouldn't think about it the way I did. I sat behind the wheel until they came over.

"I can't go in there," I said.

"Why not?"

"It's Paul Vale's parents' place."

They looked at each other a moment. Calvin said, "It's a free country."

"It's not a matter of that."

I could see Calvin didn't understand; he had a fixed idea about why somebody couldn't eat or be served in a restaurant. I thought about Mrs. Nick years ago, not serving me after the Olans had moved in.

"There's no other place open now," said Ronnie. "I'm starved.

I got to feed my face. Just sit in the back with us in a booth. Nobody will know."

"You're going to see them all sometime anyways," said Calvin.

But not in their restaurant, I thought. Still, I got out, followed them inside. Maybe I wanted to get it over with; maybe too I knew the chances of the Vales' being here were slim. They tried to be together as a family after six; I remembered this from talking with Paul.

The place was packed with the first wave of kids from the Old Mill. We found a table for two and squeezed around it. The waitress came, and we gave her our order for three cheeseburgers and Cokes.

While we waited, Ronnie entertained us with stories about the Chester Towers Pharmacy, the characters who came in. "Mrs. Lovo," said Ronnie. "Big black lady." Ronnie held his arms out to indicate army-size breasts. I glanced at Calvin; he didn't seem to mind. "She calls me over. 'Mrs. Lovo,' I say, 'what can I do for you?' 'I need somethin',' she says. 'What do you need?' 'You got somethin' to make nature rise?' 'Pardon?' I say. 'You got something make nature rise?' 'I'm not following,' I say. She nods at my crotch. 'My man want it,' she says." Ronnie and Calvin burst out laughing.

"You get her something?" Calvin asked.

"I gave her two copies of *Playboy* free. Told her to try these on him. She seemed happy."

"I know Mrs. Lovo," I said, suddenly realizing I did. Her seven-year-old son had diabetes.

"What do you know about her?"

I realized I had nothing to say, nothing funny, that is. Every time I'd seen Mrs. Lovo, she'd only looked worried about her son, who had to take insulin twice a day. "I've just seen her in my father's office with her son," I said. They waited a moment expectantly, for the joke to come and then, when it didn't, looked around for the food.

When I glanced up, I saw Mrs. Vale. She noticed me at the same time I did her—she had been in the back helping and was bringing the order out for our overwhelmed waitress—and the look that came across her face was not the same tolerant one that Paul Vale had given me in the halls at high school. It was confusion, as if she couldn't imagine this. What would I be doing here?

Mrs. Vale put the plate down in front of me—in that way it was different from the time with Mrs. Nick—but what followed was worse. "How can you come in here?" she said, in a low, empty voice whose sadness was more apparent than its anger, whose exhaustion was more evident than its meanness. It was the voice of the one person I'd been dreading, the voice that forbade me to forgive myself in any way, and I'd heard it, and I knew I'd come in here because I had to hear it.

I sat a moment staring at my plate. I think Ronnie and Calvin were looking down at theirs too. I'm sure they felt horrible for bringing me. "I'd better go," I said.

"We'll go with you," Calvin said quickly.

"That's all right," I said. "Finish your food." I stood up and smiled at them, only because tears were running down my face.

"I'll call you," said Ronnie.

"Okay," I said.

I walked up to the cash register where Mrs. Vale was blowing her nose and did not look at me when I went through the door.

S E V E N

I tried to blot out my encounter with Mrs. Vale, but it intruded upon my dreams. I don't know how often and in how many forms I dreamed about her, but I do remember one night's dream that had her watching me through a window of her house, not oblivious in the laundry room downstairs, as she had actually been, but watching me as I raced backwards down Todmorden against Crow. I saw Sarah standing in her pink bathing suit in the front yard as she had been—so many things were the same—but I couldn't reach the brake. I was too short, too prepubescent, too weak, too panicked to push the pedal, and Mrs. Vale just watched through her window and let me do it.

It woke me up, or I forced myself awake. Usually after one of these dreams I'd sit in bed and read for a while. But I got up after this one, so shaken was I, and went to the bathroom and then looked in on my mother. I just wanted to see her. She still slept in the guest bedroom. She had kicked the covers off, and even in sleep she sensed me standing there, the way mothers can do, and she woke up with a start. "David? What's wrong?"

"Nothing. I just couldn't sleep."

"Do you want some water?" She had sat up and swept her legs over the side of the bed, automatically ready to get me something.

"I'm fine. I just had a bad dream." I didn't want to tell her how bad, ashamed of repeating it. Mrs. Vale's expressionless face had been worse than if she'd been scowling or hateful, its blankness a chilling rebuke in itself: *I won't help you.* I was alone, it said, utterly alone in my action.

"Count backwards from a thousand, David." I think my mother was so tired she didn't know what she was saying, giving me a technique for insomnia. The trouble was sleeping, not my being awake.

"I'll go back to bed now," I said. I had passed my father's room or what I'd come to think of as his room. I knew I was responsible for this arrangement, two separated people under one roof. They were staying together for fear of making any drastic move that would upset me. And I didn't try to dissuade them because maybe I needed them to be in this configuration until I could get my footing again.

My mother started to get up. I stopped her. "I'll be fine. You go back to sleep." In a minute I could hear her snoring, which I let soothe me as I sat in the hallway halfway between my room and hers.

Adrian called and wanted to know if I'd like to visit and see the apartment he'd just rented in New York for his upcoming sophomore year.

School had been canceled Friday for a teachers' meeting, and I thought I could miss Monday too. I also wanted to leave because it was the first anniversary of Sarah Vale's death. The closer I got to the date, the worse my dreams became. During the day I was fine, feeling optimistic, less tense at school. I'd sit with Ronnie and Calvin at lunch and we'd plan what to write in *The Bluehead,* the two-person staff of which I'd joined. My first column had been an anonymous article about the strange sighting of a largish, pinheaded driver cruising around town in a new apple red Mustang, waving happily, his arm on a marionette string. A free ROTC scholarship had been offered to anyone who could bring us the license plate of the said vehicle. (Someone actually did, and we returned it secretly.)

It had been, if not a great literary triumph, a release for me. I'd done something rebellious, subversive. I'd once seen a picture of a hydrocephalic child, his head so swollen with liquid that it had to rest on a float around his neck for fear of hemorrhage. By writing the article, I'd let off some of the pressure, and perhaps my guilt wouldn't hemorrhage into some unexpected act as the anniversary of Sarah Vale's death approached. Calvin and Ronnie, known conspirators, had been called into Mr. Shelley's office about the article and had made a point of refusing to divulge their sources. Calvin had gotten into a screaming match with Mr. Shelley, a former basketball coach who was already furious at Calvin for leaving the team, and that had distracted everyone from the issue of my modest satire, a shunt for my hydrocephalic shame.

Ronnie and Calvin still wanted to picket the Acme; they just needed to get their organization together. The local Quakers at Pendle Hill were supposed to help them out. In the meantime, I was going to New York. There would be plenty of time to plan all this when I got back, they told me.

"You have a school picked yet?" said Uncle Stonny. He was my mother's brother, the only boy of four children.

"Not yet," I said.

"Your brother did very well. Although he could have done better than the local university."

"It's not 'the local university,' " said Adrian.

"I'm just saying, with your brains why not Harvard?"

111

"Leave him alone," said Aunt Rose. His wife. "Don't pester him."

"I'm not pestering. I'm inquiring."

"You're one to talk? With your degree from Shea Stadium?"

Uncle Stonny leaned toward me. "Twice what I made standing on my feet selling cheap suits all day."

"Now you walk up a million stairs." Aunt Rose sighed.

We were eating dinner at their house in Queens. They'd invited Adrian and me over when they heard I was coming to town. My mother's two sisters—the twins, Miriam and Marvelle—were due shortly.

"They're late," said Aunt Rose, throwing up her hands. "Every time."

"You have to eat at six o'clock on the dot? Is this a dinner theater we're running here?"

Uncle Stonny, who wore suspenders over his sleeveless under-shirt, once owned a clothing store, but when that went out of business, he'd started selling hot dogs at Shea Stadium and Madison Square Garden and continued to do so, against Aunt Rose's complaints. "They're here," he said, looking out the dining room window. "I see them."

"The food's turned back into an animal already," said Aunt Rose. "It's not worth eating now."

"I'll go down and let them in," said Adrian, jumping up.

"We'll buzz, we'll buzz!" insisted Uncle Stonny, but Adrian was already gone. He'd told me, on the subway here, that in the three times he'd been to Aunt Rose's for dinner he thought he'd developed an ulcer.

"So how you doing, doll?" said Aunt Rose now that we were alone. Uncle Stonny had gone into the bedroom, where he would sit for five minutes with his hands on his knees breathing stertorously. He had heart trouble—or maybe indigestion—he had told me as soon as Adrian and I walked in the door. But the stadium steps were good

112

for him, exercise. "Don't listen to her," he'd said before Aunt Rose even came out.

"I'm doing all right," I said.

"That poor girl," said Aunt Rose, and sighed. I stiffened. That was the thing about our New York relatives. You couldn't depend on them for any refinement or discretion. They got to everything right away.

Except Aunt Rose wasn't talking about Sarah Vale, but about her sister-in-law Marvelle, one of the twins.

"She lost Lou only a year ago. Fifty-eight, and she's a widow already."

I nodded sympathetically, relieved we were only talking about Aunt Marvelle.

"You'll give me a hand taking these plates back to the kitchen, doll, after they come in?"

Aunt Rose had already put out the food. She wanted to make a point.

"Your poor mother," she said to me suddenly. "How is she doing?"

"She's doing fine," I said. "She's taking a pottery class."

"She's always been so"—Aunt Rose tapped her heart—"sensitive. She's not like the twins. I feel so sorry for her with what happened. You're better now, doll?"

"I suppose," I said.

"Shush!" said Uncle Stonny from the bedroom. "You promised not to talk!"

"What? I'm just asking him how he's doing. He can't answer for himself?"

"You're not asking. You're snooping!"

I could hear Uncle Stonny's labored breathing.

"He doesn't have to make it a history book!" shouted back Aunt Rose. "I just want to know if he's happy. Are you happy, doll?"

"Happy?" I said.

"You're not wanting to do such things to yourself anymore?"

"Enough!" shouted Uncle Stonny.

Mercifully the door opened: Adrian with the twins—Aunt Marvelle and Aunt Miriam—and Uncle Joel, Aunt Miriam's husband.

"Oh, look at him!" said Aunt Marvelle. "David, come give me a kiss. You've grown so much, *kineahora*!" I walked over to her and kissed her cheek. She crushed me against her chest, and I smelled her heavy perfume, like beeswax. The twins were nine years older than my mother, who was the youngest in the family. Uncle Stonny was right in the middle.

Aunt Miriam said, "David, dear, we haven't seen you in so long. Look at you—like a little man!"

"I'm waiting how long?" said Aunt Rose from behind us. She stood next to the brisket. "Just so you should know." Then, with my help, as we'd rehearsed, she swept the plates back into the kitchen.

The twins had come dressed in pink and lavender pantsuits. They both had scarlet lipstick, straight capped teeth, dyed blond hair, daisy earrings, and large plastic white handbags. I sat between them at the table—they insisted—eating the same brisket that had been whisked away only minutes before and warmed up in the oven.

"How long you in town for?" asked Uncle Joel.

"A few nights," I said.

"Where do you want to go to college?" he asked.

"We've been through this already," called out Uncle Stonny from the bedroom.

"So where?"

"*Oy Gottenyu*," said Uncle Stonny, and belched.

Adrian was eating quietly. I think our relatives overwhelmed him. He wasn't prepared to fight for a place in the conversation. At our house the quiet reserve of my mother, the preoccupations of my father, and my deference to a smarter, older brother combined to push someone like Adrian onto a stage of his own brilliance. But he wasn't used to people punctuating his brilliance with *Oy Gottenyu*.

"Your scores are decent?" asked Uncle Joel. He had worked in the garment district "since I was a little pisher," he liked to say.

"Not bad," I said. They'd been above average, though compared with Adrian's eight hundred perfect scores on his SATs, they paled.

"You should come up here," said Uncle Joel. "You have a brother, you have family, why not?"

"I want to stay near my parents," I said.

"Your mother should have been a schoolteacher," Aunt Miriam said. "She was so smart."

"The only one of us to go to college," Aunt Marvelle said.

"Very sensitive. Like you, David," offered Aunt Miriam, and looked at her twin meaningfully.

"Remember we used to take her to the meadow in Central Park?" Aunt Miriam said to her sister. She turned back to me. "Mama would send us out for the whole day while she cleaned for Passover. You should have seen what went on. A carp this big"—Aunt Miriam threw out her arms—"splashing in the bathtub, for the gefilte fish. We'd take Stonny, who was five then and the baby, your mother, and we'd spend all day in the park. Nobody bothered you back then. Your mother we'd put on a blanket, and she'd kick and gurgle, and we'd kiss her all over. What a little doll she was."

"It's a shame," Aunt Rose said.

"Shush," called out Uncle Stonny.

"Stop with the shushing!"

"I have an idea," Adrian said, tensely gripping his fork. "Tell us something about the family's history."

"What's to tell?" Aunt Miriam said. "We're from the hoi polloi. Peasants there, peasants here."

"Who got us here?" said Adrian.

"God," Aunt Rose said. "Who else?"

Uncle Stonny grunted from the bedroom. "With a little help from the pogroms."

"Who was the first to come over?"

"Why do you want to know?" Aunt Rose asked suspiciously.

"He's a historian," Uncle Joel said. "He's curious, right?"

Adrian, who had let his hair grow down to his shoulders and wore a blue work shirt, said, "I'm thinking about making a film."

"Tell him about Chaika," Aunt Marvelle said. "That's a good story."

"Very good," Aunt Miriam said.

"You tell it."

"You."

"I'll tell it," Uncle Joel said.

"You're not in the family," Aunt Miriam said.

"I'm not in the family? Thirty-two years we're married and I'm not in the family?"

"Tell it, Stonny," Aunt Marvelle said. He'd come out of the bedroom.

"All right, I'll tell it," he said, and I could picture him barking out, "Beer, heeah!" at Shea Stadium and the Garden. He was a frustrated performer. "Your grandmother Chaika—you boys were both babies when she died—came over by herself. But what a trip she had. The boat was crowded like you wouldn't believe. And people coughing, with colds, and worse, but Chaika, who was only twelve, told herself she couldn't get sick. She could not run a fever. She could not cough. She could not have a rash or puffy eyes or itchy skin. She was told in Odessa by her parents, too old to make the trip themselves, she would go to Ellis Island, where the Statue of Liberty was near, and the doctors there would listen to her lungs and her heart to make sure there were no bad noises. In the meantime, she was to hold on to a fifty-cent piece U.S.A. money, never let it out of her hand. This is what she must use to pay for a telegram when she gets to America to contact her uncle waiting for her.

"When she got to Ellis Island, the doctor examined her chest. 'Breathe,' he said. She was afraid to breathe, afraid he would hear the little mice in her chest. 'Breathe!' he commanded. 'You want to turn blue and die!' She had dreamed the night before she would be sent back because she had little mice in her chest that would not be quiet when the doctor examined her. So she held her breath and tried to make them shush because she thought, With so little oxygen, who can squeak? But the doctor made her take a breath. Everything was good. He gave her a blue card to bring with her to a big room with benches. Other people sat with bundles waiting to meet relatives. 'Who is coming for you, little one?' an official said to Chaika. He was a big man and had on a uniform with brass buttons. She could trust him. Chaika gave him the fifty-cent piece and recited the address she had memorized in English. He sent the telegram for her.

"One day passed. Two. Three. No Moshe Baruch came to pick her up. Chaika slept in the dormitory. Another telegram was sent at the big official's expense. 'Where is your uncle?' they said to her. And to themselves, they said, 'If he doesn't come soon, we must send her back. Five days is the longest we can wait.' 'Give him two more days,' said the big official. He felt pity for Chaika. Meanwhile, Chaika waited. They gave her books in English to read. She looked at pictures and guessed at words, asked for meanings, please, when the officials were not busy. They brought her a ribbon for her hair and a comb. Every morning she combed her hair, and with the ribbon in it, she waited for her uncle Moshe Baruch to come. She made herself useful. She swept the dormitory and helped serve the soup. She was beginning to believe she lived here. This was America. She had not set foot off Ellis Island.

"The day came when she had to leave. The big official said, 'I'm sorry.' Chaika did not cry. She'd been told not to cry. They would think she was sick. Now when she should cry, she couldn't. If only she could cry, they might let her stay. But all she could do, poor Chaika, was make her eyes get bigger, which did no good. Inside her chest she heard the mice squeak.

"Meanwhile, you know what's doing at Moshe Baruch's? A wedding. Can you believe such a thing? Here poor Chaika is stuck by herself on Ellis Island. She will soon have to go all the way home by herself, under terrible conditions, the long voyage back to Odessa. Won't her family be sad! She had been chosen to go first. But do you know why her uncle has not come for Chaika? Because Moshe Baruch dances with his daughter at her wedding and claps his hands. The wedding couple is raised high on chairs and carried around the room. Someone shouts it is time to read the congratulations. On a silver tray are the letters and telegrams that have been arriving all week from relatives who wish the couple long life and happiness. It is the custom to open all the telegrams at the wedding, never before.

"One by one they are opened.

" 'May you both live in happiness with God's blessing!'

" '*Mazel tov*, such *naches* for your parents!'

" 'You will be blessed with many children!'

" 'I am at Ellis Island. Please come. Chaika.'

"What? What was this? The guests laughed. A joke. The musicians in the background stopped playing and laughed too. What was this? 'God help me!' cried Moshe Baruch. 'My niece Chaika, she's at Ellis Island a week now!' Then and only then did the whole wedding party rush into the streets. What a sight! A hundred people, the groom and the bride too, running through the streets of New York City to rescue Chaika."

"That's amazing," Adrian said. "Can I film that?"

"Film what?" Uncle Stonny said, affecting modesty.

"Go," Aunt Rose said. "Back into the room. You're too excited."

"Can I film you telling that story? I want to make a documentary about it. I have to do a short. This is perfect."

"We'll see," Uncle Stonny said. "Talk to my agent." He nodded at Aunt Rose.

"Leave him be now," Aunt Rose said.

"You want to know how I got my name?" Aunt Marvelle said.

"Can I ask a question first?" I said.

Everybody stopped and looked at me. "What's your question, doll?" said Aunt Rose.

"Did they get to Chaika in time?"

"Of course they got there," called Uncle Stonny from the bedroom, strolling out. I didn't understand why he was banished there every five minutes; it took more energy to keep reappearing. "You think we'd be here if they didn't find her?"

"How I got my name," Aunt Marvelle said, jumping in, everybody wanting to talk suddenly, "is that Miriam was born first."

"Sixty-eight seconds before," Aunt Miriam said.

"They had a name for her. They'd named her after our aunt, Chaika's dead sister. But they didn't expect me. When I came out, they couldn't get over it. Two for the price of one!"

"They were so stunned they couldn't think of a name for her," Aunt Miriam said. "More than they bargained for."

Aunt Marvelle opened her handbag and blew her nose.

"Why are you crying?" Uncle Joel asked.

"Lou," said Aunt Miriam. "She's crying about Lou."

Uncle Joel opened his hands, an empty gesture. "It's a year already."

"Finish, please," Uncle Stonny yelled from the bedroom.

"So for two days they couldn't think of a name. Every name they tried they thought was wrong. They wanted something with an *M,* to match Miriam. It got to be a joke after a while. There was Miriam, and there was . . . me. The other one."

119

Aunt Miriam got out a fresh tissue for Aunt Marvelle, who dabbed at her eyes.

"Finish!" shouted Uncle Stonny.

"So finally our papa is walking in Brooklyn one day on his way to the tailor shop where he works and he sees a truck. 'Marvelle Hat Company,' it says."

"That's it," said Aunt Miriam. "That was her name."

"He knew it," added Aunt Marvelle. "Right away."

"That's the whole story?" Adrian asked.

"Twenty-two years later I'm working as a bookkeeper and a new fellow comes to work for us. A sales representative." Aunt Marvelle blew her nose.

"Lou," Aunt Miriam sighed. "Poor Lou."

They were both crying now, unable to finish.

Uncle Stonny came out from the bedroom. "Lou's father had owned the Marvelle Hat Company," he said. "The funny thing is his father had the business for only three months. Marvelle was named after a truck our father saw only once, and twenty-two years later the hat man's son turns up at her workplace—of all the businesses in Brooklyn!—and marries her. That's the story."

Uncle Stonny put his hand on Aunt Marvelle's shoulder. "Enough now," he said. "He's dead. Other things are ahead of you."

Aunt Rose looked at me and shook her head. "Your poor mother," she said. "She never wanted to move away from us."

"I'm coming over Monday," Adrian said. "Can you tell the stories again just like this on camera?"

"Joel, get the car, we're tired," Aunt Miriam said.

—

Uncle Stonny had gotten tickets for us to see a game at Shea Stadium, but I told him maybe next time. I wanted to hang around more with Adrian and his friends. Adrian had a girlfriend, Naomi, from Long Island. She was Jewish, interested in film (not movies),

120

and liked to make noise when she and Adrian slept together. I was sleeping out on the couch in the living room, and I tried to cover my head with a pillow. Her parents were Orthodox Jews and would have been horrified to find out she was living with a boy, so they had two phones. When the red one in the kitchen rang, it was her parents; when the black one in the hall rang, it was for Adrian—or their friends, who used that number. Once by mistake I had answered the wrong phone, and Naomi and Adrian had come running out waving their arms hysterically. I'd said, to the thick voice on the other end, "You must have the wrong number." Two minutes later the phone rang again, Naomi picked it up, and all was rectified.

On my last night at Adrian's apartment he'd had a small party, mostly film people. In fact, that was the main event of the evening. We were going to watch a Renoir film, *The Southerner,* in Adrian's living room (my bedroom). Adrian had borrowed a sixteen-millimeter projector from the department, along with the print, and we sat down for the screening.

There weren't any snacks or popcorn. These were serious film buffs, and the very idea of food constituted heresy, redolent of the behaviors of the masses. The subject of conversation at dinner—Naomi had baked challah and made a delicious matzo ball soup with steamed carrots and celery; she was an excellent cook—was a new theater on Forty-eighth Street that exclusively showed Swedish movies to viewers who lay in black boxes so you couldn't hear or see your neighbor. Not so much as a joke as just to add something (naively) to the conversation, I had asked if the films were dubbed in English or had subtitles. The look I'd gotten was somewhere between amusement and horror. "They're in *Swedish,*" said Adrian. These were purists, and I gave up trying to say anything intelligent about "film" the first day I was there.

On the other hand, nobody knew me or cared about what I'd done. The subject didn't come up with Adrian, somewhat to my dismay. I was finding out that was the thing, the new thing, about

Adrian. Whereas he had once been alone for large parts of his childhood, he now surrounded himself with people, a condition that had
started back with Scott's Hi-Q. He'd gotten a taste of being a star,
and he wasn't willing to let go of it so easily. So he had these little
soirees at his house, or the phone was constantly ringing, his—their—
phone, or he was popping out the door to meet someone at a museum
or coffeehouse.

I dragged around after him, studying the subway map so I would
have some autonomy if I wanted to explore the city alone. But I
didn't. For whatever reason I was afraid to go out on my own. Not
afraid of muggers or getting lost but of being alone. It made it that
much harder to come back to his apartment, filled with energetic,
talkative students, discussing films and books and politics and New
York. I was irritated, jealous, I suppose, that they could sit around so
freely, joking and gabbing, while I had this thing, this problem, this
life that I had to carry with me everywhere. It seemed the wrong
time, the wrong generation to be part of with this burden. While
everybody experimented with new ideas and drugs, smoked pot, listened to *Surrealistic Pillow* and *Sergeant Pepper's,* I had to sit on my nest
of charred, blackened eggs. In some ways I fit better into Uncle
Stonny's world, that anxious, fretting, nagging world of Aunt Rose,
where disaster was right around the corner and where behind every
smile, behind every "sit sit sit" was a solid worry. But even there the
legacy proved to be one of rich stories with happy endings, timely
rescues at the last minute, future husbands magically glimpsed in the
name of a passing hat truck. Disaster might befall you, but after all
the hand wringing, kvetching, and keening, 51 percent of the time
life was ruled by the god of good coincidence. A majority. It wasn't
exactly what I believed. Where did I belong in all this?

Try as I might, I couldn't, like Naomi and Adrian in their surplus
army jackets and tinted granny glasses, cut loose. Not on grass at least.
I had discovered an opened bottle of cheap red wine in the refrigerator, and I'd proceeded to finish it off the first night I was here, the

first night the usual assortment of guests crowded into Adrian and Naomi's apartment on Amsterdam Avenue. I drank slowly, inconspicuously, but thoroughly, and by the end of the evening, when the conversation had turned to the socialist regime of Alexander Dubček and how much longer it would last, I was, if not happy, submerged, like Chuckie Halbert in his basement, alone with his trains and poker and ant farm.

The next night I found a corner grocery and bought with the spending money my parents had given me a loaf of rye bread, some gum, a few bananas, oranges, *The New York Times,* and then I went across Eighth Avenue to a liquor store and got some wine. A sweet wine. I had the same feeling as I'd had at the Old Mill: warm, melting comfort. I could add something to the conversation (or not); I didn't care about the result. I was behind one-way glass. Nobody could see me, not *that* me.

Naomi had tried to take me aside and talk with me, find out how I was doing at school, what I was interested in pursuing (assuming I'd go to college), if I had a girlfriend. She was chatty and had a huge, friendly, wide mouth and dark, springy curls that flopped forward when she laughed, as she did often, clapping her hands. Her chin was sharp, and she was absolutely in love with Adrian, as he was with her; they crawled over each other. For some reason he called her Dooglie Girl and she called him Dooglie Boy, endearments that I could never figure out, arising, I'd decided, in the mysterious ways couples come up with ludicrous pet names for each other. He had learned how to play the harmonica to accompany her on her guitar. They had sung "The House of the Rising Sun" for me the first night I was there, a duet mustered with great mutual passion, and the glance Naomi gave Adrian afterward might as well have had a bubble above it that said: *I love you, Dooglie Boy.*

Meanwhile, Naomi looked at me so earnestly (I wished she wouldn't) that I tried to make inane conversation, about anything from the cockroaches in the apartment to a black man I had seen juggling bagels in front of a deli, but she obviously wanted to hear about "what happened," and I was apparently going to resist her interest. Perhaps she thought (her fallback plan was to be a psychologist, if directing didn't work out) she could help me or make me like her. But what I felt was invaded, dabbled with. I had traveled out of my area and now was a sideshow, heard about far and wide.

Of course, when I drank my wine, I didn't worry about this, and on the last evening, when Adrian had his party, I sat in the corner of the apartment, under a barred window, and watched *The Southerner* with enormous sympathy for the penniless farmers whose land had just been wiped out by floods. When it was over, Naomi flipped on the lights. "I have to say this," Adrian declared. "The dissolves are truly amazing. Each image just flows into the next, yet he has these remarkable close-ups of the family, almost portraits. He's painted one of his father's masterpieces on film."

A black-and-white film, its grainy contrasts only lent it authenticity, in the view of everybody present. Renoir was a master to take this rural subject matter and make it his own through a French sensibility, and in doing so, he had contributed a classic American film. I had thought to add that I could feel the barren dirt sift through my own fingers. But I kept silent. I was just happy to have a bottle to myself that had lasted throughout the movie.

There was a movement to go barhopping in the Village. Surprisingly, I declined to join. It wasn't just that I was under eighteen and might have trouble getting in; it was more that I could stand only so much company.

Adrian shuffled everybody, including himself and Naomi, out the door except for the person who had brought the film. His name was Graham, and he was from New Orleans, he told me. He had been up here three years and was glad to get out of the South. We wound up talking at the kitchen table, after he had packed up the four separate reels of the film. He wore a sport coat and an open-necked white shirt, a well-dressed guy in the midst of T-shirts and patched jeans.

"Did you like the movie, David?" he asked. I was impressed he'd cared enough to learn my name.

I said I did. I didn't say much more, afraid to err in the ways of cinema studies.

"I loved the story," he said simply. I liked that he spoke about the film this way, in such fundamental terms, plot. I could deal with plot.

"Mind if I have a glass?" he asked. I (reluctantly) poured him a glass of my wine, which I'd brought to the table.

"What's New Orleans like?" I said.

Graham told me: Bourbon Street was touristy, but the Quarter was wonderful if you could find the right places. There were some terrific bars that let you get really wild. He looked at me a moment, then added, "You like oysters?"

"I've never had them."

"Very slimy," he said. "But with the right sauce they're delicious. You develop a taste for them, especially if you grow up there. Ever have crawfish?"

I shook my head.

"We used to have them by the bucketful at my parents' house in Arabi. We'd all go down to the river and catch them. Now I'd be afraid to eat anything from there." Graham drank his wine. "You have any other brothers and sisters?"

I'd been trying to figure out during our pleasing and easy conversation if he knew about me. It didn't seem he did. I had guessed he wasn't a close friend of Adrian's, and I realized that for the first time in a long while I was talking with someone who wasn't looking at me through that lens.

"Just Adrian," I said. "He's enough."

Graham laughed. He got up and came to stand beside me. I saw that he was taller than I first thought. His sandy hair hung in his eyes. He had blue eyes and a thin nose, sharp cheeks shaved clean as fresh-sliced cheese. He spoke in a soft voice when he asked, "Can I kiss you?"

I don't know that I can say I didn't see this coming. I probably knew what was going on, but perhaps I kept it from myself, unsure what to do, what I'd do. Maybe I didn't know and wanted to find out.

"I guess," I said, and let him kiss me. He did it gently, his lips flat against mine, leaning into me, his right hand braced on the table, then looking at me, his left hand on the back of my neck, cupping it there a moment like cool water. I'd never kissed anyone, not since it mattered, not since reaching puberty, and I knew something of what I wanted after he did. I had that feeling of somebody paying me attention, noticing me, somebody who didn't know anything about me and wasn't revolted and couldn't see how far away I felt and how reckless I had been, how careless I was being now, lost in my wine cloud, everything easy.

Graham put his hands on my chest and started to unbutton my shirt, my button-down shirt, neat like him, and I put my hand on top of his to stop him. I didn't like it. I don't mean I didn't like his unbuttoning my shirt. I don't even mean I didn't like him. I didn't like the mise-en-scène, a term I'd picked up the past few days: the whole placement—his lips on mine, his rougher skin and strong hands and squared shoulders. Something in me was looking for a different degree of strength, a tensile force that would resist me, and it was all bound up with smell and the quality of light on skin and the timbre of a voice, Naomi calling *AAAA-drian,* and whatever other subtle, intricately threaded elements made up femaleness as opposed to maleness, and none of it had much to do with my having a choice. Despite how much I wanted to lose myself in any other world, any existence that promised love and tenderness and distraction and that could supplant my own hellish tunnel of one, I couldn't fake this. It was clear that it wouldn't work, and I could never make it so.

"I'm not really, you know . . ." I wanted to say queer or homosexual, some term I'd grown up with. But that wasn't it. "I'm not who I seem."

Graham knelt beside me. It was funny, when he got close to me, just stayed close to me, not sexually close but just near, I liked the heat from his body, the comfort. "That sounds foreboding," he said. "*Not who you seem.* Who are you exactly, CIA?" He laughed.

"It's hard to explain," I said. And I realized I was drunk, or getting there. "I'm not really interested anyway."

And Graham stood up, pulling all that lovely comfort away with him, packing it up instantly, the price I paid for rejecting him. "Just thought I'd ask," he said, and shrugged.

He gathered up the four encased reels of *The Southerner.* "Tell Adrian I'll check this in for him. I'll come back for the projector on Sunday."

"I'll tell him," I said, relegated to being a messenger. I couldn't wait until Graham walked out the door, which he did in a moment, so I could take a long drink of sweet wine.

E I G H T

Nobody in our house drank except for my father, who had an occasional beer after work. Then there was Mr. Richardson, my
mother's friend, and he drank frequently and insistently, but he didn't
get sloppy (indeed, as I said, his speech improved), and he was an
outsider anyway, and Irish, whereas Jews, as I knew from the old joke
around Hebrew school—if a bar mitzvah begins with four bottles of
wine, how many will be left when it ends? Five—drank very little.
So, in my mind, I wasn't really drinking, since I wasn't a wino, since
I was Jewish and not Irish, since I wasn't even eighteen.

I got money from my mother whenever I asked. I don't think
she questioned what I was doing with it. If anything, she was relieved
to give it to me, seeing that I was going out more now and seemingly
having fun. As for getting the liquor, that wasn't hard. My old lunkhead pal Corky Innes, still with his Kongmobile, played pool at Ray's
on the edge of the project, and I would simply go down there, ask
him to make a milk run, and tip him two bucks, which he was glad
to have since he had been laid off at Scott Paper. My only obstacle

was avoiding Crow, who hung out there also. I'd wait until I saw Corky come outside for a smoke—that is, grass (inside Ray allowed everything but)—and I'd wave him over to the car.

"Mr. Nachman," Corky would say, "what can I do you for today?"

He'd drive into Chester, Media, or Springfield, pick up the fuel, as he called it, and deliver it to me in back of Ray's (it was a service he provided for other kids too, not just me). His once-glorious Kong-mobile now smoked along. Its set of silver exhaust pipes had rusted and hung by a wire. The polished black chassis had turned a lusterless primer gray. The aerial was attached with electrical tape. No longer called Kong, Corky had been stripped of the title by a new generation that saw him simply as a jobless man with a beer belly who hung around Ray's and bummed cigarettes and drove an old beater. When he got into his car, he had to lift the dented driver's door up and out.

"Anything else, Mr. Nachman? Thank you, thank you very much," he'd say, stuffing the bills in his pocket with whatever additional he'd stolen from me; I knew he charged me more than the wine cost. He had gotten in the habit of "losing" the receipt. And I didn't ask.

I felt revolted every time I saw him, how obsequious he'd become, how much he depended on the few dollars I gave him every week, how eager he was to get in his faded Kong and rush to the liquor store for me, how humiliated I was to have *him* doing it, as if a nattier, more mannerly deliveryman would make me feel better about my drinking.

On the other side of this, the other side of my drinking, because I'd actually created another side where I could forget that I did it to excess—wasn't Ray's filled with kids my age who liked a beer?—I hung around with Ronnie and Calvin. More to the point, we planned our latest strategy. We had started distributing *The Bluehead* on the street corners of Media and at the Springfield Center. Occasionally, someone, usually an older person, a veteran, would actually throw the paper back in our faces. Since school was out, we'd turned to more global issues and were regularly protesting the bombing of Hanoi by Johnson. We had no money to print photographs, but Calvin had some drawing skills, and he would feature cartoons such as U.S. planes strafing villagers at harvest in their rice paddies. "*Their* fruited plains," the caption read. He did one "cartoon" of a North Vietnamese boy fleeing a burning thatched hut, his shirt in flames: "Children should not play with fire."

I thought it was in poor taste. That wasn't exactly what I thought. I hated it. I hated anything that showed a child hurt, and I couldn't be reasonable. "We can't run this," I said.

"Why not?" Calvin asked. We were in his basement in South Media. His parents both worked, and we'd set up a mimeograph press down there. Ronnie, from managing at the drugstore with his mother, drew a regular salary and funded us. But he wasn't here this night, having to work late.

"It's too harsh," I said.

"That's the point," Calvin said. He'd let his Afro grow out even fuller and now had a mustache, definitely against the dress code our high school was hanging on to. There was some talk that he wasn't coming back to school at all his senior year, couldn't stomach it. He had pictures on his wall of Angela Davis and Huey Newton with rifles, and I thought he was getting increasingly desperate to make something happen. But then again, I was desperate too, just in a different, unsober, secretive way.

"I don't think it does any good to shock people like this," I said. "It doesn't wake them up. It just makes them angry and disgusted. They can never get by that to hearing our message."

Calvin ignored me at first and continued getting the drawing ready for the mimeograph machine.

"So can we put something else in instead?" I said.

He clipped the mimeo to the edge and proceeded to crank. "If this was a white boy, you wouldn't be saying this shit," said Calvin.

"What's that have to do with it?"

"I'm saying if this was whitey burning up in the picture, you wouldn't be so quick to shove it under the table. You'd all make a big fuss about it, get the fire department and the police and the National Guard out there to stop this shit."

"What's that got to do with him being a child?"

"It has everything to do with it. You think you'd cry 'bad taste' if this was happening to your brother? You'd want everybody in the whole damn world to know about it."

"Calvin, I don't care that he's not white. I just don't like to see any child burn up. It's using them to make a point. Don't you understand that?"

I think it finally dawned on Calvin what I was talking about because he stopped cranking, sat down again at his father's workbench, and went back to silently drawing. I don't think he agreed with me. I suspect he just realized I was talking with some authority from personal experience and the light went on.

We'd show up at parties where nobody expected us, or wanted us, and stand around, make our presence known, receive hostile looks from the all-white groups dancing by the swimming pool on the patio. Ronnie was particularly good at finding out who was having a party, and he liked to walk through the door with his arms akimbo and announce, "Party time! Your darkest fear is here," and then Calvin would come in with white face on, his eyes wide, an Aunt Jemima rag on his head, a Stepin Fetchit gait, and Ronnie and he would launch into an Amos and Andy routine. I would stay in the background, very much on the periphery, near the edge of the door. I held the props—tap shoes, a banjo, a watermelon—which Calvin and Ronnie would work into their performance. For the finale Calvin withdrew a big knife (terrifying everybody) and sliced the melon, offering pieces, with a smile, to people before we left.

The whole "goof" lasted ten minutes, and we were out of there before anyone called the police or started a fight. Then too nobody was willing to take on Calvin. Close to six-three, no longer playing sports, he'd gained weight and looked intimidating. Once Ronnie and Calvin started the show, you could see the relief on people's faces; it was only a skit, a prank, a goof. Until Calvin pulled out the knife. We'd talk about that moment afterward in the car, or rather Calvin and Ronnie would, how quickly everybody changed their tunes, just the way it was in real life. "We okay as long as we on the winning team," Calvin said, "but put us out there jumping for the same job as them and then they say, 'What you doing here, nigger! Get away from me with that knife! I thought you was here to do some shuckin' and jivin' and make me laugh!'"

I had to fortify myself for these occasions, and since neither Ronnie nor Calvin seemed interested—I'd offered them some the first couple of times, but they'd told me not to open the bottle in the car—I would slip off and have myself a few pulls. Every once in a while I'd catch one of the partyers glancing my way, as if to wonder what I was doing, wasn't I the guy who . . . and I'd force myself to stare back. I was part of *The Bluehead* now, part of guerrilla theater, part of life outside the artificial world of Rose Valley summer lawn parties.

We didn't just crash parties. We also went to the Wallingford Swim Club, with Calvin. As far as I knew, no other blacks had gone there, and when I mentioned this one afternoon to Calvin and Ronnie, they jumped on it. We went in on my pass. My family, though they no longer attended, were still members of the swim club. So the three of us packed our swim trunks and towels and went through the gate. "Two guests," I said.

"You can only bring one guest at a time," the girl at the window said without looking up at Calvin. She had seen only Ronnie.

"I'll sit out," said Ronnie.

We pushed Calvin ahead. "A dollar twenty-five," she said, without giving Calvin a second glance. It evidently wasn't a first, or nobody cared enough to give us a hard time. We did get some looks sitting on our towels, Calvin and I, but largely it was a dud. In fact, one lifeguard, a former teammate of Calvin's, walked by and called out, "You coming back to play B-ball next year?" and Calvin said he didn't think so. He was as confused as I was by the indifference here, and in the face of it we quietly soaked up the sun and floated in the pool, barely making a ripple of protest.

It was different when we went to the Springmore Golf Club. The caddie manager informed us they had a lot of golfers today in this nice weather. Which of us wanted to caddie first?

"We're not here to caddie," said Ronnie.

"Pardon?"

"We're here to play," said Ronnie, and took a swing, like Johnny Carson. "We can carry our own clubs," he said seriously.

"All three of you?" said the caddie manager. The golf pro came over and started listening.

"That's right," said Ronnie, who wouldn't back down from anyone. He carried himself more like an adult than a teenager, as if losing his father had made him grow up quicker. He had to shave twice a day and had exceptionally hairy hands and a thick way of moving. Like many of the older Jewish businessmen in Chester, he'd stand in front of you with his chin on his chest, looking at you from over his glasses, tolerant, but impatient; he'd seen it all, at seventeen.

That was the way he was looking at the caddie manager now.

"I think we're all filled up today," said the caddie manager.

"I think you better ask your boss," said Ronnie. "And by the way tell him Ronnie Horowitz is asking for him, that's H-O-R-O-W-I-T-Z."

The Springmore Club didn't admit Jews as members either.

In two minutes the club manager appeared. A big man in a white, short-sleeved shirt and blue necktie, hair combed back in oiled strands, and a class ring on his finger, he had a name tag on that said "Vernon Saunders." "What can I do for you, Mr. Horowitz?"

"We'd like to play a round of golf," said Ronnie. Calvin was mulling about in the background, looking over the merchandise in the display cases, the golf gloves, the drivers, the sparkling white balls. But he was listening, as was I, standing next to Ronnie, conscious of being a fellow Jew at this moment.

"This is a private club, Mr. Horowitz. You must be aware of that."

"I'm aware that today is Tuesday," said Ronnie, "and the course is open to the public on Tuesdays."

"You're welcome to play."

Ronnie paused a minute. Was this going to be another Wallingford Swim Club encounter—a lot of puffing on our part and no fire to put out, or start?

"The two of you," added Vernon Saunders, nodding at me.

"Excuse me, but I count three of us," said Ronnie.

"I'm sorry," said Vernon Saunders, politeness still in his voice, "but that just won't be possible."

"Why's that?" asked Ronnie, inflating his square chest and giving his best exasperated, I'm-a-busy-man sigh.

"Because I see only two people here," said Vernon Saunders.

The caddie manager walked away to check in golfers. We'd brought along my father's clubs. I'd golfed with him once, in Wynnewood, a father and son charity tournament for doctors. We'd done so badly that after the first five holes we went back to the clubhouse and had Cokes and giggled about hiding out. It was one of my best memories of being with him.

I couldn't believe I was standing here now. It somehow seemed disconnected from everything, but my nerves were tense, excited to see what Ronnie would do.

It wasn't Ronnie, though, who did something. It was me. Or my father in me, my father picking himself off the ground after a brick had knocked him down, then going inside the Olans' house anyway. I heaved the golf clubs over my shoulder. I nodded at Calvin to follow me, and he did, surprised. He wasn't used to my taking charge either. Ronnie's look, on our way past him, said, *Whose plan is this?*

"Why don't you let the press know about our golfing?" I said to him.

I walked out toward the first hole. A party of four women were getting ready to tee off. They looked at us, at Calvin in particular, and glanced around to see whom he was a caddie for. "Excuse me," I said, and walked past them. I wasn't exactly sure where I was headed. But I nodded to Calvin, and he followed me onto the fairway.

Vernon Saunders and the caddie manager started to come after us, calling out that we were trespassing. I kept walking. "Where you going, man?" whispered Calvin.

"Trust me," I said.

"I don't," he said.

"You should," I said. I walked to the first green and sat down on my father's clubs. Calvin sat down too. The ladies shielded their foreheads with their hands to see us in the distance.

⁓

Fifteen minutes later we heard sirens, and three hours after that, after being booked at the police station, we were telling our story to the Chester *Times*, which ran it on page one with the headline BOYS WHO COME TO PLAY, DRAGGED AWAY, with a picture of Calvin and me being yanked by our legs. For whatever reason, the police had decided to handcuff Calvin and not me, and this was obvious in the picture, the image reminiscent of southern lynchings as Calvin was pulled facedown across the green with his hands shackled behind his back.

What no one could see—and perhaps it had been for the best— was Calvin's face shouting out vicious remarks about the pigs and motherfucking honkies. Calm beforehand, while Vernon Saunders and the caddie manager stood over us like bagged moose, Calvin went berserk when the cops touched him. He fought them until he and they, all four of them and their backups, were exhausted. When the Chester *Times* photographer arrived—good old Ronnie using his powers of persuasion to convince them it would be worth their while to come out—Calvin had just been turned facedown with a boot on his neck.

It was that boot on the neck, the shackled hands, and Calvin's legs in the air that brought to mind the southern lynchings. I, by comparison, a small (and willing-to-be-moved) lump in the corner of the picture, was incidental.

My mother was panicked at first, not understanding why she'd gotten a call to come get me from the police station. She'd managed to get hold of my father and have him meet her there. So relieved were they to find out it had been only a protest of conscience that on the way home my mother confessed, "We thought . . . we were thinking it was more serious." My father nodded at my mother's words. I loved too much seeing them this way, together because of me, and proud of me too. My father put his arm around me when we got home and said, "I've never liked that damned country club. Bigots through and through."

Our arrest started a chain reaction of events. The Philadelphia *Inquirer* came out and took pictures of us—Calvin, Ronnie, and me— standing in front of the entrance to the Springmore Country Club, which, ironically, had a black lawn jockey holding up the sign. The next day the jockey was gone. A week later the Springmore Country Club opened its doors to blacks and Jews. A brief announcement in the Chester *Times* let the public know that the country club was now "a facility serving members of all races, religions, and nationalities." This was part of a settlement with the attorney general's office. The picture of Calvin and me had made its way around the country, it seemed. Cousin Larry in Chicago, son of Aunt Miriam and Uncle Joel, called to tell us he'd seen me in the *Tribune*.

For once Adrian called to congratulate *me* on something. He wanted to know when I was coming back up to New York. Naomi got on the phone. She shrieked, "David! It's so exciting!" People were going overboard to give me a pat on the back, but I wasn't going to argue.

I could hear in the background, "Dooglie Girl, tell him the news!"

"You tell him," said Naomi.

Adrian got back on the phone. I thought he would tell me that they'd decided to get married or (was this good news?) Naomi was pregnant or maybe something had happened with one of Adrian's short films.

"I've decided to go to med school," said Adrian instead.

I couldn't speak. This wasn't what I was expecting to hear, and though it wasn't intentional, perhaps unconscious in that delicate way siblings have of upstaging one another, it took all the pleasure out of my own recent events. I knew, despite whatever else happened, I wouldn't be going to medical school. I wouldn't be a doctor. It was incontrovertible. It wasn't only that I'd forbidden myself that option as a punishment but also that I didn't have the confidence to care physically for others. I didn't believe I could entrust anyone's life to me. After I got off the phone with Dooglie Boy and Dooglie Girl, I sat in Adrian's closet and opened my bottle. Thinking and drinking, I eventually made myself happy for my brother.

It wasn't long after this that Calvin's family decided to move. They were going to Houston, where they had relatives and where Calvin's father hoped to get a better job. Ronnie said he wanted to have a farewell party for Calvin. It wasn't unusual for Ronnie to throw parties. What was unusual was that other people would be there besides the three of us. In particular, he'd invited three girls, not dates, just friends or friends of friends. I had known one of them, Myra, from Hebrew school. She went to a different high school, Swarthmore, and maybe that immediately gave her some allure for me. She was one step removed. Not that she didn't know what I'd done. I could tell she did when we sat in the kitchen talking about our parents. She was a little too sympathetic and nodded a little too fast when we got on the subject of driving and I told her I'd had to wait awhile before I got my regular license. She didn't ask why, of course, since she knew.

Her father owned a shoe store in Chester, so we had something in common to talk about, the town. Ronnie was upstairs with Calvin doing an exclusive show for the two other girls, Robin and Nancy, Calvin with white face, Ronnie imitating Amos, or Andy maybe. I wondered if Calvin ever got offended at Ronnie's crass imitations, if he, Calvin, could always justify them as being social commentary rather than indulgent ridicule. In any case, I was tired of the shows, sick of looking for new targets. We were scheduled to picket the Acme soon. Negotiations between the Delaware County NAACP and the Acme, after proceeding through the summer, had recently broken off, and the Quakers from the meetinghouse in Chester were supposed to march with the NAACP in Media, joined by Ronnie and me and anybody else we could recruit. But it looked now as if we'd wait until the fall.

That, I thought, might be it for me. The activism was wearing thin, and I wondered how much good it did. Ronnie and Calvin had kept wanting to look for "bigger fish to fry" ever since our Springmore venture had gone so well. They'd even talked about going down South. It didn't seem to scare them that three civil rights workers, one Jew and one black among them, had not so long ago gotten killed in Mississippi. Now that Calvin was moving I had the feeling Ronnie would lose interest too. There had been some sort of rivalry between them, to see who could be the boss of our three-person organization. The only thing that had been clear was that I was the staff and they were the management fighting over ultimate authority.

I'd decided I would live at home and commute to Temple University, concentrate on college. I'd already looked into a program in hospital administration. It was what I wanted to do. I hadn't been to my father's office much lately. The one day I'd gone there, I'd hung around somewhat aimlessly, speaking with Alice, the receptionist, about my summer and our protest at the country club more than office matters. Things had evidently continued very well without me the last couple of months, and for the first time I admitted to myself that if I left, I wouldn't be missed as much as I feared. Even my childhood dreams of coming back here as a doctor and taking over for my father in Chester seemed naive now. Chester might need him, but it didn't need me. He didn't think of himself as a hero, as I imagined myself to be when returning victorious from medical school to sacrifice my life for the poor. He wasn't aware of sacrificing anything, and that was the difference between us. It was just a job that had to get done, day by day, with lots of hand washing and alcohol swabbing. I wasn't sure what needed me.

"So what do you do as a hospital administrator?" asked Myra when I told her, the first person I'd mentioned my decision to.

"This and that," I said.

"This and that, huh? Would you be a doctor?"

"No."

"A nurse?"

I laughed and shook my head. I'd made Myra two whiskey sours. I had found I felt comfortable as a bartender, fiddling with the bottles. "The program trains people for administrative positions in the hospital."

"Ohhh," said Myra with mock sincerity, "a secretary!"

I laughed harder. We were having a good time. I could see she wanted to stay here with me.

"What then?" said Myra. "An orderly?"

"No," I said.

"Gift shop?"

"No, no, no."

"Describe, then, in convincing detail, your future job, David."

I liked hearing my name from her. She had a high, slightly nervous voice, reedy but not a whine, more like a long silver thread that trembled a bit. She reminded me of my mother when she talked. Her hair was in dark bangs almost down to her eyes, and she had braces that she tried to hide with her lips but couldn't very well because she liked to laugh too much. Her cheeks had flushed from drinking, and I forgot everything laughing with her.

"David," she said. "Tell me."

"I would oversee hospital staff and functions."

"But what would you *do* exactly?"

"I . . . don't know," I said, and laughed at myself. "It's just an administrative position. You administrate. That's what I would do."

"Cafeteria?"

"Don't start!" I said.

"Hey," she said. "You want to dance?" A slow song had come on.

"I don't dance," I said.

"I'll teach you." She stood up and led me to the living room. She placed my hand on the small of her back, held my other hand between our shoulders and gave me a nudge to go, as you would a reluctant work animal. I smelled her hair and relaxed into her compact body, which fitted snugly against mine. Her ease was enough for the both of us to move almost fluently. I found when I didn't think about it, I could make my body tilt and bend in interesting ways.

In a while we were flailing our arms to "Paint It Black," Myra spinning and twirling; she danced with quick changes in tempo, with odd little kicks of her legs and pumps of her arms, and I could see she enjoyed my watching her. It struck me that she wasn't afraid of moving her body suddenly and unpredictably but that I was.

Somewhere during another slow song, Ronnie came downstairs and sotto voce said, "*Oy,* look at the love monsters." I was kissing Myra, standing right where we'd stopped dancing. I couldn't do both at once. Every hurt, lonely, despised feeling in my body had shrunk to the place where our lips met, dissolved by her soft, wonderful mouth. Myra pulled away for a moment and said to Ronnie, "Don't you have some homework?" and then went back to kissing me.

3

N I N E

I carried a sign that said ACME UNFAIR TO BLACKS. Myra and Ronnie were supposed to be here but hadn't arrived yet. A group of blacks from the Delaware County NAACP in Chester had shown up, as well as the Quakers, ten of them.

Coffee and doughnuts were available in the back of a station wagon that some of the Quakers had come in. It was fall now, and chilly in the mornings before the day warmed up.

"My name's Arthur," said a man in a blue windbreaker. He was close to my father's age, with handsome lines on his face, a blond beard, and wire-rim glasses. He looked like a professor from Swarthmore College.

"David," I said.

"We appreciate your coming out so early."

"Hope it does some good," I said.

"It's frustrating," said Arthur. "You try to make things happen, and they go a lot slower than you hope. Sometimes you think you're going backwards."

I nodded. We passed over the subject. Backwards. I drank my coffee. I'd gotten up last night, taken a bottle from behind the clothes in my closet, and transferred part of the contents to an empty jelly jar, screwing the lid back on. "What am I doing?" I'd said out loud. I was holding the jar upside down over the kitchen sink to see if it would leak. I'd tried figuring out how I could bring something to drink without anybody's knowing. The thought had woken me up at three A.M., and there I was, conniving a way to quench my thirst the next day. Looking at the jelly jar filled with sweet red wine, I suddenly felt disgusted. I thought of Corky standing out front of Ray's with his big beer belly. I'd been doing this for months now.

I poured the wine down the sink, then lay awake until six A.M.

Now I drank a second cup of coffee and asked Arthur if he thought we'd get the management to hire more blacks and pay equal wages.

"I don't know, David. If we stand in front of this store day and night for the next ten years, maybe they'll lose a little business, maybe a lot. Or maybe none at all. But we're going to make our presence known."

"Do you live in Media?" I asked.

"At Pendle Hill," he said, without elaborating. I knew that Pendle Hill was some kind of center, a retreat for Quakers.

"Do you teach there?"

"I'm on the staff. We all teach, in a manner of speaking. I'm giving a seminar this semester, 'War, Segregation, and the Uses of Nonviolent Resistance.'"

I didn't know what to think of Quakers. Despite their presence in the area, I couldn't say I really knew any or much about them. There was a Friends meetinghouse not more than two miles up the road from us, on the corner of Chestnut Parkway and Twenty-fourth Street. I'd gone by it all my life on my way into Chester to my father's office. It was a white stucco building with a simple front porch supported by hand-hewn beams. A small cemetery with thin headstones was in back of the main building, and next to it a garage that appeared to be a converted horse stable. My mother had once told me that the meetinghouse had been there since the late 1600s. "People sit on benches," she said, "and pray in silence." I'd pictured grim men and women in dark clothes, motionless on hard benches in forbidding quiet.

"I'd better check on a friend," I said, thinking I'd give Myra a call to find out where she was. "It was nice meeting you." I put out my hand, and Arthur took it gently.

I half expected him to invite me to a service, try to recruit me in some way, but he simply said, "See you out front in a while."

We kept a few steps apart, all fifteen of us walking in a small circle a hundred feet from the entrance (the management had moved us back).

"Getting tired?" I asked Myra, who had come shortly before lunch.

"A little," she said.

Ronnie hadn't shown up after all, and I wasn't sure Myra really wanted to be here. It was something she'd fallen into through Ronnie, Calvin, and me.

"You want to take a break?"

"Okay," she said.

We stepped out of line and sat in a triangle of grass between the parking lot and the market. Next door was the 111th Infantry of the National Guard, headquartered in the Media armory, a building that had squatted here since 1908 with its buttressed walls and broken battlements and low flak towers. Soldiers in fatigues stood out front watching us. Arthur waved to them, but they didn't wave back.

Meanwhile, the Acme's customers, after initially being surprised when the first ones showed up at eight A.M., had gotten used to us, and passed through our moving circle as easily as sand through a sieve.

That, I suppose, was the point, according to the Quakers. Nonviolent confrontation. We were not supposed to harass anyone. If anyone harassed us, we should just ignore them and keep circling in front of the store.

"I should have worn better shoes," said Myra. She wore high leather boots, a new style from her father's shoe store.

It was September, a Saturday, and the leaves on the willows had just started to turn. Myra and I had been together almost every day since Ronnie's party five weeks ago. I'd meet her after school and we'd stroll up to Swarthmore College, which owned extensive woods honeycombed with trails in back of the campus. We wouldn't get very far before we stopped at a tree and kissed, talked some more, and then went a little farther, losing track of time. I had no desire to go home, to be anywhere else than with her.

Myra pulled her boots off and propped her feet up across my legs. We watched the Quakers move in a slow, silent circle, carrying their signs, while we took our break. The handful of blacks who'd come from Chester had left after lunch. It was almost dinnertime, and I wondered how long this was supposed to go on. Occasionally I stopped to talk with Arthur; two or three of us took a break at once. He told me he worked in his spare time as a draft counselor in Media. He'd been surprised to find out I was still in high school (a flattering mistake). I felt comfortable talking with him, his earnest regard for my answers. It was the way I imagined adults would take me seriously when I got to be a certain age but had never actually experienced with any of my teachers.

"Do you think Ronnie skipped out on us or just forgot?" I asked Myra.

"Suits," said Myra.

It was one of Ronnie's sidelines: selling suits. At any given time he had an inventory of between twenty-five and fifty cheap suits he sold to customers at the pharmacy and to teachers up at school. He'd carry them in over his arm and lay them out across the desks, going classroom to classroom with his samples before and after school. How he got away with this . . . well, he gave them a good price, the principal included. He wouldn't tell us exactly where he got the suits, only that they weren't stolen.

"A hundred percent cloth," said Myra, imitating Ronnie's pitch. I whistled. "A hundred percent?"

"A hundred percent. Guaranteed."

"Cloth, you say?"

"All cloth, every one."

"No aluminum?"

Myra leaned over and whispered, "My competitor. There you'll find aluminum, plastic, tin, Saran wrap! And bauxite and tungsten."

"What exactly *are* bauxite and tungsten?"

"I don't know," said Myra, "but they always go together. We don't sell them separately."

"And you're sure of the quality?"

"These are no ordinary suits, my little *shmeckl*. These you can wear. A hundred percent cloth! What more can I tell you?"

"I'll take three," I said.

"The hundred percent cloth? Or the other?"

"What's the other?"

"The *shmatte* material."

"The *shmatte* material? Is that durable? Will it breathe?"

"Will it *breathe*? Durable?" Myra rubbed the back of her neck the way Ronnie did. She was a good mimic. "The *shmatte* material wears like you wouldn't believe. It's underrated. But—*but*, if you want the hundred percent cloth . . ."

"No, no, I'll take the *shmatte* material."

"You'll be very pleased with the *shmatte* material."

It irked me that Ronnie hadn't shown up, and I enjoyed making fun of him behind his back. Now that *The Bluehead* was defunct and Calvin gone, he had backed off from social causes (and, more to the point, me), as if he'd sold that concern like a business.

Myra leaned over and kissed me. She stroked my cheek with her hand. "You should grow a beard, David. You're a senior now. I think you'd look distinguished."

"I'd be expelled."

"God, what a backward school."

Myra's high school, Swarthmore, was much more liberal and had abolished its dress code long before 1968.

"We should get up," I said. The Saturday afternoon shoppers were coming by, trying to read our signs while avoiding eye contact. Myra grabbed my hand. She'd worn one of her father's old flannel shirts and some wrinkled white painter pants. She had expected to be roughed up, beaten with nightsticks, bitten by police dogs, and dragged away to the Media jail. Nothing, in fact, had happened to us. Several Media police had slowly cruised by and then not returned. Our experience at the Springmore Country Club had been an anomaly, I was finding out. Protests for the most part turned out to be steady drudgery, met not by violence and rage but by indifference. The Quakers accepted the monotonous pace, keeping with their purposeful, determined stride, which seemed to promise they would still be here long after this Acme or any other closed its doors.

We slipped back in the circle and walked side by side for a while, holding hands. Myra leaned her head against my shoulder. I touched her hair once just to make sure she was really here. Light brown, it fell around her cheeks and made of her face a small oval. It had the sweet, damp smell of Swarthmore woods in it.

"Are you happy, David?" she asked.

I thought of the slippery wet leaves on our walks through the woods of Swarthmore College; how we would search for a dry place to lie down; the whistle of the train in the distance as it pulled into Swarthmore Station; both of us blinking in the cold, grainy light of dusk on early fall evenings, our faces pressed close together; Myra beneath me, her breath warm and excited on my cheek—everything under my fingertips.

I said I was, and I meant it, an extraordinary truth.

⁓

Perhaps because things were going so well, I decided to jeopardize them. Or maybe I just thought they couldn't go this well, so I'd test out their staying power.

I dropped Myra off at her house on Vassar Avenue. Swarthmore's residential streets were named after fellow and sister liberal arts schools, and there was something charming and naive, Myra thought, about growing up in a town with such idealistic foundings.

As for myself, I realized I'd gone through the whole day without drinking and hadn't missed it. The thought exhilarated me, and then I had the idea that I could drive by and see if Corky was out front, just look. But I knew I'd stop and Corky would swagger over to the car and lean his beefy body inside the window and say, "A little petrol today, Mr. Nachman?" I couldn't stand to see his happy leer, his crushing my money in his hand. So I did something different enough to pull me away from him. I drove over to the Vales'.

I knew they were likely to be home. The diner was closed for remodeling. I'd drive by it occasionally, hoping to catch a glance of Mrs. Vale. I just wanted to see her face, see if it was still set in grief, or if it had softened, maybe not happy but preoccupied and thought-ful, distracted by common worries of shopping for groceries or getting to the cleaner's before it closed or making one of Paul's track meets, anything that might show she'd forgotten about me. Maybe I thought I could convince myself their lives looked normal enough from the outside that mine could someday be that way too.

But I'd been afraid to look too closely the one time I did see her pull into the diner parking lot, turn off the engine, and drag out a box. New menus? More salt and pepper shakers? My heart had thud-ded, the blood pounding in my ears, and I'd driven away, afraid to be caught spying. I didn't have enough of the right words to explain that I just wanted to see her, Sarah's mother.

I turned off Brookhaven Road into Todmorden. In the year and a half since the accident, I'd avoided even looking down the road, let alone driving into the subdivision, all built up now, no longer just the Vales' house standing alone among empty lots. Lawns spread out on either side of the street. Small oak and maple trees, still staked down with guy wires for support, formed a junior arbored boulevard. The wide street, which we'd found so desirable for racing, stretched around the bend to the curb at the Vales' blue clapboard house with its white shutters.

Some children suddenly appeared from behind the house, not Paul or his brother, but younger, two boys and a girl. They were carrying a large cardboard box from a refrigerator, and I watched them set it on the front yard adjacent to the Vales'. The little girl—she looked about five, the age I realized Sarah would almost be now—got inside, and the two boys tilted the box over and rolled her around the lawn. I could hear their squeals of delight, and then their mother, a woman with dark hair and long bangs like her daughter, came to the front door and called them inside for dinner and the street was quiet again.

—

"Yes?" said Mr. Vale, and I knew he didn't recognize me. Why would he? I'd seen him only once in my life.

"I'm David Nachman," I said. There was silence. Not ordinary silence. A stretched-out silence that extended behind me, down the road around the bend, on and on, until I thought I could stand here no longer, my knees would not hold.

"What do you want?" he said without bitterness or surprise, just utter confusion.

"Could I speak with you?"

"My wife's not here."

I nodded. I had wanted to speak to Mrs. Vale too, but I couldn't come back. I could never get up the nerve to come back now that I'd been here and understood what I had done, how unthinkable it was I was standing here.

Mr. Vale remained in the doorway. He had a light blue short-sleeved shirt on, and his arms were muscular.

"Can I speak to you now?" I asked.

His shoulders gave a slight shrug, not so much a no or a maybe as tension, apprehension: What would his wife say if she found me here? What did it mean to let the killer of his daughter inside?—a small shrug of repulsion, get out of here, please.

I saw his son Russ come up behind him, a small boy for fourteen, who had neither his brother's height and lean frame nor his father's bulk, small, I think, the way Sarah would have been. He looked the most like her of anyone in the family. His eyes went wide at the sight of me. He put his hand on his dad's arm, alarmed, as if I were an intruder, which of course I was, the worst kind.

"You can come in for a moment, I suppose," said Mr. Vale, and turned his back on me, leaving me to open the screen door myself.

An umbrella stand with nothing in it and a grandfather clock stood in the foyer. Mr. Vale went into the living room and sat down in an easy chair.

"You can sit," said Mr. Vale. He'd buttoned his shirt in the meantime. I saw on the wall behind me before I sat down pictures of the family, and of Sarah. Out of the corner of my eye, I glimpsed a flash of pink—Sarah in a dress—and my throat tightened up, my head got dizzy.

"Could I have a drink of water, please?" I said. Mr. Vale nodded at Russ, who was standing in the doorway of the living room, to get me a glass of water.

I sat down with my hands between my legs and dropped my head slightly. I felt faint. This was far more difficult than I imagined it would be, but I absolutely couldn't get sick here or pass out or do anything that would make them have to call somebody, my parents, or, worse, take care of me. I took a deep breath, and by that time Russ was back with the water, which I gulped down. When I glanced up, Mr. Vale was staring off to the side, as if not wanting to look at me in the privacy of my torment, as if it shamed him to watch, like seeing a school-age child soiling himself.

"Go upstairs and do your homework," Mr. Vale said to Russ.

"I did it."

"Check it over then," said Mr. Vale.

Russ shrugged and started to leave but gave me a slight smile before he did. I think now looking back that it was his smile, involuntary and nervous as it might have been, the middle child who had become the youngest, that enabled me to find the strength to go on.

After he left, I said, "I never wrote to you and Mrs. Vale. I wanted to explain things better in person."

"I don't think I should be talking to you without my wife," said Mr. Vale. "She'd want to hear all this too. You have something to say to us, you should say it to us both."

I shook my head. It was an odd sensation. I hadn't expected to argue with him. But I knew I couldn't come back, and I wasn't sure I could face Mrs. Vale anyway. "Can I please just talk to you?"

Mr. Vale pressed his lips together. He was unshaved, and he'd gained weight since the time I'd seen him. Paul had shown me a picture of him playing baseball for Chester High in 1948, at the age of eighteen, a handsome man with his hair combed straight back and a strong, full face, a broad smile as he posed for his athletic picture. He'd been only a year older than I was now.

"What the hell happened?" he said, and it just seemed to explode from him. "What the hell were you all doing out there?"

"We were racing," I said, and perhaps because he saw I was going to make no effort to lie to him, he relaxed and fell silent, sunk into a kind of helpless quiet, and waited. "We were racing backwards, and my car jumped the curb. I couldn't control it." I had thought to say,

"The wheel leaped out of my hand," but I realized this was what I always told myself, and it wasn't true. *The wheel leaped out of my hand,* a phrase I'd used to put myself to sleep on some tormenting nights, had no *I* in it.

"You were racing backwards?" said Mr. Vale.

"It was to even out the race."

He shook his head. "Goddamn," he said. "Backwards. I didn't know that. I knew you were racing, but not backwards."

I tried to look at the ship's compass on the wall, the polished mahogany captain's wheel. They had a boat, I knew, and a small cottage down the shore at Mystic Island. I tried to think about them there.

"Backwards," he said, and I wished he would stop repeating it. Then I realized something. I realized, looking at the walls, the nautical theme of the living room, the promise of adventure and relaxation and distant shores, that Russ was at the top of the stairs crying. That the sound I heard and couldn't place was his whimpering and that he was crying for his sister—this was what the missing and love for her sounded like in their family.

I heard Mr. Vale say, "I've got to tell my wife. She still thinks it was an accident." It was as if he were talking to himself, reasoning it out, whether he should tell her.

"It was an accident," I managed to say.

"It wasn't that kind of accident. Not the kind you led us to believe."

I started to say what I had rehearsed, that I didn't want them to hate me. Instead I blurted out, "I wanted you to know the truth," which I understood was why I'd come here.

He sat a moment, then went over to the cabinet. He took out a package wrapped in white tissue paper and slowly and attentively peeled away the layers until he held a pair of child's pink ballet slippers. He brought them over to me and stood above me for a moment, trembling with rage, his fist clenched around the slippers so tightly

155

they were crushed in his hand like balled-up paper, and then he loosened his fingers, and the slippers sprang onto my lap. They were the shoes she'd been wearing when I hit her. They'd been left behind at the point of impact, as if she'd vanished.

———

I don't know how long we sat there, ten, fifteen minutes. It was in silence, and I had the sensation of time being turned inside out. I was dizzy enough to forget for moments where I was, the slippers weightless in my lap as I'd once held Sarah Vale. Mr. Vale sat across from me in his chair, softly weeping, his fury dissipated into the vastness of mourning between us as if we both were sitting shiva.

I got up and placed the slippers on the couch beside Mr. Vale. I stood a moment indefinitely, then walked to the front door. Mrs. Vale and Paul were just pulling up, and when Paul got out to open the garage, he saw me at the front door. His face registered surprise, then alarm, and he jerked his head, as if telling me to go before his mother saw me. As he drove the car into the garage, I hurried across their lawn.

———

The next day my father was up early, dressed in a suit and tie even though it was Sunday, his day off.

"David," he said, coming into my room, "do you want to go to services with me?"

It was Yom Kippur. I'd forgotten about it.

I hadn't gone for years, not since I was bar mitzvahed and had decided to keep my distance. Adrian had always attended with my father. But he was staying up in New York with Naomi's family, going to shul with them on Long Island.

"I suppose," I said. I couldn't refuse a direct request from my father. He so rarely asked anything of me like this.

"I'll make you some breakfast." He seemed cheered by my willingness to go. "What do you want?"

"Whatever you're having," I said.

"I'm fasting."

I'd woken up thinking about Sarah's slippers. I swallowed dryly. "I'll fast too."

"That isn't necessary," said my father, nodding at my pajamas, which were suddenly too short for me and came up past my ankles. "You're a growing boy."

"I want to," I said.

My mother came into the room. "You're going, David?" I nodded. "I'll try to come later," she said, but I had the feeling she wouldn't. She'd never been very observant, even on the holidays like my father. He put his hand tenderly on her back. I could see them as a couple just meeting at the University of Pennsylvania: how attracted he was to her; how he wanted to take care of her—and she would have to make up her mind whether to let him—how the war had intervened and they wrote letters for three years, an engagement that spanned the seas; and perhaps they fell in love through their letters and never had a chance to know each other in person; and how once married, she hadn't expected to feel so alone as a doctor's wife in a strange town.

We took seats in the back of the synagogue. This was actually a new one that I'd never been in before. My experiences had been with the place in Chester, before it was closed and the congregation, along with many of Chester's Jews, moved to the suburbs. I'd had some fond memories of the temple in Chester, a large brick building next to the Chester *Times*. On the second floor had been the classrooms, and above them the sanctuary, with its stained glass windows and rows of immobile theater seats. I would spend hours getting up and sitting down as the ark was opened, praying in Hebrew, though understanding very little of it. Occasionally I would glance at the translation on the left-hand page and see passages about God's wrath and vengeance and all the blessings to thank him for his mercy in not smiting us— his poor, lowly creations—with a single fed-up lightning bolt.

I came away frightened of disturbing a very temperamental God who had enormous expectations for His people and was not one to suffer their ignorant mistakes. You could do better, seemed to be the message, especially for Jews. In short, he reminded me of Chester "Chet" O'Connor sending out his Goon Squad and barking orders at us in gym class. Try as I might, I could not see God as merciful, kind, omniscient, fair, peaceful, or wise. I was aware that on Yom Kippur, the Day of Atonement, when we admitted our sins against God and, if lucky, were forgiven, my fate was being sealed in the Book of Life—or death—as to what would happen to me for the next year. It was all decided and most likely not very promising, because I could never live up to such high hopes. Years later a rabbi would explain to me another interpretation of Atonement: At-one-ment. What was once broken could now be whole. A single undifferentiated moment of unwavering forgiveness and compassion.

But nothing could have been further from my mind as the rabbi presented his sermon on the lack of Judaism in our community: Jews assimilating and forgetting their heritage. The message was clear. God was getting mad, very mad, watch it, watch it . . . that pen being lifted to write one's name in the book of death with a shake of the head, the heavens thundering, the angels bowing their heads, my running over Sarah Vale. If it hadn't been written, foreordained by God— Yom Kippur, the day when God seals our fate—then why had it happened? It seemed the logical conclusion of everything I'd been taught in Hebrew school: The wicked are punished, the blessed rewarded. Or more to the point: God works in mysterious ways and works especially hard at perplexing the suffering Jews. You must study and learn and educate yourself, I would hear the rabbi say, but this was no guarantee you'd understand anything but the ways of man, certainly not the suffering of your own people, or your own life.

Now let us say Kaddish.

This was the part I always remembered vividly because Ronnie would stand in the synagogue and say Kaddish for his father. Ten years old, he was lost among all the adults, a tiny figure in a mass of stooped bodies praying for the dead, and I'd felt both embarrassed for him and awed by his courage to stand as the lone child among older mourners.

But on Yom Kippur it wasn't just the Kaddish but yizkor that was said, the special prayer of remembrance recited only four times a year. We, the children, would be ushered outside to the hallway while the yizkor service was conducted inside, the doors shut, the mourners screened from view.

What did I imagine? Old men and women wailing as they said their prayers for the dead. We, the children, were not to witness this spectacle, this display of grief, this congregation of orphans. While we chased one another through the hallways, ran to the vending machines and shook up our sodas, jumped on desks in unsupervised classrooms, and pulled down our pants to moon one another, our parents wept before God. We were protected. Such keening was to be hidden from our eyes. Only God's sight could endure such collective sorrow. Only His eyes alone could take all this in: adults who remained strong and took care of us year-round breaking down and crying out for their lost ones.

But today I didn't leave after the appointed time came. My father glanced at me when the doors were opened and the ushers stood by to lead away the children and the fortunate ones never to have known a dead parent. Or a dead child.

The rabbi said, "Let us rise for the yizkor service, which begins on page one hundred and seventy-eight. Please read silently."

I found the page. There were yizkor prayers in memories of a father, a mother, a husband, a wife, a son, a daughter, and for victims of the Holocaust. I found a yizkor prayer for relatives and friends and decided this was the closest I would get. It had a blank to fill in the name of the person I wanted to remember. I read to myself, moving my lips silently to say Sarah Vale's name. *May God remember the soul of Sarah Vale. . . .*

Her name remained on my lips a moment. I repeated it again. I struggled to get by it. I squeezed my eyes shut, then forced myself to read on: *"And of all relatives and friends who have gone to their eternal home. In loving testimony to their lives I pledge charity to help perpetuate ideals important to them. Through such deeds, and through prayer and memory, are their souls bound up in the bond of life. May they rest eternally in dignity and peace. Amen."*

The rabbi said, "Now let us recite the Mourner's Kaddish. Please continue standing."

Yit-gadal v'yit-kadash sh'mey raba ba'alma di v'ra khir'utei.

I found that I was weeping as I prayed. I did not see others weeping. My images from childhood were not true. Jews did not beat their chests or fall on the floor or sob piteously or call out for their dear, departed parents. I could hear my father pray for his mother and father and for his sister, Bea, in quiet, dignified tones. The Kaddish, after all, mentioned nothing about death. It was affirmative and two thousand years old and praised the glory of God: "Magnified and sanctified be God's great name in the world which He has created according to His will. Glorified and celebrated, lauded and worshipped, acclaimed and honored, extolled and exalted may the Holy One be. Let there be abundant peace from Heaven, with life's goodness for us and to all Israel. *Y'hei shlama raba min sh'maya v'hayim aleinu v'al kol yisrael, v'imru amen."* But I did weep, perhaps because it was a prayer of life. I tried to get control of myself and concentrate on the words, but tears flooded my face, as they had the night I'd seen Mrs. Vale. I wiped my eyes with my suit sleeve and said Kaddish for Sarah Vale, for God on this day to look at a Jew who had killed a non-Jew and to do something to help me make sense of it. *Oseh shalom bi-m'romav, hu ya'aseh shalom aleinu v'al kol yisrael v'imru amen.*

And as I stood there an extraordinary thing happened. My father took his tallis and wrapped it around my shoulders. We shared his prayer shawl, and while we prayed together, he took me under his cover.

Afterward the doors opened and people filed back in. I stayed with my father through the mincha and neilah services, my legs shaky from fasting. I was lightheaded enough to have to grab the back of the seat in front of me a few times. And then at the end of the day, when the sun was setting, the shofar sounded. Its single, arced blast struck me square in the chest as if a tiny fossil were being chiseled from my breastbone.

T E N

It seemed that Ronnie's store and my father's office were the only places left in Chester still breathing. The town had just lost Speares department store, a landmark for decades. All the kids I'd gone to school with had shopped at Speares for their school wardrobes. Now when I walked down Market Street, many of the stores were boarded up. Tollin's furniture was gone, along with the newsstand under the train tracks where I once bought comic books that I read for hours at my father's office. The Boyd Theater had closed. So little was left, in fact, that I wondered how the town could go on. What would pay for the police and fire, the schools, the other municipal services? That my father was still working hard on the redevelopment committee was a testament to his faith in the town. "Where are these people going to go?" he asked one night when my mother and I went out to dinner with him at a Chinese restaurant on Welsh Street. "They can't just pack up and leave and find a better life in the suburbs. It's the end of the line for them unless something is done."

So his committee had tried to lure shoppers back to town with a free shuttle that ran up and down Market Street. They even changed the name of the street to Avenue of the Americas. And put fancy satin banners on each street corner. They added free parking, and all the merchants, the ones left, had sidewalk sales on Saturdays. But little changed. The shuttle went largely unridden. The free parking offered no advantage because few people drove into Chester anymore from anywhere else. Whites, for the most part, the ones who could afford to leave Chester, had become afraid of the town, afraid of the crime there, even in broad daylight. And beyond the pull of the suburbs and the dying of the city's obsolete economy, whites just didn't want to be associated with the place. The suburbs promised progress, prosperity, security, quality education. What Chester had to offer was decaying nostalgia, a main street with boarded-up windows.

It was curious then that Ronnie, as shrewd a businessman as any three times his age, stayed in Chester. He yelled at his mother (I'd discovered he was the real boss); he yelled at the customers. He could have picked up his store and moved it to Springfield or Upper Merion or Newtown Square or any number of places where other Chester businesses had fled, including Myra's father's shoe store just a month before. But he remained. He was, though he wouldn't admit it, devoted to the town and its people. He complained about profits, about nobody writing down in the ledger at the tobacco counter register what was sold, about bounced checks, about food missing from the fountain, about the shvartzers—employees and customers alike—robbing him blind, but he drove to their houses to drop off the prescriptions personally when they couldn't come in for them. He cashed their checks. He extended credit when they pleaded low (or nonexistent) funds. He hired five kids at a time to sweep up in front of the store. More than once I'd seen him comp a meal at the lunch counter for Chester's poorest, the people who would come by with their possessions in a shopping cart from Food Fair. He looked for ways to throw money at them and then complained about it. It was irritable, generous behavior, but I'd begun to think it was all an effort to keep the drugstore open as a sort of mission.

Meanwhile, he'd given Myra and me the key to his house. His mother never came home until after six, and though I felt guilty about using Ronnie's house for our illicit sessions, I felt too good to worry about it.

One day when we were alone in Ronnie's room, Myra turned to me and said, "I have something to tell you."

We hadn't been using anything. We'd been practicing the rhythm method, what Chester "Chet" O'Connor had informed us in health class was to be used once you were married.

We had, however, been careful. I had pulled out, and though Chet had warned us that coitus interruptus—in his gravelly smoker's voice it came out "Quoits Interrupted"—was the most unreliable of all the preventive methods, I possessed a good deal of control. This itself had surprised Myra, who, unlike me, wasn't a virgin. She'd slept with a counselor at Camp Archmere when she was sixteen. He'd been "older" and experienced, and though he had dropped her at the end of the summer, they'd "done it" quite a number of times, and she had to admit she loved it. She shouldn't, she knew, her parents would die, she'd be considered a slut, she'd get VD as much as she liked it, but she couldn't help it, she loved fucking. She'd thought it would hurt all the time, and she hadn't thought she could like it more than with the camp counselor.

"He didn't have a lot of staying power," she'd said, "but I didn't really care because we did it enough to make up for that. You don't have hiccups," she'd said to me. A hiccup was what the girl counselors called premature ejaculation, which seemed to be epidemic among the boy counselors they were having sex with that summer. "This is better. I didn't know what I was missing exactly," she said. We were lying side by side, stretched out on Ronnie's bed, his crisp white sheets, which we washed and changed every time. His room was a mess, but Myra always straightened it up before we lay down. She was holding my hand against her breast and lightly scratching my leg with her toenail.

"I think it has to do with puberty," I said.

"What?"

"Puberty. It took me a long while to get there. When you take that long, you learn patience at a young age."

"David, you're so silly. How long did it take you anyway?"

I was embarrassed to remember. "Awhile," I said.

"Seriously, how long. I mean, were you sixteen or something?"

"Yes," I said. Myra looked at me aghast, just the way I had imagined would happen when a girl discovered the little parakeet in the backseat of a car.

"You're joking?"

"I'm not."

"God, David, I reached puberty at *eleven*. I was having all these sexy thoughts about you at Hebrew school and you weren't even, you know—"

"I know," I said.

"Anyway, I think you're a great lay," she said, and laughed. She cocked her head. "Am I?"

The fact was I thought about Myra all the time. I'd think about her at school, at home, at my father's office, in the shower, when I slept—I wasn't having nightmares anymore—and I was afraid of how much I did think of her. Sometimes I'd take a rubber ball and slam it against the garage door of our house as hard as I could and count up to five hundred just to free my mind for a moment. I saw her slipping out of her panties, unhooking her bra, curling her fingers around my penis and saying Up! Up! (which it instantly obeyed); I saw her straddling me and smiling while she bucked her hips, and I marveled at this kind of bliss. "Yes," I said, "you're a good lay," as if afraid to say anything more for fear of releasing a flood of overwhelming emotions.

"What?" I said now, braced for the news. I would get a full-time job, go to college in the evenings, marry her.

"It's really something more I have to show you than tell you. But I don't know how you'll feel about it."

It took me a moment to realize what she wanted to show me wasn't a baby inside her stomach. "Sure," I said.

"Okay, wait here," said Myra, and hopped off the bed. She wrapped the top sheet around herself, the excess dragging on the floor like a train. Despite the constant protest about her weight and need to diet, Myra liked her body and enjoyed showing it off. She wiggled for me going out the door, and I could see—feel—her buttocks outlined under the white sheet and her sturdy hips, which indeed would serve her well one day in making a baby. She shuffled back into the room, the sheet pinned with one hand up at her throat, a shoebox in her other hand. She had brought it inside with her when we got to Ronnie's. I'd joked that she must have some fancy shoes from her father's store to model for me, but she'd said she'd show me in a while what was in the box.

"I don't know how you feel about this," she said, "but I saved all these."

She opened the box and removed a handful of faded newspaper clippings, spreading them on the bed. They were all about Sarah Vale's death. Most of them had come from the Chester *Times*, but a couple were from the Philadelphia *Inquirer*. I had known about them, but I'd never read them. I glanced at the headline of one: CHILD IN COMA AFTER BEING STRUCK BY FIFTEEN-YEAR-OLD DRIVER.

"Why do you have these?" I said. My legs had begun to shake.

"I don't know," she said. "I just kept them all. I started cutting out the articles because I knew you." Tears were on her cheeks.

I moved one of the clippings aside gingerly, as if with the lance my father used to burst a boil, not my finger. I felt sick to my stomach, as I hadn't in months. My eyes skimmed the headlines to see if any of them cast blame. CIRCUMSTANCES OF FATAL ACCIDENT REMAIN UNCLEAR, one said.

"Why'd you keep these?" I kept asking the same question, unable to understand why she'd bring these here. I had foolishly believed I'd never have to see them. My mother had taken care of screening me from them, whisking away the paper for months until it wasn't necessary anymore.

Myra sat cross-legged on the bed, the sheet over her legs, her breasts small pears hanging down as she hunched her shoulders and cried. "I'm getting all this pressure from people, David."

"Pressure from who?"

"Everybody!" she burst out. "Everybody has something to say. My girlfriends wonder how I can go out with you. 'How can you *do* stuff with him after what he did?' they say." Myra spoke in a high mocking whine, but she didn't sound sincere in her ridicule. "They don't know you. If they knew you—"

"Who else?" I said. "Who else is pressuring you?"

"Everybody." She turned away. "My parents. They think we're spending too much time together." She wiped her eyes with the back of her hand. "What am I supposed to tell them? I'm starting to lie about where I go."

"Do they think that because of this?" I said, and nodded at the box. I saw another clipping: DRIVER CHARGED WITH VEHICULAR HOMICIDE ATTEMPTS SUICIDE. I could feel my voice shifting into a familiar monotone, my body floating away or wanting to float away, to find something that would put a cloud between us.

"They're afraid we're getting too serious. That's all they'll say."

"We *are* serious."

Myra looked at me. "When Ronnie first asked me to come over to a party, I didn't want to go. Did you know that?"

"No," I said quietly, barely loud enough for even my own ears.

"I don't know why I'm telling you this."

"Because you have to, I suppose."

"Ronnie told me it would be a mitzvah."

"A mitzvah," I said. "Ronnie and his mitzvahs."

"He said you were really depressed and needed company, and he wanted to cheer you up. I had this sick curiosity to see you. To see what you looked like after—"

"Stop," I said. "Don't tell me anymore."

"I have to. I have to because that's not the way I feel now. Can't you see what I'm saying?"

"No," I said.

"I didn't expect all this to happen, David."

"So what are you telling me?"

Myra looked down at her legs. We were both sitting cross-legged on the bed, our knees almost touching through the sheet. I had a sudden desire to cover myself up, to drape my penis that stretched toward her in dumb, accordion confusion. "I don't know why I saved all the clippings. I just kept them and then felt really guilty that you didn't know."

The phone rang. It sometimes rang twenty times, usually one of Ronnie's many suit customers. Myra put her hands on my face. "I feel like if it happened to you, then it happened to me too. David, do you know what I'm saying?"

"I don't think so," I said.

Now that I knew the shoebox existed, I wanted to see what was written about me. That could have been, I suppose, a healthy sign: I cared enough about my reputation to investigate what had been said. But it was more that Myra had produced the very situation I dreaded; somewhere somebody kept my horrible secret in a box, like the skeleton under Adrian's bed.

At home I took the top off and found the earliest article. Myra had been reluctant to let me have the shoebox at all. "It's just going to make you feel worse, David," she'd said to me on the otherwise silent drive to my house. "Why do you want it?"

"I just do," I said.

She'd let me have it, worried, I could see, about what I planned to do with it.

"Are you going to be okay?" she asked when I got out of the car. Tomorrow Myra was leaving for five days with her parents to look at colleges in New England.

"Sure," I'd said, cradling the shoebox. "Have fun looking at schools."

"I'll call you."

I scanned now the first article quickly for my name and then realized I wasn't going to find it: that as a juvenile my identity had been successfully kept out of the paper. I was "the youth" or "the minor" or "the teen driver" or "the driver responsible." The facts were all there: I'd been driving my parents' car late one afternoon in May through a section of Wallingford. Three other boys, "friends of the driver responsible," had been riding in another car. A little girl—Sarah was mentioned by name—had run out to her yard through an unlocked screen door and encountered the vehicle. You could see the reporter didn't know how to present the facts in this first article: the bizarreness of a car winding up backwards deep on someone's front lawn. There was even the impression that Mrs. Vale had somehow been negligent in not locking her screen door. A photographer captured the askew angle of the F-85, as if it had been intentionally placed on the lawn for display, like a show car.

I found a clipping dated May 17, one day later:

An investigation continues into the circumstances surrounding the automobile injury of a 3-year-old Wallingford girl in front of her home by a local juvenile. Drag racing is suspected in the accident. Three other boys involved in the case, all juveniles, have claimed that no racing occurred. The driver responsible for the injury has been unavailable for comment. The girl, Sarah Vale, of 4200 Todmorden Drive, remains in a coma at Chester-Crozer Hospital.

Followed by May 19:

The 3-year-old injured Wednesday in an automobile accident died Friday evening of head injuries. The victim, Sarah Vale, had remained for two days in a coma until her death. Charges are being considered against an underage Garden City driver. The district attorney has declined comment on what the charges will be, if any, pending further investigation. A funeral service for the child will be held at Nacrelli's Funeral Home in Chester on Sunday.

I picked up a longer article from the Philadelphia *Inquirer* dated June 2, two days after my birthday. The headline said: DRIVER CHARGED WITH VEHICULAR HOMICIDE.

A 16-year-old boy was charged Tuesday in the death of a 3-year-old Wallingford child. Controversy has continued to surround the case, with parents and community groups calling for stricter enforcement of traffic laws and appropriate penalties for vehicular offenses. The victim, daughter of Adele and Jack Vale, owners of the Media Diner, died May 18. The child was in her front yard when she was hit by an out-of-control vehicle. Driving without supervision on a learner's permit, the youth responsible told authorities he was backing up when his car jumped the curb. The district attorney's office, after pressure from the victim's family and other members of the community, finally charged the teen on Tuesday with vehicular homicide. Reports had been circulating that the driver, the son of a prominent Chester physician, was receiving privileged treatment, an accusation that Chief Deputy District Attorney Morton Bell forcefully denied: "We are carefully and diligently going about this case as we would any other.'' No pleas to the charge have yet been entered. The driver remains in the custody of his parents.

I held this one in my hand for quite a while, reading, and rereading the sentence "the son of a prominent Chester physician" and had some idea finally of the misery my parents had also gone through.

I skipped a month and a half to an article about my suicide attempt, which I had to force myself to read: "The youth responsible for the death of a 3-year-old girl in a driving accident attempted to take his life yesterday afternoon. . . ." It was only the facts: I was rushed to Chester-Crozer Hospital and reported to be in stable condition. Nothing was mentioned about Sarah Vale other than a quote from Lance Schnabel that he hoped the case could finally be brought to a quick resolution in light of the pain this tragedy had caused everyone involved.

I found a series of short articles reporting a plea bargain was in the works and then one stating an agreement had been reached with the district attorney's office. A new hearing was expected in two weeks. After that there followed an announcement of the plea and then an article reporting my sentencing and probation. And a reaction from the Vales, a brief statement that although they were disappointed, they had accepted this possibility as a means of securing an admission of guilt, without which they could have found no rest. Myra had dated each clipping, cut the borders neatly, and stapled the longer ones together, all without comment. I held the pile in my hand, testing the weight of them, and I remembered the time I laid Sarah Vale against my shoulder, the same lightness, the same immensity.

Unable to sleep after thrashing around until two A.M., I got up and looked in the closet to see if a bottle of wine was still there. It was. The same sweet grape wine I liked best. But after a few good swallows I didn't want it anymore and put it away. Perhaps I knew then I wasn't alcoholic, not physically addicted at least, not the wino on skid row, or the closet drinker in the secluded Main Line home, or the school kid desperate enough to drink NyQuil for its 12 percent alcohol. I should have enjoyed some relief from this, but I felt worse. It scared me that there wasn't something to fall back on now, no tonic to heat the lumpy, formless paraffin that composed my ego and re-shape my fear and loneliness and sorrow into a pretty holiday shape, all scented with purple grapes and oblivion.

In the morning I went to school, ate lunch with Ronnie. He was largely distracted with his various business interests—school was just another office to him—and I longed for someone to pal around with during the day, strongly missing Calvin, who had been more available. Despite the routine of school, the year and a half it had been since Sarah Vale's death, I was still wary of making friends, of getting close to anyone. The possibility always existed of getting knocked in the back of the head with a geography book, or whatever it had been, but more important, I trusted few people with my immense shame, monolithic again by reading about myself all night. And Myra's re-mark about her Swarthmore girlfriends' astonishment how she could be with me had remained in my head and made me worry, as I had when I first returned to school, that people were thinking about me all the time. I found myself getting angry at her, having fierce argu-ments with her in my head about why she'd done this—the shoebox, the whole issue—and then flipping to the other side and thanking her for getting everything out in the open.

That afternoon, by habit, I drove up to Swarthmore and walked around the college's woods. I took the same path that Myra and I did, and I tried to reassure myself that everything would be fine when she came back from investigating colleges. I had no reason to believe otherwise. Aside from the shoebox, which had always been there anyway, things were looking better, not worse, and I attributed my massive anxiety (I had started sweating on a crisp fall day) to my usual apprehension that everything would end badly for me.

I passed two students on the path, a couple. The boy gave me the peace sign. He wore bellbottoms and a headband, and the girl, I noticed—couldn't help but notice—was braless; I realized I'd startled them and that they'd probably been doing what Myra and I did here.

I walked on farther west and for some reason decided to cross Crum Creek, which marked the boundary of Swarthmore College's property. I stepped over a hollow log, then found a shallow place in Crum Creek to hop across the rocks. I followed a ravine up a steep hill, crunching my way over dried leaves and through brush and ferns and tangled ivy until I came to Rogers Lane and the beginning of a large estate, which I realized was Pendle Hill, the Quaker retreat and study center. I'd known it was around here somewhere. It covered a relatively vast area of twenty acres but had always been tucked away in the township and discreetly hidden by tall trees. I walked out of the woods into a clearing with a large garden: the yellowing vines of squash, trellises and tepees for pole beans, and spent tomato plants. In a few minutes I came to a two-story fieldstone building. A couple of men stood on the porch talking and paid me little notice as I approached. I hovered there for a moment, trying not to listen to their conversation, which was about a Quaker committee they both served on. Finally I interrupted. "I was wondering if you could tell me"— I realized I didn't know his last name—"if Arthur is here?"

"He's at the barn," the man said. They smiled at me.

"Thanks," I said, and they went back to talking.

I walked down a gravel driveway in the direction they'd pointed me and soon saw the barn, a yellowish brick building that had obviously been added on to over the years. I tried one door, found it led to an empty room, then went through another and saw Arthur behind a large wooden door on wheels—evidently the old barn gate—changing lightbulbs in the ceiling fixtures. Several rows of long benches faced one another in a square.

"Hi," I said.

He looked down from his ladder at me, then said, "David." It pleased me that he remembered. "How *are* you?"

He stepped off the ladder, wiping his hand on his jeans, then extended it to me.

"I just thought I'd stop in," I said.

"That's great you came by."

"I walked from the college."

Arthur looked impressed. "That's quite a jaunt."

"I sort of lost track of time." It was true, and the steady walking, fording Crum Creek, forging through sticker bushes and underbrush, had distracted me from thinking about Myra—or anything else. "I've never been here before. It's practically in my backyard."

"How about a tour?" asked Arthur.

"I'd like that," I said, and he put his arm gently on my shoulder, guiding me out.

ELEVEN

I tried calling Myra when she returned from her trip but only got her mother, who said Myra was at an orthodontist appointment.

I waited two hours, then called again. "She's still not back yet, David," said Mrs. Berman, who was always unfailingly polite and asked after my mother and father, even if she had just inquired the day before. "I promise to have her call you."

I waited two more hours by the phone. By this time it was almost eight o'clock, and I couldn't imagine where she could be. I called again. Her father, far gruffer than his wife, barked hello. Myra wasn't back yet. He didn't know. He just got home. He hadn't even read the paper. What was my number?

I told him she had it, I was sure. He hung up.

I became frantic, began pacing around the house. My mother was out looking at places to rent in Swarthmore, to find a space to do her pottery. It didn't mean anything else, she had told me. She just needed some studio space, and Swarthmore seemed the ideal place. The paper had a few possibilities advertised, and she'd driven over to look at them with Mr. Richardson. She'd been gone more than six hours, and I felt deserted by everybody. When I needed her most, she wasn't here, and the old anger and resentment and impulse to do something drastic came back. I paced in front of the house, as if someone, Myra in particular, might notice me. Finally I went inside and called again, praying it wouldn't be Mr. Berman who answered.

It was Myra.

"Where were you?" I asked, not giving her a chance to explain anything. "Why haven't you called me?"

"I've been so busy, David. It's really been hectic."

"When did you get back?"

"Yesterday."

"Yesterday? When yesterday?"

"What's it matter?"

"I can't believe you didn't call. You said you were going to call from Boston even."

"Talk about busy. I hardly had a moment to think up there. I'm in love."

"What?"

"I'm in love with Wellesley. David, it has the most wonderful theater program."

I sat silently, brooding about this a moment.

"I can't wait to tell you about it," said Myra.

"When can I see you?" I said.

"Okay," she said. "We should do that."

" '*We should do that*'? What's that mean?"

"It just means I'm busy, that's all. I've missed four days of school! I have all this work to make up."

"Myra, you're a senior, you're supposed to miss school. And it's never worried you before."

"Come tomorrow after school, okay? I'll meet you at the train station."

I felt enormous relief, as if my skin had reattached itself to my bones, jumped from the wire hanger it had been suspended on while I'd been waiting to hear from her. "Can we talk a little now?" I asked.

Myra put her hand over the receiver, then came back on. "My dad wants me to get to bed. I stayed up till two every morning hanging out at the colleges when we were in New England. I'll see you tomorrow. Promise." She blew me a kiss through the phone.

I met Myra at the bridge by the train station in Swarthmore, next to the college. I hugged her, but she pulled away after a moment, not yielding to my kiss. It took me by surprise because I didn't know Myra this way. I knew a girl who drew me toward her soft breasts and whose mouth was loose and wet on my own and who didn't protect herself. I wasn't much of one to crack hard shells, and I found myself walking beside her with a considerable space between us.

She told me about her trip to New England, the campuses of Brown and Wellesley, her interviews, a night she'd spent on the floor of a girls' dorm, while her parents stayed in the motel. I had a hard time concentrating. I wanted to know what all this meant for us.

We started to walk toward the woods, and Myra said, "Let's just talk here." We sat in front of Clothier Hall on a wood bench dedicated by the class of 1929. On the chair's back, on a small brass plaque was inscribed, "Day, You are old, will You forget songs that we sang the morning we met?"

"Day," said Myra, clutching her heart, "You are old!"

I tried to laugh. The bell in Clothier Tower chimed four times while we sat in silence as if waiting politely for it to stop ringing.

"You're shivering," said Myra. I had hardly noticed, but it was November and cold as soon as the sun dropped. I'd rushed out of the house without a jacket to meet her.

"I'll be okay."

"We can go inside."

I shook my head. I didn't want to be where anyone could hear us or see us. I was afraid I'd lose my composure. "What's going on?" I said.

Myra wrapped her arms around her legs. "Nothing," she said. She put her chin on her knees. "Everything."

"Tell me."

"I don't know what to say, David."

"Why didn't you call me when you got back?"

"I needed some time to think." She looked at me. I was trying to bite the inside of my cheek to keep from shivering. It was as much from nerves as the cold. I pictured myself as a large blob of Jell-O on one of those motorized tummy belts. I had hoped to appear terse and hard, the Marlboro man, and instead everything was becoming ge-latinous. "I wanted to see if I still felt the same way when I got back," Myra said.

"The same way as what?"

"As I did up in New England. I liked being able to stay out and not worry about anything. I could see how it would be next year."

"When you're not with me."

Myra hesitated. "I guess," she said, and suddenly I saw her sleeping on a dorm room floor not by herself but with somebody. Whether this was true or not, I don't know. It felt true. It felt as if she could forget me, and some howling ache began inside, as if the last hinge of a shutter had blown off, letting the wind rush fiercely through. "I think we should try to be on our own for a while."

I turned to the side, holding back tears. White Adirondack chairs dotted the expansive lawn in front of Parrish Hall. Students strolled down Magill Walk, under an endless row of hundred-year-old oaks whose branches formed a voluminous canopy.

"I don't want to lose you as a friend, David."

"Why can't we continue?" I said. "Do you think I'm going to tell you what to do at college? That I'm going to insist you never see anybody or have any fun?"

"Aren't you?" said Myra.

"Of course not," I said.

Myra put her head in her hands. "You're just confusing me, David. You say I'm free to do as I please, and then you tell me that we should just continue on as always. What do you *want* from me?"

"I want you not to run away because you're afraid."

Myra's face was streaked with tears. "Everybody else is afraid for me. I don't even have a chance to be afraid for myself."

Myra and I agreed to talk on the phone after two weeks. If I really was being truthful about not trying to control her, then I'd give her that time. I said I was. She kissed me deeply, her tongue thrust hard into my mouth, and I was the one who became confused.

I drove to Pendle Hill. Arthur had invited me to dinner, and I went in search of his room. He was at Upmeads, one of the older buildings on the grounds and the place where tea was served every afternoon at four, he'd told me, a nod toward Pendle Hill's English roots. I knocked lightly, and he came to the door with a book in his hand.

"Am I early?"

"Right on the button," said Arthur. "I'm glad you could come by."

His room was sparsely furnished: a pine dresser, a simple desk, and a reading chair by a single window. A bookcase stacked two and three deep with books stood against the far wall.

"Is this where you sleep?" I didn't see a bed.

Arthur laughed. "I have a cot in the closet. It's tight in here, but I don't spend a lot of time cleaning, on the other hand."

I went to dinner with him. We ate in Main House at a long pine table the color of dark honey. Arthur introduced me to the director, Elton, and a few of the residential students who were here for the eleven-week term, which had just begun. And the sojourners—they were called that, seekers who had come to study, meditate, or pursue a project or just be part of the working community for a brief period. Not everybody was a Quaker, or an American Quaker at least. There were three people from Japan, two from South America, a Canadian, two Buddhists from Thailand, and a student on semester leave from Oberlin College. Pendle Hill, I learned, had enjoyed an illustrious list of visitors, including T. S. Eliot, Aldous Huxley, and Christopher Isherwood. I felt immediately comfortable, unlike among Adrian's group of friends. "What do you study here?" I asked Arthur at dinner, and he rattled off a list: Quaker studies, religious thought and spiritual practice, peace and social concerns, literature and the arts, and I realized while he was answering that I'd already begun to think of myself as a seeker and could imagine myself sojourning here.

When I got back to my house, I picked up the phone to call Myra, then put it down, remembering my promise. I wanted to tell her about having dinner with the Quakers. The last time we'd talked about them, after we'd picketed the Acme, Myra had said she thought they seemed earnest and dedicated but a little too quiet for her. She liked noise. She liked exuberance. She liked cacophony and kvetching and some spicy naughtiness and the occasional bad temper. She wanted to be an actress. What great Quaker actress did I know? None, I had to admit.

And she liked gossip. She loved to talk about people, especially adults and their messed-up lives, which fascinated her endlessly since her own parents were so boringly predictable and stable. "I think they have sex once a week because the aspirin bottle is always out on the sink every Saturday evening. I never want to become like that," said Myra. "I can't imagine it ever being such a chore."

I doubted my own parents had sex anymore. As for my father having affairs since Josie, I wasn't sure. I suppose he might have, away at medical conventions or even here in town. But I had long since stopped looking, afraid of what I might see. On the other hand, I wondered if he and my mother had struck some kind of deal, as I had that day when he rumpled my hair and said I needn't tell anyone about seeing Josie and him embracing. Perhaps my parents had made an agreement of their own: my mother's presence here for my father's fidelity.

The fact was I knew nothing about my parents' sex lives. I suppose my father could have sneaked into my mother's bedroom or vice versa, but it was more than likely they had no contact of that sort between them, and surprisingly, it bothered me now—now that I had started having sex. Were they still doing (or not doing) this for me?

I fell asleep in my clothes. When I woke up, it was after midnight, and there was a light on downstairs. I thought it might be my father getting in late from the hospital. But as I passed his bedroom, I heard his rhythmic snoring.

It was my mother, reading on the living room couch, with her legs tucked under her.

She looked up startled. She had on her bathrobe. Her hair was down, unusual for her, since she so often tied it up in back. She no longer visited the beauty parlor to have it dyed brown, but had let the roots grow out gray. Her birthday was coming up in December, and she would turn fifty.

"Are you unable to sleep, David?"

I nodded and sat down on the green velvet wing chair across from her.

"Aren't you tired? You have school tomorrow."

"I'll be all right. Can we talk awhile?"

My mother sighed, cornered by the late hour, by both our sleepless ways. "Yes, I suppose. I'm just concerned that you get enough sleep."

I looked at the closed drapes by the picture window. My mother's bottle collection was long gone. She had a few pieces of her early pottery along the ledge, some bowls and mugs, but mostly she'd packed it all away to take to her new studio. She'd found a carriage house to rent in Swarthmore in back of a retired professor's home.

My mother stared at me for a long moment.

"What?" I said.

"Is something wrong?"

"No," I answered, a little too quickly.

"Is this about you and Myra?" my mother asked. "She hasn't called here lately."

"We're just taking a breather from each other," I said, wanting to believe it.

"Did you have a fight?"

"No. Not really."

"Not really," repeated my mother. "What's that mean?"

"It means she's worried about her freedom. And as I said, we're taking a break."

"David, can I ask you something?"

"I suppose," I said, uncomfortable at the wide-open possibilities.

"Do you and Myra talk about your accident?"

"Just recently," I said.

"What did she say?" asked my mother, more than a little curious. She'd untucked her legs from the couch.

"She didn't say anything. She had a shoebox of clippings about what happened. She'd kept them."

"Kept them?"

"She'd just saved them." I shrugged, thinking about them in my room. I'd put the box in the bottom drawer of my bureau among old tie clips, cuff links, and an identification bracelet that had always slipped off my wrist.

My mother was silent a moment. "Myra cares for you very much, David. It's been wonderful for me to watch."

She must have been thinking about this for some time now:

Would I find a girl who would understand? And how every parent must worry about such a thing. Whatever cruelty, whatever handicap, whatever deformity or failing or lacking—slurping soup or killing a child—somebody will have enough perseverance and reason finally to overlook it and love your child.

"Sometimes, David, I think it would be easier if you could talk with your father."

"What do you mean?"

"I'm saying he might understand feelings you have for Myra, and your confusion, better than I do."

"I don't think so," I said. I couldn't imagine talking with my father about girls. I looked up at the scalloped yellow glow from the porcelain shades of the two brass sconces on the wall and thought of Josie's hand on the back of my father's neck.

My mother came over and stroked my hair. After a minute she said, "Your father can be a difficult man, David. I won't deny that. But he's amazed me in the past."

"What do you mean?" I said carefully. I did, and didn't, want to hear what she might say.

"Two instances come to mind. After your accident I asked him if we could move. Adrian was going off to college. I thought it would be best for everybody, take the pressure off. I wanted to leave the immediate area, at least for a while. He wouldn't do it."

"What was the other thing?"

"I don't think you know this, David. Your father went to Sarah's viewing."

"What?"

"He insisted on going. He waited in the long line and filed past her open casket and then expressed his regrets to Mr. and Mrs. Vale."

"Are you sure?"

"Of course I'm sure. We didn't want to tell you at the time."

"What did the Vales do?"

"I don't believe they spoke back to him. He was in line with two hundred other people, and he moved on past, without incident. I found it hard to believe he had done this."

"You think he shouldn't have?"

"I didn't say that. I just said I found it hard to believe. I couldn't have done it myself. He's a very stubborn person, your father, once he makes up his mind about something."

"So what are you saying? That's good or bad?"

"I don't know, David." My mother laughed. "I honestly don't know. I guess I'm very tired, more tired than I thought. Come upstairs soon. Please."

When I came home from school the next day, I went upstairs and took out Myra's shoebox, this repository of my history that we shared custody of. Whether she'd forgotten about the box, which I doubted, or was just embarrassed to bring it up, she hadn't asked for it back, as if there were no graceful way to want something like this returned. It was questionable whom it really belonged to anyway.

I opened it again and took out the one clipping I'd been avoiding. It was an article about the Vales, shortly before my sentencing. They'd allowed themselves to be interviewed by the Philadelphia *Inquirer*. The article's headline said, FAMILY STRUGGLES TO STAY FAITHFUL AFTER TRAGEDY, and there was a picture of the four of them standing out in front of the Media Diner, with an inset of Sarah, her hair in pigtails. The Vales had dedicated their luncheon room to her. It was the place where the Lions Club and the Rotary met, and it was to be called Sarah's Room from now on. In the picture Mrs. Vale had a slight, forbearing smile, Paul looked solemn, Russell nervous, and Mr. Vale unfocused, his gaze away from the camera. They had, they said, been trying to spend time as a family at church. Neighbors and friends had been wonderful. They'd received more than three hundred cards and sympathy letters. The hardest thing was coming home from work and not hearing Sarah's voice in the house. She'd been the noisy one of the family, full of silly songs and insistent calls to play dress-up at ten o'clock at night. Her brothers had lavished attention on her, in between calming her down. "It doesn't seem fair," Mrs. Vale said, "that the very youngest and most alive of us should be taken first." It was a line that I found depressingly honest. I read it over and over and over, with punishing regard.

———

"When Jesus said, 'I am the way, the truth, and the life,' early Quakers interpreted this statement to mean that the life of Jesus was a pattern to be learned from and emulated," Arthur said.

I sat in a group of about fifteen at Upmeads around a crackling fire in the hearth. Arthur spoke to us of George Fox and his spiritual growth. George Fox, whose journals and those of other Quakers formed the basis of the course Arthur taught, had preached that Jesus lived in all of us, a heretical idea at the time, for which Fox was accused of trying to make himself equal to God.

Arthur read: " 'Now I was come up in the spirit through the flaming sword into the paradise of God. All things were new, and all the creation gave forth another smell unto me than before, beyond what words can utter.'

" 'Beyond what words can utter,' " said Arthur, repeating the last line of the text. "Fox's writings were preoccupied with the transcendent moment beyond which words cannot take us. John Woolman, an early American Quaker, had a similar experience he recorded in his journal. He wrote of one of his dreams: 'I saw a mass of human beings in as great misery as they could be, and that I was mixed with them. I then heard a soft, melodious voice, more pure and harmonious than any voice I had heard with my ears before; and I believe it was the voice of an angel. . . . The words were, *John Woolman is dead.*' "

Arthur took his glasses off. "How do you think Woolman interpreted such a dream?"

The student from Oberlin raised his hand. His name was Francis, and he had a shock of red hair and a patchy straw gold beard. I wondered what I'd gotten myself into. A small alarm had gone off in my head that I shouldn't be here. When I'd told my mother where I was going, she'd given me a slightly uncomfortable look, as if to question why I, as a Jew, would be going to a Quaker center. Though she wasn't devout by any stretch of the word, she shared the same wariness as I did that somebody out there was waiting to convert us, or any Jew, an especially good catch. There were places where Jews would be taken and brainwashed and converted, and then afterward we would betray other Jews. My mother's slightly puzzled look was because she couldn't fit Quakers into the scheme or not readily so. She, like me, knew little about them. But somewhere along the line I'd been told and gotten the message "You are a Jew, and you must never forget it. When they start talking about the Messiah, flee."

But I stayed.

Francis, the Oberlin student, said, "I think Woolman is saying that he suddenly found himself part of the great mass of humanity and his life had no meaning apart from their suffering."

"He's unable to separate his fate from that of others," said Arthur.

"It's a true political calling," Francis said.

"Service, would you say?" asked Arthur. "He's going to form a committee?"

Everybody laughed. The Quakers evidently had hundreds of committees, a committee for everything.

There was silence. I'd noticed that the discussion sometimes flowed, sometimes completely stopped, and although Arthur was supposed to be nominally leading it, I don't know that he actually was. He would wait for minutes sometimes before posing another question or adding a comment. We'd been sitting for two hours. At least half that time had been spent in silence mulling over what had been said. These silences hung with crystalline sharpness in the air.

"I wonder about something," said a girl with blond hair. She wore a long blue skirt and had sat as quietly as I had, listening, though her eyes had been bright with interest. "I wonder if John Woolman's dream has simply shown him the death of his ego and his merging into a divine unity."

There was an especially long silence, and then Arthur said, "That's a fine note to end on for today."

I found a phone. I wanted to check in at home before dinner in Main House and see if Myra had called. I had this idea that she might. My mother said she was waiting for Mr. Richardson to come over. They were going out to see a movie. My father was at the office and then off to a meeting with the governor's representative for the redevelopment of Chester. "Were there any calls for me?"

"No," my mother said. "Were you expecting any?"

"Not really," I said.

"Are you coming home now?" she asked.

"After dinner."

"Is everything all right there, David? What are you doing exactly?"

"We've just been talking so far."

"Is it . . ."

"What?"

"Is it very religious?"

"I don't think so," I said. "Not in that way."

"I think your father would be disappointed if it was, if you were there for the religious part."

She meant Jesus. Was I about to be swept away by Jesus? I'd already been told that not everybody who was a Quaker believed in

Jesus, but some part of me took a perverse pleasure in not giving my mother this piece of information.

"I have to go," I said. "I'll be home about nine."

I went back to the dining room and sat next to the blond girl who had spoken so succinctly about John Woolman's dream.

"I'm David," I said.

"Helen." She had gray-green eyes with flecks of gold in them.

We bowed our heads in a silent grace, and then the food was passed around, a stir-fry dish that a Japanese couple had supervised making.

"Do you agree with the action of sending *The Phoenix* into the waters of Haiphong Harbor?" Francis asked Arthur.

Helen said in an aside to me, "*The Phoenix* was a Quaker ship with medical supplies that was sent to North Vietnam."

"I'm not sure, Francis," said Arthur. "I was not part of the committee that made that decision."

"But you're expressing some reservations about the action," said Francis. "In your voice."

"If I'm expressing that, I am unaware of it. It was an action with which I agreed, in part."

"In part?"

"I think the action might have warranted more planning, that's all."

There was a moment of silence. Then people went back to eating, leaving the question in the air. Helen whispered to me, "The subject of the Mid-Winter Institute was 'The Gap Between the Generations.' Fitting, no?"

I nodded.

"Are you a sojourner?" she asked.

"I'm still in high school," I said. "I'm just sitting in on some classes. Are you?"

"A sojourner? Yes. I'm a freshman at Swarthmore College, but

I'm taking some time off." She smiled at me and touched my hand with hers and seemed as surprised as I did that she had.

After dinner the Japanese couple came up to me. "Hideko," the woman said, bowing. She was dressed in a brightly embroidered kimono and obi.

"Akio," her husband said, bowing too.

I bowed back and felt enormously relieved to be here.

T W E L V E

I went to morning meeting every day before school. I'd get up at six, take a shower, make my lunch, and then drive my mother's car over to the center. She had been generous about letting me use it, but lately she'd complained, though I suspected it had more to do with my spending so much time at Pendle Hill than with taking her car.

My father had asked, at my mother's bidding (it was interesting how in spite of their other problems, they still functioned as a parental wall), if he could come visit the study center with me sometime. I'd said certainly, though neither of us mentioned a specific date. I thought he'd actually enjoy the center—he had the inbred spirit of a Quaker from what I was coming to understand of them—but on the other hand, I didn't want him intruding on my world.

I parked in the visitors' lot and walked past Main House and the volleyball courts to a favorite spot, a three-hundred-year-old beech tree that I liked to lean back against in the morning before meeting for worship. The oldest tree on the grounds, the beech had been here since the time of William Penn. I found comfort in its enormous span

190

of branches stretching skyward and the mighty girth of its thirty-foot-round trunk.

I saw Arthur coming across the lawn with Madelyn, the resident dog. Niles, the resident rabbit, followed them. It was a different world here, almost make-believe: rabbits and dogs merrily running and hopping along; ancient guardian trees; people cooperating in all aspects of living—household chores, the office, the garden, the grounds—an abhorrence of war and bigotry; vigorous self-questioning; and new ideas that I couldn't even keep up with.

I had brought Howard Brinton's *Guide to Quaker Practice* home with me and read it cover to cover in one sitting. I was barely able to control my enthusiasm and wanted to take all the courses offered. It all tasted sweet to me, hopeful. Contrary to the perception of Quakers, mine included, that they walked around in gray frocks saying thee and thou and rejected music and festivity, they were not gloomy or dogmatic. Arthur, in a spirited Monday night lecture, had quoted a Quaker, Jack L. Willcuts: "To be one in the Spirit is true togetherness. Not that we look alike, dress alike, sound alike, or even think alike. . . . Unity is spiritual, uniformity is mechanical."

I had told Arthur I wanted to enroll for a term.

"When would you come?" asked Arthur.

"This summer."

Arthur smiled. I'd caught up with him right after morning meeting yesterday. He was cleaning the gutters of leaves. "We don't have sessions from June to October. We have our special programs then, retreats, conferences."

"Then in the fall," I said, standing next to his ladder. He scooped out a thick brown sludge of decomposed leaves.

"David," said Arthur slowly, "you should take your time with all this."

"Why?" I said, hurt by the rebuff. "I'm interested. I'm very interested."

"I know you're interested. My question is, are you ready?"

"Ready for what?"

"To involve yourself so much at the center. You're here every spare moment." Arthur laughed. "Don't you have some other friends you'd like to see? What do your mother and father think of your spending so much time here?"

"They're fine about it," I lied. "They're glad I'm doing something educational with my time."

"Look, David, I'm not trying to dissuade you from coming here. I'm delighted you're so interested. But I've seen the signs before. People fall hard for this place, and they use it as a retreat from the world, for all the wrong reasons. I'm asking you to question that in yourself." He dropped a handful of leaf crud into a bucket. It was to go into a compost pile behind the barn.

I slunk away, or if not exactly slunk, then retreated, chastised. Arthur hadn't been stern, but I'd felt the sting of his remarks in a different way: *for all the wrong reasons*. I didn't like to think that I was using the place as an escape. That wasn't it. I'd found something that made sense. I'd gone to see him later in the day, after school.

"I think you're being too hard on me," I said. "I know what I'm doing here."

Arthur rubbed his wrist, looked down a moment. "Maybe I am being hard on you, David. I'd planned to tell you that as soon as I saw you."

"I'm very interested in all this stuff," I said.

Arthur laughed. "This stuff *is* very interesting, I have to admit. Want to walk with me while I pick up some deliveries at the entrance?"

———

I took my seat on one of the benches. The barn was where attendees and members met every morning for meeting. I didn't know which of us were actual Friends, which just visitors. Half the people at Pendle Hill weren't even Quakers, just the curious, like me, though I wanted to think of myself as more than just curious.

I sat with my hands on my knees. I stared at the mullioned windows, the narrow benches, the exposed brick walls. No stained glass. No organ. No bema or pulpit. No ark with a thousand-year-old Torah. No leader. The meeting would just begin, out of nowhere. Everyone would suddenly become silent.

My first time I'd waited tensely for someone to speak, and when no one had, I'd felt disappointed, as if the experience had been one large blank, like a test with no answers. I don't think that was the way others felt, however, because after about an hour the members abruptly rose to their feet, grasped hands, and began talking animatedly, enjoying the coffee and doughnuts. They appeared to be revitalized.

It wasn't until the third time that I did hear somebody speak, and the voice slipped from the quiet as easily as a loose thread being pulled off a sweater: "It's been laid upon my heart to leave the shelter of school and make a stand against the war." It was, I realized, Francis who had spoken. The statement stayed in the air, each word framed by the lack of any reaction other than total silence: *heart, shelter, stand, war.* I had not, despite *The Bluehead,* thought much about the war. I had even been looking forward to registering with the draft board at eighteen, a sign of manhood I could claim with a card. The possibility that I would go or be drafted I hadn't taken seriously. College would keep me out, and then the war would be over. It was stunning to me that someone would reject all that assurance and protection.

I sat listening now for myself to speak, for some message I might be moved to impart. I knew, however, I wouldn't. Arthur had been right. I was trying too hard. My mind wandered. I thought of Myra. I was hungry, having rushed out of the house (the meeting started at

8:00 A.M.). I worried about a paper I had due for English class on *Crime and Punishment,* a book I'd read twice, looking to see what really motivated Raskolnikov in the moment of killing the old lady moneylender. "The central themes of *Crime and Punishment* are the redemption of man from sin and darkness and the crushing forces of poverty on the human spirit." I crossed this out, disgusted. Somewhere between this tired idea and some feverish confession of my own must lie a sensible, intelligent understanding of what I'd read. But I couldn't find the middle ground, couldn't offer up any insights with assurance.

I tried harder now to "center down," the Quaker practice of opening to the spirit and the presence of God. But I had no idea what that meant. Did God want to hear my problems? Did He want to know how I couldn't write a paper on Raskolnikov in *Crime and Punishment* because I was Raskolnikov in my heart? Did He want to know how I had suddenly concluded that I needed to leave the world and live at Pendle Hill for the rest of my life? Did all this no longer matter because I, David Nachman, was part of a boundless Truth that erased all distinctions between my individual will and God's?

I listened to the occasional cough around me, the patter of the rain as it hit the roof, the slight shifting of bodies on the benches. My back and neck muscles felt particularly stiff, and I thought it was harder today, my tenth time, than it had been all the other nine. I was *more* conscious of myself. I had so much to get done. My mother wanted me to help her move into her new studio in Swarthmore. Myra had called and said she couldn't wait the full two weeks until Monday to see me. Could we meet tonight, Friday, instead?

A woman spoke. "As I ponder the difficulty of prayer, I have come to think about that old joke, the one about the man who keeps asking God to help him win the lottery. 'Oh, Lord, please let me win,' he says every week, and every week he doesn't win, he says the next week, 'Oh, Lord, please help me win,' and he goes on saying this, week after week, month after month, year after year. Until one day he hears the Lord speak to him, and the Lord says, 'For heaven's sake, you have to buy a ticket first.'" There was laughter, the one time I'd heard any in a meeting. "I find that first step toward God very hard," said the woman after a pause.

A few minutes later someone else spoke, "In all the hustle and bustle of the season it's nice to have a moment of peace."

I recognized neither speaker and took some solace in their anonymity, and mine.

Nothing more was said, and when the meeting ended, we stood up and shook hands.

I picked up Myra that evening to go see *The Graduate*. It was Myra's favorite movie. I'd missed the film when it first came out, as I'd missed much of what was happening during that period, but now it was on a second run at the College Theater in Swarthmore.

Myra had on blue jeans, her first pair of hip-hugger bellbottoms. She twirled around for me when I came to the door. I hadn't seen her since we'd decided to part company for two weeks.

The collar of her white blouse peeked out of a butterscotch-colored cashmere sweater. She smelled freshly of apricot soap. She threw her arms around my neck, and I hugged her lightly, aware of Mrs. Berman watching us in the background.

After the movie Myra said, "I want to be Katharine Ross."

"You want your true love to come steal you away at your wedding?" I asked.

"No," she said, "I want to play her role in the movie. I don't care what happens to her. I just love her part."

We drove out of the parking lot. We'd gone to see an early feature, so we hadn't had much time to talk. I was tired. I yawned. "You want to get something to eat?" I said.

"Sure, if you do."

We went to HoJo's, sat in a booth, and talked about New England. Myra was definitely leaning more toward Wellesley now than Brown. It had a better theater program anyway. She was confident she could get in both places. "Are you still planning to stay around?" she asked me.

"I think so," I said, and looked down at my place mat, a map of the United States with bright orange roofs designating all the HoJo's in capital cities.

"David, is something wrong?"

"Nothing's wrong," I said.

Myra leaned back in her booth with her arms folded. "Did something happen while we weren't talking?"

"No."

"Why do I get this feeling you're hiding something?"

"I'm not," I said.

"This has to do with the shoebox, doesn't it?" said Myra.

"Not really." I fiddled with my knife and fork. I'd ordered a cheeseburger and dipped it in too much ketchup. It lay there half eaten and used, ragged with a gummy cheese border. The waitress came by and asked if everything was all right, then left when I said yes. "You're going away," I said. "Doesn't it make sense that we should be thinking about splitting up?"

"Ten months from now," Myra said.

"You wanted to break up two weeks ago yourself."

"So this is to punish me for that?"

"No," I said. "It isn't."

"What's wrong then?"

I shrugged. "I don't know what else is wrong," I said. "Something did change. With us."

"I knew I shouldn't have shown you the clippings," said Myra. "Can't you just think of that as a stupid mistake? And forgive me?"

"I'm not blaming you—"

"You *are*, David. You are blaming me. Why else would you change overnight like this?"

"Look, everybody thinks this is a bad idea. Your parents are worried, your girlfriends are appalled, your teachers no doubt wonder why you're hanging around with me—"

"What do *you* think, David? I don't care about them right now. I want to know what you think? Do you love me?"

I took a breath and slumped down in the booth. I kept seeing Myra with the sheet up in one hand and the shoebox in the other, and I didn't know where to look.

We drove to Rose Valley and pulled into the parking lot of the Hedgerow Theater, found a back corner away from the street. It was a popular parking place, if you could escape the cops who drove by and searched the front of the lot with their lights. There was another car near us, with its windows fogged up. It was a few days before Thanksgiving and cold. I kept the motor going and ran the heater.

"This beats Ronnie's, doesn't it?" said Myra.

"Yeah, who needs a bed?"

"God, we're lucky. We could be lying on sheets right now."

Myra took off her sweater. "Look what I got for you." She unbuttoned her white blouse and showed me the sheer black bra she was wearing. "I found it on my travels. I was thinking of you when I bought it. It's quick," she said, and turned her back for me to undo the single hook.

I took it off and kissed her and thought over the speaker's comment in meeting about the lottery ticket and taking a step toward God. I wanted to tell Myra. But she'd have a puzzled look on her face: *Why are you telling me this now?*

She put her hand on my fly, unzipped my pants. "Want to go in the backseat?" she said.

"Okay," I said, and we climbed over.

Myra unbuckled my belt, then pushed her new jeans down past

her hips. "I've missed you, David," she said. "Do you know how much?"

"I missed you too," I said, trying to match her tone.

I slid into her. After a few minutes I pulled out, or, more accurately, fell out, and Myra said, "Did you . . . ?"

I shook my head. I'd never had this happen before. "I guess I'm just off tonight," I said. Every part of me felt weighed down, sagging into the earth.

Myra looked at me a moment, then, as if embarrassed by her nakedness, fastened her bra and buttoned her blouse. A car drove by and turned in toward us, though it wasn't a cop. I pulled up my pants.

"Maybe we should go," said Myra.

We drove around, talking about school and Ronnie and avoiding anything about ourselves, and after a while we came back to Myra's house on the corner of Vassar and Yale. She said goodbye quickly, with a peck on the cheek, and I knew she'd given me all the chance she could.

THIRTEEN

I spent a quiet Thanksgiving with my parents in Amish country. We went to Zinn's Diner, where we used to go when I was a child. My mother kept asking if I wanted to invite someone and then finally came right out and asked what had happened with Myra. She looked pained when I told her we'd just "drifted apart." I couldn't alleviate her anxiety by giving her any more reason than that, because I really didn't know why myself. I was surprised by the swiftness of my indifference.

Zinn's wasn't actually a diner. It was a restaurant with a formal dining room, where we ate a very quiet Thanksgiving dinner. On our drive here we'd passed a family of Amish walking along the roadside. Unlike Quakers, they dressed in plain dark garments and had solemn, private faces. The children, a group of brothers, it looked like, with Dutch haircuts under straw hats, hurried to keep up with their parents. For some reason I waved. They looked at me with polite disinterest.

Adrian was having Thanksgiving with Naomi's family on Long

Island. He'd be home for the first time this year at Christmas break. My mother kept up a conversation about her new studio. She had put on makeup and worn a red skirt and navy blue sweater. Her eyes always shone when she talked about her pottery. It was a big step for her to declare herself good enough to have her own studio. "I'll need more shelves," she said. "Don's going to help me pick out material for curtains—and a new paint color. Those brown walls. Ugh."

My father made a few jokes about how much this was costing him, but I could see he was pleased, delighted my mother was so excited. Once again I wondered why they couldn't get together, and then I thought about Myra and how I had no good reason for withdrawing from her. A door had just closed. I couldn't pry it open, and perhaps that was what had happened for my parents long ago, the best intentions sealed shut.

One morning after meeting, Arthur took me aside and said he wanted to talk with me. "Are you still interested in coming here for a term next fall, David?"

I said I was.

"You'll want to get your application in soon."

I said I would.

"Are you sure this is where you want to be?"

"Yes."

Arthur sighed. "You knock yourself out working here. I'm starting to feel guilty about having you contribute so much." I worked in the kitchen helping prepare dinner, even when I couldn't stay to eat. On the way from school I stopped and picked up the mail at the Wallingford post office. I answered the phones for an hour every Wednesday and Friday afternoons. I chopped wood, hauled brush, cleaned stoves, scrubbed pots, and turned compost.

"I don't mind," I said. "I'm glad to do it."

"Are you sure, David?"

I suddenly detected something in his tone. Arthur, whom I so admired, more than I could tell him, was trying to explain that he wasn't sure we were a good match, Pendle Hill and I. "Don't you want me around?" I said.

"That's not the question. I'm not sure you have a project here. It's a study center, David. People come here for a specific purpose, even if it's just to find a quiet place to meditate and go inward for a while. I'm afraid you're trying to make yourself a servant here. It's not serving *you*, however."

"It is," I said, not wanting to plead but afraid to be banished.

"Just slow down, David," said Arthur. "Take in what's meaningful for you, not for the whole universe. More patience, less devotion."

I decided I would bring my father to a meeting.

He sat with me on a bench and folded his hands in his lap. He had his tie on for work, his long wool overcoat. The barn was cold in the winter, more so when you sat so quietly in one place. A few people rubbed their hands together. Elton, the director, made a joke about someone finding a bunch of frozen stiff Quakers and not knowing if they were still having meeting. The people at Pendle Hill, I'd discovered, had quite a good sense of self-deprecating humor.

And then, like every other morning I'd been here, the meeting abruptly started. I tried to keep in mind something Arthur had said. That I should let my thoughts go where they wanted and not chase after them with the scolding broom. As for being moved to speak out, I shouldn't worry too much about that. Such openings came when one was ready, and no amount of individual will could force the process. If I happened to experience an opening, it would flow right back into the silence, gentle as a leaf landing and sailing up again. I'd recognize it as my natural spirit, quiet in its grace, familiar as a cup of milk. I should keep in mind, if it helped, that the best description of prayer was that God yearned for me as much as I yearned for God.

I closed my eyes, aware of my father next to me. I tried to clear my mind, not to have any expectations outside of centering down and enjoying the gathered meeting. That was, after all, what distinguished Quakerism: the connection with others while we sat. It was not a religion of loners, though we sat silently. It was the bonds of the community that mattered, and I longed so to be part of this community. "We're just as anxious, hateful, smug, depressed as any other people," warned Arthur. "Don't mistake us for missionaries," a joke that in my fervor for absolute goodness went right by me.

"I've been given the joy of a granddaughter," spoke Arthur in the meeting, and I realized I'd never asked about his family.

The announcement made everyone breathe more deeply.

What was the great revelation here? But it filled the room—*given joy.* I wasn't even willing to allow for such a thing. I was looking too hard, trying too much to prove God existed somewhere, temptingly inside me. He hadn't deserted me after all. I wasn't as alone as I feared. Given joy. A simple statement about birth, a child of Arthur's child. Given joy. It echoed, clamored in my head. I'd completely forbidden such an occurrence, shut it out, tacked it up like burlap over a bright window. Why couldn't I have joy? Why couldn't *I* be given joy? It had been there with Myra, and I'd thrown it back, afraid it would be stolen away, turned against me: the shoebox, the lid off the box—

"I have taken a life and want to give back what I have."

The words flew out of me. A message, an opening, God's throat pressing sounds upward in my own, a cry, an outburst, a whisper. I don't know how loudly or softly I spoke. I don't know what I expected, gasps, sighs, snorts, outrage, pity, sympathy, wonder, curiosity, amazement, horror . . . nothing. Just silence. My father sat still next to me.

When I glanced at him, I saw his eyes were red, from lack of sleep perhaps. He'd been woken up three times last night by patients. His skin looked grayer. I understood suddenly. Me. He was worried about me. I was still suffering, and he was afraid for me. He couldn't do anything to help his son out of his pain, an awful sorrow for a parent. *I saw myself through his eyes.* This sudden view was my opening, and quiet as a leaf falling and rising again, it passed.

The accident had been like that, Sarah Vale falling down, passing on.

⁘

Ronnie called in the afternoon. He wanted to know why I hadn't been in school. I'd asked my father to bring me home after the meeting. He'd done so without question, as if realizing the experience had left us both weakened, depleted of will. "I couldn't face school today," I told Ronnie. I'd been reading George Fox's journals. He'd had no trouble speaking out. He'd told a judge trying him for heresy that he should tremble before the word of God. "You are the Quaker, not I," the judge had responded, thus the religion's name. I trembled now, shook in bed, feverish, I realized.

"So how are things going?" he said. "Your brother home yet?"

"A few days," I said.

"You want to see a Sixers game? I got a couple free tickets."

"For when?"

"For anytime."

Ronnie always had free tickets, free passes to movies, a free card for a gas fill-up. Somebody always seemed to owe him a favor.

"Sure." I shifted the phone to my other ear. I pretended to be annoyed by his busy life, but on the other hand, I wasn't sure I wanted to spend any more time with him than I did. "How about next Friday?" I said.

I heard Ronnie flipping through pages, his appointment calendar; he was the only kid my age who carried one, and it was as thick as a telephone book for a small town. "Can't swing it. I've got a gig for the Earwigs in Spring Valley, New York. I'm driving up there with them." Ronnie now managed the Earwigs. "They're breaking out of the bar mitzvah circuit," he said. "I bought them some headbands and wild purple satin shirts like Hendrix. What a difference! We canned Marty on drums too. They got a new guy who can blow out the windows. That's what's been holding them back. You wouldn't believe their sound."

I thought about Pendle Hill. I'd told Ronnie once, when he asked why I was always late in the mornings for school, that I'd been spending time there, to which he'd said, "It's an ashram or something, isn't it?" I tried to imagine Ronnie sitting still in a meeting. Impossible.

"So you going to be home for a while?" asked Ronnie.

"Yes," I said. "You want to come over?"

"Can't today," he said. "I'll put us down for a Sixers game, though. Soon."

Five minutes later Myra called and I realized that Ronnie had asked if I'd be home so he could tell her.

"Hi," I said. We hadn't spoken since before Thanksgiving, our date in the parking lot of the Hedgerow Theater.

"I was just thinking about you and decided I'd call. Everything going okay?"

"Fine," I said.

"I'm at my dad's store," Myra said. "He's got me working here after school now."

"Are you going to be there for a while?"

"All evening, until El Slavemaster releases me."

"I'm coming out," I said.

＊

Myra's father's new store had a huge front window lit up with a neon green, pink, and blue sign that said SHOE GALAXY. In Chester it had been called Berman's Shoes. I parked in front of Korvette's. A grand opening sale was in progress, much like the continuous sale Myra's father had had in Chester for the thirty-five years he'd been there. People moved up and down the self-service aisles, picking shoe boxes off the shelves like library books, putting them back after a look, going on to the next one. The store felt entirely different from the personal service in the old Chester location. Mr. Berman, pleasant as always, was behind the cash register.

"Is Myra around?" I asked him. He stared at me, trying to figure out where he'd seen me before, the context.

"Nachman, right?"

"Right," I said. He was blindly ringing up sales with one hand, talking to me over his shoulder. "She's in the back. Don't distract her. If you're here for more than five minutes, grab a price gun and pitch in. I'm drowning in business."

Myra sat on the floor surrounded by boxes of mismatched shoes. When she saw me, she looked up once, then back down. She was lacing up a pair of Red Wing work boots. "People take all the shoes out of the boxes and then just throw them any old place," she said. "I have at least fifteen shoes that absolutely have no mates. I cannot find them anywhere. I hate this place."

"Your father says he's doing well."

"More than well. He plans to buy me a car for college."

"You should be happy."

"Thrilled," said Myra. She pulled the laces tight on the work boot as if strangling the shoe. "And you? Would you like to see something in a brown oxford?"

"I just wanted to see you. I'm sorry about what happened."

"I'm not really sure what *did* happen," said Myra. "Is it really bad between us or just sort of stalled?"

I wanted to say "sort of stalled," but I knew this would mislead her. *I* was stalled, not Myra.

"So what have you been doing?" she asked when I didn't answer quickly enough. I could hear in her voice the pride covering the hurt—as if hurriedly throwing a sheet over the top of it. She was a good actress, someone who could project numerous complicated moods at once. I admired this ability but knew it was completely the wrong moment to tell her.

"I'm going to move out," I said. The idea had just come to me lately.

"What?"

"I'm going to move out of my parents' house in the fall."

"To where? That place?"

"Pendle Hill? No. Just an apartment somewhere near Temple. I think I'm holding them back from something, or they want me gone but don't know how to ask."

"I've never heard you talk about your parents like this before," said Myra. She stood up. She wore a baggy burgundy sweater; the sleeves bunched up at her wrists, and the high-ribbed collar swallowed up her chin. "Are you serious about leaving? What are you going to do for money?"

"I'll get a night job, go to Temple during the day. I'll figure something out."

"You make it so hard on yourself, David."

"About what?"

"About *everything*. Can't you just have a normal freshman experience somewhere and sneak girls into your dorm and go on panty raids and do whatever healthy, horny young college men are supposed to do?"

"I guess not." I put out my fingers and touched the tips of hers.

"I think I hear some shoplifters," said Myra, turning away from me. "Don't you?"

"I'm not sure. What do they sound like?" I kissed her above her eyes.

"One person distracts you with noisy questions while the stealer runs out the door with our shoes. They're all over the place out here. We didn't get that problem in Chester, surprisingly. It was such a small store it would have been like somebody taking a toaster from your kitchen. David, please go, okay?" She pulled away from me, and stood by a post with a fire extinguisher. "Let's just say goodbye now, all right? It's starting to make me crazy."

"Myra!" her father shouted. "Up front. Now!"

"Igor calls," she said, and limped by me in hunched servitude toward her father, careful not to brush up against me.

F O U R T E E N

Adrian arrived home. He'd come in late, almost midnight, but we'd all waited up for him, including my father. He stood tall in the doorway, in a double-breasted pea coat that came down past his knees. He had a full beard, a mop of hair, and his eyes blazed despite the hour. He threw out his arms and shouted, "Welcome!" as if we were the ones visiting him. He gave my father a bear hug—the easy intimacy between them was striking—and put his other arm around my mother, kissing her cheek. He was full of cheerful, hearty greetings, and I realized that for all his complaining about Uncle Stonny and company, Adrian belonged with them, robust and exuberant talkers and gesticulators that they were.

"David," said Adrian, and reached out his hand over my mother's shoulder. He was like a returning hero, an astronaut, a burly vodka-drinking cosmonaut, a conquering mensch. He squeezed my hand warmly. What had he done other than go away and come back? He didn't carry tragedy with him, for one; he carried only promise, and in some twisted mixture of love and envy I felt hot tears in my eyes, and I ducked my head down so he wouldn't see.

The next day my mother took Adrian and me over to her new studio. Mr. Richardson and I had helped her move here three weeks before, but I'd never realized how much she'd produced in a relatively short time. She had started painting her pots with small roses and miniature tulips, radishes and pears; irregular, rounded shapes attracted her. I'd been listening to her explain all this to Adrian, who picked up an oblong plate and brushed his finger along its curve.

"When you work, do you depend more on your eye or your hands?" Adrian asked, and our mother, as if conducting her first interview with the aplomb of a veteran artist used to such academic questions, answered, "If I were suddenly blind, I could still make pots, and if I could feel no more, I could still do it, but if both happened . . ." She drifted off into a laugh. "Well, we won't go that far into my nightmares."

Her pottery was displayed on the shelves. She had plates, mugs, pitchers, bowls, serving platters, and then an assortment of abstract shapes with which she was experimenting, little bowls with huge handles like elephant ears, mugs with tapered tops small as a child's mouth, a water pitcher with three flaring handles like the spread wings of a deformed bird that couldn't fly. She called these her "mistakes," but I couldn't stop staring at them. They reminded me of the odd-shaped bottles she used to collect, and I thought that even back then her artist's eye was absorbing the world, getting ready to produce her own work.

She'd fixed up the studio with curtains and a daybed. In the corner by one of the two windows, she'd placed her wheel, which Mr. Richardson and I had struggled to lug in, puffing away. Mr. Richardson had turned so red in the face that I was frightened for him. Her kiln we put, with the help of two truck drivers Mr. Richardson had enlisted from Freed's Furniture, outside in a metal shed. She had a desk and shelf with art books that she studied for designs. The small bed was neatly made. She spent six hours a day here but returned home promptly at dinnertime, and it, her pottery, her work, had kept her from having any more breakdowns. This both thrilled and worried me: Did it take something like this to be happy? What if I never found it?

———

Adrian invited me out to dinner—just him and me, on our father's credit card, our father, whose idea I guessed it to be, trying to get us together as brothers, his two different sons. We decided on D'Ignazio's Towne House.

Everybody came to D'Ignazio's for proms and to celebrate birthdays or anniversaries. The waiters wore red vests with white ruffled shirts and looked as if they resented not being in New York City, where they could make some real money for how snooty they had to act. They rushed around serving the big Christmas parties. We sat at a small table in the corner, with green Christmas napkins and a kerosene lamp on a red tablecloth. We'd ordered, and Adrian was telling me about our cousin Eddie.

"Nobody talks about him," said Adrian. Eddie was Uncle Stonny and Aunt Rose's only child. "So I decided I would spend a weekend tracking down Cousin Eddie. I found him in upstate New York. He lives in the woods and has long hair down to the middle of his back, and he spends about three quarters of every day in a sensory deprivation chamber that he's built. He wanted me to get in."

"Did you?" I asked.

Adrian took a bite of garlic bread. "Are you kidding? I was afraid Eddie would lock me in there. He's a fanatic. His latest project was investigating something called the ganzfield. If you get inside the chamber and put halved Ping-Pong balls over your eyes and shine red lights down, you can induce a uniform pink ganzfield. The ganzfield will have no breaks in it. It's boundless and smooth and, above all, unified, with no pattern or distracting detail to mar it. It's the closest we'll get to oblivion on the planet. Eddie said he could hear this loud buzzing when he did it, which at first he thought was extraterrestrial communication. Then he figured out it was his nervous system, which is the whirring sound it makes when you eliminate all other noise in the environment."

I'd met Cousin Eddie only once, at Adrian's bar mitzvah. He'd been seventeen then, with terrible acne. At the reception he'd sat making miniature paper airplanes out of everyone's place cards. By the end of the evening he'd created an airfield of a hundred fighter planes and never left his seat except to quietly pick up another person's place card and say, "May I? Thank you"—the only words he said the entire day.

"What do Uncle Stonny and Aunt Rose say about all this?" I asked.

"Nothing. They shush anyone when the subject of Eddie comes up. You'd think they were paragons of mental health themselves."

"I thought I had problems," I said, and we both laughed, awkwardly.

"We have an odd family," said Adrian, and glanced at me sympathetically. I wondered how he described my own history since it didn't lend itself to the comedy of Cousin Eddie, who was remarkably like the child of Mr. Potato Head (Uncle Stonny) and Silly Putty (Aunt Rose), an offspring of elastic and mutable characters. Cousin Eddie's experiences might rearrange his nose, ears, and mouth on the wrong side of his head, but he'd basically remain intact through it all, like Uncle Stonny triumphing over a bad heart to sell hot dogs.

I leaned back to let the busboy take my empty plate. "How you doing, Dave?" he said.

I stared at him a moment, the face not registering instantly in the bow tie and white shirt. Crow.

Adrian stood up.

"This is Crow," I said. "My brother, Adrian." They shook hands, and Adrian sat down.

"So, you playing ball this year?" asked Crow, an old joke.

"Nope," I said, and smiled.

"Me neither," said Crow, and laughed at himself.

I wanted to leave suddenly. I'd had some idea I would never run into him again, a foolish notion. Crow's hair was perhaps the only change in his appearance. No longer in a ducktail, slicked back with glue or whatever it was he had used, it was more shaggy like the Beatles, but tucked behind his ears in a greaser version. He was still thick and muscular, dense as a bale of hay.

"You been working here long?" I asked, because Crow was hanging around our table. Maybe he thought we were still friends in some impossible way.

"A few weeks," said Crow. "I'm married now," he said.

"You are?"

"Lorraine Novis. We're having a baby in a couple months."

I nodded. Adrian, I saw, was folding and unfolding his green Christmas napkin. He knew of course all about Crow. And what could you say anyway to someone who just told you he was married to another teenager and they were having their first child and neither of them even had a high school diploma? I felt, much to my surprise, sorry for him and was aware of how much had really changed. "Congratulations," I forced myself to say.

"Vic's working for his father's auto shop," said Crow. "I don't see Chuckie much. He's going to some business college after he graduates."

"I think I heard that," I said, trying to make polite conversation. Still he stood there. "I got called up," said Crow.

"Called up?"

"The draft."

Adrian looked at his fingernails. I couldn't think of anything to say. "I'm glad to go," said Crow, as if trying to convince himself. "Got to serve your country, right? You guys want coffee?"

We said no.

"I'll tell your waiter you want your check," he said, and lumbered away, looking as if he were in a costume in his bow tie and crisp white busboy's shirt that fitted him too tightly, the buttons straining across his chest. The uniform diminished him somehow, his stature, his past threat.

In a few minutes our bill arrived, and I put my father's credit card on it. We didn't say a word until we got outside.

"Wasn't that weird?" Adrian asked me once we were in the car again. He wanted to drive around for a while, what we used to do long ago when he first got his license.

"What do you mean?"

"The simian fellow," said Adrian. "Crow." And he shook his head.

I shrugged.

"You've got to get out of here, David," said Adrian. "This place might as well be a million miles away from New York."

"New York isn't the answer for everyone, Adrian," I said, irritated with his predictable response. He didn't live here anymore. He didn't know the place. What right did he have to judge everybody here?

"You don't still see those guys, do you?"

"Of course not," I said.

"Just checking," said Adrian. "Mom says you've been spending time at Pendle Hill."

"Not recently." I hadn't returned since I'd brought my father.

"It's a great place. I've known some people who have studied there."

I didn't want to talk about Pendle Hill. I'd decided that my time there had been a failure. I could see what Arthur had been trying to tell me: The members of the community used the center not as a means to avoid the world but to go deeper into it. I had wanted to go the opposite way.

"Mom says you've been seeing Myra Berman."

"Not anymore," I said.

"I'm striking out all over the place, aren't I?"

"It didn't work out."

We drove past the Media Inn and onto Providence Road. We would have, at one time, gone into Chester, but now, afraid like everyone else to be there at night, we headed in a different direction.

"You want to come up to New York again soon? We didn't really get to spend much time together. Naomi felt bad about always being around."

It was true: I'd felt deserted by him, but I couldn't say why. "Maybe," I said. "I'm going to try to find a job soon. I want to move out of the house."

"Did you tell Mom and Dad?"

"I will. I'm just waiting for the right time."

We slowed down near the high school, the site of Adrian's Scott's Hi-Q triumphs. It seemed he'd left so long ago.

Adrian turned around in the high school parking lot, and we headed back down Providence Road toward Media. "David, do you ever think about how different things would have been for everyone if the accident hadn't happened?"

"What do you mean?"

"Different for the whole family. Not just you. Do you think about that?"

"I wasn't really aware it ever affected you."

Adrian squinted at me. I could hear Naomi saying, Dooglie Boy! "It did affect me. I think about it all the time too. I feel guilty that I didn't try to do more for you back then."

"You could have stayed around. You ran off every chance you had."

"I was scared too. I didn't know what it meant. People were asking me if you were going to get the electric chair."

"What?"

"One person asked me that."

"Who?" I said.

"I don't remember."

"So you're telling me I should feel sorry for you?"

"I'm telling you to stop feeling sorry for yourself only. It could ruin your life. There's little room for anything else."

"Do you think that's what it is?"

"Yes," said Adrian. "That's what I see."

"You're wrong. It's not self-pity. It's hate. And you have no idea how it feels or how much I hate myself." I stretched out my leg and rested my foot on the glove compartment, wanting to slam it with my shoe.

Adrian reached over and put his hand on my shoulder. I stiffened. "David, don't push so hard, okay? I want to do better by you, but you've got to help a little."

The conversation was killing me, filling my bones with sand. I hated analyzing myself this way, hated hearing words that offered so little answer to my action. No wonder I was attracted to Pendle Hill with its calming silence.

"Let's get some dessert," said Adrian as we pulled into HoJo's. He still liked to eat, and frequently, despite his thinner frame.

He patted my knee to come on, just as a father might, and I followed him inside.

The next evening I waited in the parking lot of the Media Diner. The restaurant closed early on Sunday, and I saw Mrs. Vale come out by herself at six P.M. and go toward her car. She had on a winter coat, red with oversized black buttons, and her hair was tucked under a green plaid scarf that she had pulled tight around her chin. I got out of my car and went up to her. "Can we talk?"

Her eyes didn't look as they had that night in the diner, a mixture of despair and shock. Now she just looked at me blankly; in some ways that was worse than if she'd recoiled.

"We have nothing to talk about," she said.

"Please," I said. "Just for a moment." I was shivering again, as I had the time with Myra on Swarthmore's campus, even though I'd worn my heaviest coat.

I don't know how I knew it was all right exactly, maybe the slow manner in which she moved away, but I understood I was to follow her. We sat in her car, the Buick Riviera. She turned the motor on, then the heat full blast. We didn't speak for several minutes, and it became clear I was going to have to begin. Somehow I'd never imagined getting this far: She would turn away, spit at me, call for her husband, shout that she was going to call the police, or just walk off, clearly not permitting me to follow.

Now I had nothing to tell her. Nothing new.

"You don't know," said Mrs. Vale, her voice coming out of some lost place. I could see her eyes from the light of the parking lot, smeared with mascara. She'd been crying on the way out of the restaurant. "You don't know what this has done to us all. Jack can't work anymore. Oh, he comes in and tries to help get the orders out, but he's useless back there. I'll catch him just staring down at a ticket. He can't keep up, even when we're not busy. He used to be a good short-order cook. And it's not as if we can afford to hire anybody else either." She turned the heat down. "Russell is getting in trouble every day at school. The police showed up at our door last weekend. He and a couple friends shot out the windows of parked trolleys in Media. Jack won't set his foot down," said Mrs. Vale, and she turned and looked out her window, her face away from me. "It's all on my shoulders, all of it now."

"Paul," I said, and she turned back, startled to hear, I could tell, the way I said his name, as if I knew him, knew her family through him and was close to him. "Isn't Paul helping?"

"Paul," said Mrs. Vale. "You should see how he looks at his father when he comes home, his father just sitting there watching the TV. He hates his father now, but he would never say it. He just goes up to his room and does his homework and is gone the next day to school before any of us even get up. Practicing. He runs all the time. He won't stop."

"Is there something I can do?" I said, because I had this idea— this hope—that Mrs. Vale was asking for help, but she turned to me and said, "You?"

I said nothing, looked down.

"You came to our house. You came here now. What do you want from us?"

"I wanted—I wanted to explain."

"Explain what? That you were racing backwards? That it wasn't even an accident?"

"It was," I said.

Mrs. Vale slapped me. I froze. "Don't," she said, "*don't speak to me about accidents,*" and she drew her hand away, holding it with her other hand as if it were a glove that she might pull off. Her body began to heave with sobs. "You can't know what this is like. You can't know how much I miss my baby. You can't know," she said, and each time she repeated it, I felt her slap.

She leaned over the steering wheel and cried for a long while and then said, "I wasn't going to ever do that if I saw you. I didn't want to do that. Nobody wants to be brought down to doing that."

I nodded, afraid to speak.

"I don't know what to do," she said. "I have to take care of the boys first. I have to do something about Russell. Did I hurt you?" she said.

"It's all right," I said.

"It's not all right," said Mrs. Vale, and touched the place on my face where she'd slapped me, a mother's touch, curious, concerned, wanting to feel for herself the damage. "It will never be all right," she said, and then she asked me to leave.

4

F I F T E E N

Ronnie and I shared an apartment in West Philadelphia, close to where he went to school at Drexel University and not too far from Temple. Five mornings a week I drove across the Spring Garden bridge, passed by the art museum, and then went up Broad Street to Temple. I had signed up for a program in hospital administration, but my first year was mostly taken up with required courses: freshman composition, history of Western civ, French. I met few people as a commuter student and concentrated on my studies. Ronnie was rarely around. He was majoring in business at Drexel, but he had a thousand things going, as he liked to say. No longer suits. He still managed the Earwigs, but he also booked concerts for local colleges. Sometimes when the phones rang (we had three extensions in our small apartment), as they did frequently, I wouldn't answer, knowing it was for him. I'd given my parents a signal to call, one ring and then hang up and call back. They seemed to be the only people I talked to frequently.

Unlike my plan that after I moved out, they'd get divorced, nothing in fact happened. My expectation that I'd free them of their servitude to each other had gone unrealized. Now, by spring semester, they still showed no signs of changing anything about their lives.

I worked at Maxie's Shirt Store in Overbrook Park. Maxie, who had known my father many years ago in the army, had been glad to hire me. Unfortunately he paid little and shouted too much, complaining about how the customers were killing him with these low prices he had to charge. He reminded me not so much of Ronnie as of Uncle Stonny, the older mercantile class that was passing out of existence, Uncle Stonny throwing doggies out from his hot box, and I felt at home.

The store—more a large hallway—was filled with tables of shirts that we had to squeeze by. I was constantly sorting and folding shirts and trying to keep them under their right signs: two for five dollars, two for ten dollars, etc.

We sold only dress shirts in stripes and solids, basic colors—yellow, tan, blue, pink, white—and I had mentioned more than a few times to Maxie that he should update his inventory, that the market was changing. People were dressing wildly. Hadn't he seen any of the groups? Janis Joplin, Steppenwolf, Hendrix? He didn't care. His customers wanted these shirts, and he got them cheap and that was that. Every once in a while he'd lift up his own shirt and show me where his skin had been stitched together. Folded in on itself under the nipples, a huge pink scar ran across his lower abdomen. "Aggravation," he'd say when I asked him what he'd been operated on for. This was by way of telling me not to press too much with new ideas for the store. He was happy selling cheap shirts. Nobody robbed him. He lived by himself in a little apartment in West Philly. He ate well, even with his operation.

Usually I went home on the weekends and stayed with my parents in Garden City. I made it through the weeks okay, but on the weekends I found I became tired of my own company. In the beginning—

of my first semester—I had stayed away from the house completely, only calling, as if to prove I could do it. But as the semester wore on, I drove home more and found I would draw out dinner and stay overnight. Even if no one was there, and they frequently weren't, my mother at her studio, my father at work or away at a medical convention, I still felt better staying in the house. By contrast, my apartment with Ronnie had few amenities besides the four phones that rang frequently.

One Friday evening, early in the second semester, I decided to stay at my apartment and work on a paper for my final sequence of freshman composition. Our instructor, Mr. Rosenberg, had suggested that my writing was too stiff. "Nothing is wrong with it technically, David. It just needs to flow better. Why don't you loosen up and try something more creative—as an exercise?" I did. And what I wrote scared me.

Unlike the report on *Crime and Punishment* for Mrs. Sellig's class, this one jumped out of me, with its claws on the paper, ready to shred anything in its way, unrestrained in its intent, slashing away at any pretense of normalcy or polite explanations. It had screamed, as Mr. Rosenberg was always trying to get us to do by playing Big Brother and the Holding Company in class and having us listen to Janis belt it out.

When you kill a child, you don't sleep like other people. You wake up suddenly and remember what you've done. You don't pause a moment in that envelope between sleeping and waking to wonder if it's true or not—your dream. You get up as quickly as you can and find something to do, to keep busy, to make your life methodical and harmless—to yourself. The pain comes in the form of a dread that you'll wake up and forget and then you'll suddenly have to remember what you've done all over again, anew. So you never really let yourself forget, not even when you're sleeping, because you don't really sleep anyhow, not like other people; you sleep as if you're guarding something, something important and strategic and endangered, and you are: You're guarding the child you killed.

And because it had burst out of me and shaken me up so much, I couldn't be alone. So I called home. My parents invited me for dinner, as I hoped that they would.

I didn't want to be by myself with such thoughts as I'd just put down because I realized I could go on, and on, and that something vitriolic, powerful as Corky Innes's old Kongmobile in its glory days, was trying to get free. I had the image of Maxie lifting his shirt and showing me his tucked and stapled skin folded over the pieces cut out of him, zipped up with a pink scar.

—

Dinner was ready when I arrived. My parents tried to eat together at least once a week. My father still had his tie on from work, and my mother wore a pearl bracelet and a stylish tweed dress. I had on jeans. "I didn't know it was anything fancy," I said.

"It's not," said my mother.

We sat down, and my mother asked how was school this week.

"Great," I said, though I never thought of it that way.

"What are your courses again?" asked my father.

I rattled off composition, American literature, a one-credit course on human sexuality during which we had maturely watched a movie about clinical approaches to intercourse, a very different experience in a lecture hall of five hundred from taking sex ed with Chester "Chet" O'Connor and having everyone hoot in the back. The movie had succeeded, however, in making me feel lonely, and horny.

"Are you staying here tonight?" my mother asked.

"I think so," I said. "Is that all right?"

"Of course," my mother said. I went back to eating my salad, but something in the way my mother had said "of course," a little too quickly, didn't ring true.

"Are you sure?" I asked.

"Is it all right if you're here alone?" my mother asked.

My father reached for his water glass. "We're playing bridge tonight with Ben and Madelyn Hersch."

"Oh," I said, then: "That's fine." I knew now why they were dressed up.

"You sure, David?" asked my mother.

"Absolutely."

I saw my mother give my father a worried, guilty look. They were still careful around me, afraid to make a mistake. "Really," I said.

My mother pushed a plate of hot rolls toward me. "We could play another night."

"Don't be silly," I said. "I called you on short notice. Why should I have expected you wouldn't have plans?" They looked at me as if this were true.

I must have sat for several moments without taking a bite.

"You're not hungry, son?" my father asked.

"I am," I said, and forced myself to eat and make conversation, feeling suddenly that I did want to go back this evening to Philadelphia.

Mr. Richardson died early the next morning. He had died in his sleep of a heart attack.

I drove in two days later for the funeral. My mother, I saw, had been crying hard. Her eyes were puffy, her face was pale, and I watched her take several sedatives during the afternoon. I don't think that until that moment I realized the full extent of her friendship with and attachment to Mr. Richardson. "I loved him," she said to me as soon as I came in the door. She looked frightened, panicked about his going, as if she wouldn't be able to stand on her own without him. Her recovery, the strongest part of her recovery, like a train getting up to speed, had occurred since she'd known him, and I think she looked to him to fill in all those spaces that lurked during the day.

I sat with her for a long while on the couch while my father made final arrangements with the funeral home. Mr. Richardson had an elderly sister in town, his only living relative. My father called the furniture stores where he had worked to let his fellow salesmen know of the death. Most of them said they would try to come to the funeral, and my mother picked up a bit at this news. I think more than anything she didn't want him to be lonely in his death. He had done such a good job of keeping his spirits and hers up during his life, covering whatever profound loneliness he felt with quips and manners and punctuality and, of course, drink that she couldn't bear to see him ignored in death. He had spent large portions of his retired day over at my mother's studio, reading, listening to music on a small transistor radio he carried everywhere, playing solitaire, doing crossword puzzles, and glazing her pots, the job she had assigned him. Her life had been occupied with great big chunks of his steady, sure presence, and now, in a sense, she was a widow to that.

The minister—Mr. Richardson had been Methodist—delivered a eulogy based on Mr. Richardson's career as a salesman, his loyal work record, his fondness for his customers, his place in the Chester business community. The minister hadn't really known Mr. Richardson, who attended church sporadically, and so was forced to dig deep for meaningful connections to this world. He said Mr. Richardson had been a good brother, glancing at Mr. Richardson's elderly sister, who suffered from enough memory loss to make her appear puzzled about why she was here. The minister noted Mr. Richardson had been a good friend to my mother and to my father, who had liked Mr. Richardson but had never quite appreciated him until he saw my mother weep over the man's death.

My mother had to be supported during the burial, and I think it surprised all of Mr. Richardson's colleagues from the various furniture companies where he'd been employed. Who was he to her? they seemed to be asking with their eyes. Wasn't he homosexual? As if that might limit the anguish my mother felt, her open sobbing, her mourning on behalf of him—his only real mourner. If it was possible for one lonely person to find another and truly make the other happy, then it was possible for my mother to have loved a fastidious, stuttering, alcoholic furniture salesman from the depths of her heart.

After the service I delayed leaving the cemetery. I had brought my own car. I kissed my mother goodbye and told her I'd be home soon. "Drive safely, David," she said. "Please." She seemed especially nervous about and solicitous of me, a measure of her shakiness over Mr. Richardson. Nothing else could happen to anyone, ever, her parting look appeared to say. I've had enough for one lifetime.

I walked through the cemetery. The gravestones showed little uniformity. Missing were the rocks on top of the headstones found at Jewish cemeteries. I remembered visiting my grandparents' graves in Wilmington—dead before I was born—and listening to my father say Kaddish for his parents and sister, all his family, putting a rock atop each headstone.

I wasn't just idly walking here, though. I knew this was the cemetery where Sarah Vale was buried. After half an hour, when I couldn't find her gravestone on my own, I went across the street to the small brick building that served as the cemetery office and asked the woman behind the desk if she could locate Sarah Vale's grave for me. She didn't hesitate to look through a thick binder of names and gave me the location: row 8, plot 26.

I walked to row 8, left of the big oak tree, as she'd told me, and counted off twenty-five plots, until I came to Sarah Vale's unadorned stone. I saw the dates first—February 1, 1964–May 18, 1967—and then I raised my eyes and saw her name carved in stone. I began to weep. I hadn't planned to, or wanted to, but I couldn't control myself.

I sobbed with the same force with which my mother had cried for Mr. Richardson. I crouched down and held my sides because they ached so much from crying, as if my ribs were being hammered out like old walls. I put my hands flat on the ground and tried to stop the quaking, but it would not be stopped, and every time I lifted my eyes to her name or the dates of her life I began all over the racking sobs. I said my prayer again, for it had once meant something to me and perhaps me only. *This is the secret of the unity of God: No matter where I take hold of a shred of it, I hold the whole of it.* I don't know how long I stayed, but the sky gradually clouded and people came and went and I remained crouched at Sarah Vale's grave and wouldn't release myself until it was dark and the gates were closing.

SIXTEEN

Mr. Rosenberg read my paper in class. He didn't say who wrote it; still, I felt as if every eye were on me. At the end of class, when he handed back the papers, I grabbed it and hurried out the door, avoiding eye contact with him. I didn't want to be praised or questioned. I just wanted to get away.

One girl had said, "Wow," almost involuntarily it seemed, after Mr. Rosenberg finished. He'd saved it for last.

"This is what I've been talking about," he said. "Can you hear the intensity of the language all mixed up with the turmoil of the speaker? It makes you sit up and pay attention."

Nobody asked if it was true. I think they were afraid to. Mr. Rosenberg wouldn't have known anyhow, and he'd prefaced his reading of all the papers by reminding us these were creative exercises, but I'd had the impression he'd said that specifically to reassure people about my submission. The others had been tame by comparison: a rowing competition on the Schuylkill River, a humorous camping trip with a mischievous bear, a day in a Mexican village, and then mine: *When you kill a child . . .*

I went to the student center afterward and bought myself a cup of coffee and a bagel. I had stuffed my paper deep into my backpack, after having read Mr. Rosenberg's comments:

David—

This is powerful writing. You really let yourself go here. I'd be glad to talk further with you about this or other projects. Congratulations.

I should have felt proud—an A+ was circled in red—but rather I worried I'd exploited Sarah Vale's death for personal gain.

"Can I sit down?"

It was a girl I recognized from my class. She had been the one to say, "Wow."

"Sure," I said, and moved my book bag from its flopped-open position across the large round table. I was used to taking up a whole space myself, not expecting anyone to join me, studying here for hours until I finished classes and went to work for Maxie.

"I'm Becky," she said, and extended her hand. She had long strawberry blond hair, a thin freckled face with light blue eyes, and a small mouth with a beauty mole on the right corner. She wore stove-pipe jeans and a blue kerchief and had a garland of flowers—real, I think—as a headband. She looked, on the one hand, like a farmer's daughter and on the other, like an aspiring hippie.

"I'm David."

"How do you like Mr. Rosenberg?" she asked.

"Quite a lot," I said.

"It's my favorite class. I love when he goes on about the tragic, decadent lives of dead poets."

"Dylan Thomas, Rimbaud, Byron—the immortals!" I said, imitating Mr. Rosenberg.

Becky shrugged shyly. I had the feeling she was intimidated by my actually remembering their names.

"He has a certain attraction to reckless living," I said, "probably because he does so little of it himself."

"I keep seeing him searching for his glasses when they're on top of his head."

"I imagine," I said, "him wading into the ocean with an inner tube around his waist, reciting, 'Do not go gentle into that good night. . . . Rage, rage against the dying of the light.' "

Becky laughed. "You're funny," she said, which was not something a girl, or anybody, had told me lately. "Are you from around here?"

"Near Chester," I said. "How about you?"

"Circleville, Ohio. Impressive, huh? My aunt lives out here in Philadelphia, and I was desperate to get out of Ohio and go to a real live city. This was the only place my parents would let me go and pay for it too. So, in other words, I live with my aunt or, as I like to refer to her, my full-time guardian."

"You want some coffee?"

"I'll take a pop. Here," she said, and started to dig into her huge purse.

"I'll get it for you," I said.

"No, really, you don't have to." But I was already on my way to find her something to drink.

I began to see Becky every day. We went out after Mr. Rosenberg's class and sometimes for dinner. I think she was beginning to wonder, after the third week, if I'd ever touch her. I was too. It wasn't that I didn't find her attractive; it was more that I found us so different I couldn't see how we'd ever ultimately be together. She asked me one time if I'd ever heard of Bob Dylan.

"Pardon?"

"Bob Dylan—have you heard of him?"

I smiled. "Yes, I've heard of him." It was an endearing comment.

"Oh," said Becky. "I just thought . . . anyway, he was just getting big in Circleville when I was leaving." Her face had flushed red. She was wearing bells around her neck, with clappers so big they didn't chime as much as thunk. Mostly, well not mostly, but sometimes she hit the right note in her attire and looked young and radical and free or whatever was the effect she strove for. But often, as when she wore a vest made from crocheted potholders, the result proved more ludicrous. She took all my teasing good-naturedly, and it wasn't really her clothes so much as this feeling that she was just too good, too innocent, too accepting, too irrevocably straight that I couldn't abide. I didn't know how to explain my family to her for one thing. About Adrian she had said, "I used to know a kid like that in school. He had polio and he walked around in braces all the time, but he had this really amazing brain, and the teachers kept trying to enter him in all these contests." Which wasn't how I liked to think of Adrian, clunking along in polio braces down a lonely hallway, pushed to enter some state fair contest where they'd weigh his brain.

And of course I couldn't bring myself to tell her about what I'd done. I could hear her one-word response of "Wow," said with such disbelief it made me shiver.

Still, I was drawn to her, as if her normalcy was exactly what I craved, long conversations about why people in the Midwest used so much ketchup on their food or said "please" instead of "pardon." I was not on a lofty plane here seeking higher wisdom, as I had been at Pendle Hill. It was true that Becky liked to listen to Mr. Rosenberg drone on about famous, romantic, mad poets, but this was entertainment to her, out-there stuff. Real life was the twenty dollars a week she got from her mother for "pin money" or our trips to center city to shop for bargains in the basement of Wanamaker's. "I love the organ," Becky would say as we entered the department store on Market Street. She'd pull me by the hand, and we'd stand underneath the organ in the loft while it played patriotic melodies. "We have to come some December for the light show," said Becky, but she wasn't talking about anything psychedelic projected on huge screens behind rock stars, who stomped on their immolated guitars in Dionysian frenzy. She was talking about the Wanamaker's Christmas Light Show, which accompanied the organ: different patterns of light dancing merrily across the department store walls and illuminating the soaring fountains of the atrium.

We spent much of our free time like this, shopping in center city, strolling in parks, looking in pet stores, and even though kids my age were having adventures hitchhiking across country, crashing in communes, dancing topless at rock concerts, or more urgently getting clubbed in the streets of Chicago, I wondered if I couldn't make a whole and passable life out of quiet lunches in the Crystal Tea Room on the ninth floor of Wanamaker's. I was passing again as something I was not—or was I? Could there be such a thing as good passing? Were disguises always so bad, and at what point did they meld to the hidden self and lose distinction? I had to admit that in some way it was mindlessly entrancing: I was just an ordinary person going about the business—with Becky's guidance—of buying lemon-scented soap and fragrant sachet pouches for my apartment bathroom.

I'd been invited to Becky's aunt's house to have dinner. Her aunt lived in Conshohocken. She had two young children, both boys under five, and a husband who drove a Sunbeam bread truck at night and would not be joining us. Becky's aunt had similar features to Becky's: the strawberry blond hair, the thin frame, the sunken eyes that Becky was always working on to make less like two "moon craters"—the reason she couldn't go without makeup entirely. She was basically, she explained over and over, a sensible girl, as if to excuse too why she wanted to go see the Fifth Dimension this evening instead of The Doors, as I had thought we might do; both were in town.

Her aunt served meat loaf with peas, and though meat loaf was my least favorite food, I ate it politely and made conversation at the dinner table about my father, whose profession as a doctor always drew respect and whom I had learned to use as an icebreaker in these situations. About halfway through dinner I felt something poking my crotch and looked down to find Ricky, the two-year-old, sticking a gun in my groin. I jerked my chair backwards, but he followed with his toy pistol. "I think Ricky is poking me with a gun," I said finally. It was starting to hurt.

"What was that, David?" asked Becky's aunt, who had just come back into the dining room carrying a side dish of macaroni and cheese.

"Ricky has a toy gun stuck in my crotch," I said.

"Ricky!" shouted Becky and her aunt simultaneously. They dove under the table to drag the screaming child out of his assault position.

We did go to the Fifth Dimension, and when they sang their big hit, "Up, Up and Away," Becky leaned over and took my hand and said, "Now aren't you happy we came here?" It was the kind of thing Aunt Rose might say to an intransigent Uncle Stonny about a Broadway musical she had dragged him to, and I found myself thinking it *wasn't* so bad. I could play this role. When the group got to "Stoned Soul Picnic," and the crowd applauded wildly for several moments into the song, I had no reluctance about leaning over and kissing Becky full on the lips, the first time I'd done that. We'd had an old-fashioned courtship, just as she was used to and, despite the elephant bellbottoms she wore and the incense she burned in her car, probably preferred. And I wasn't above taking advantage of the dazzled, in-love look in her eye when the Fifth Dimension sang what Becky later said, in bed at my apartment, we should make the theme song of our relationship—"Go Where You Wanna Go"—because it expressed our reckless, romantic nature and how things were just so wild these days, you had to go with the flow or drown, and she talked herself through this loss of her virginity—I was surprised to find out—talked the entire time nervously until she asked me if this was it, and I said, yes, this was it, and she said, "David, I think I'm pregnant," and corrected that a few moments later to "I mean, in love, are you?"

We talked about getting married. While everybody else lived together, called each other their old man and their old lady, Becky and I discussed whether we should have the wedding in Circleville or Philadelphia. "I know so many people in Circleville," said Becky, slipping up, as she did occasionally, about what the town meant to her. I said Circleville would be fine.

We spent a lot of time at my apartment. Becky had added a few womanly touches, such as curtains and lightbulbs. Ronnie and I just ducked under windows, if we ducked at all. As for the bathroom light, we'd explained that it wasn't really necessary if you left the door open to the hallway. Becky had just smirked at this. Ronnie, though he enjoyed teasing her, truly wondered why I was with her. I raised my eyebrows meaningfully and let him misinterpret this. Sex was fine. Becky disliked having the lights on, but she let me coax her into a steamy shower where we soaped each other and tried various positions and approaches she hadn't permitted herself lying on her back in bed. I took more pleasure than I should have in pretending to be widely experienced. When she asked me about former girlfriends, a frequent conversation, I waved away the multitudes of previous admirers and lovers as if it were impossible to calculate. I had decided that I would be someone else entirely, with a whole different past, and as we got to know each other and recounted our younger years, I simply filled in the blanks with my happy family life, my many dates at sixteen, when I got my driver's license without event. Yes, I'd had a normal childhood: happy stay-at-home mom, protective big brother (sans polio and iron lung), close father, and loyal, law-abiding buddies. No wonder Becky kept saying, "I always had this idea you were going to be different once I got to know you. Did I ever tell you I thought that paper Mr. Rosenberg read about the child being run over was yours? That's why I came up to the table that day. To see if you'd really written it."

Me? I laughed. Amused. Incredulous. We went back to talking about the wedding, how many people we'd invite, our separate guest lists, who would marry us. Her brother, Mike, an Episcopalian seminary student about to be ordained, might be able to do it.

"Would that be all right?" Becky asked.

"Sure," I said. Why not? It all felt a bit like a big stage production anyway. Anything for the show.

"Do you love me, David?" she asked one evening at my apartment. Sometimes she could cut right to the heart of things. She had moved in, amazingly without objection from her aunt, beleaguered by her two children. Becky's parents didn't know, "and what they don't know won't hurt them," her aunt had said.

Becky had pulled the sheet up over her small breasts. Despite our erotic foreplay in the shower, our venturing into the kitchen one hungry night and my showing Becky, via a Popsicle, what she could do to give me more pleasure, despite pushing the boundaries of Circleville, Ohio, into the Atlantic Ocean and letting me reciprocate "the unimaginable" to her, she was still a shy girl from the Midwest and I was a liar, although a soon to be married one. "Yes," I said. "I do love you."

I had, it seemed, since leaving home, abandoned all the frames that cemented my identity, and now any far-flung thought could become me, as long as no one like Ronnie tripped me up. I'd coached him to keep quiet about anything in the past. "It's off limits," I'd said, "as far as Becky goes," and he tried to say once, "But you're going to marry her, David, shouldn't she know?" "I'll tell her eventually," I said, but of course had no intention. I didn't even know whom I'd created for Becky. I assumed she kept a record of all the bulletins about myself. ("Sports? I ran track," I'd say, and think of

Crow, Vic, and me puffing around the track in our leather jackets with their jingling zippers, cigarettes dangling from our mouths.)

"I love your hair, David," she said to me another night. We were on the couch making out during a show about NASA's flight last summer to the moon. She ran her fingers through my thick curls. I'd given up trying to beat my hair down into poodle ears and had let it balloon out. The sleek dark ringlets vibrated in place, all charged and connected. What had once been a liability was suddenly sexy, for Becky. "It's so lush," she said, her hand lost in my private topiary, her eyes watery with staring and fascination. I was the other to her too, not just her to me. Jewish, exotic, East Coast: Only a few of these approached just how other I was in my heart and actions, but she seemed to want this—me—for reasons of her own.

At spring break in March, I was supposed to go home to meet Becky's family in Circleville, but at the last minute I came down with the flu and took to bed. Becky played nurse to me. It was, if modern dance didn't work out, and it didn't look as if it would, what she wanted to do. She gave me sponge baths; my fever had gone as high as 105, and this is what my father had advised. She brought me fresh lemonade to drink, changed my sweaty pillowcase frequently when my fever broke, sat by my bed and watched me sleep and was there dozing a bit and smiling when I woke up. I felt almost that I wanted to confess everything, that I wasn't the person she should marry and that she deserved to know the truth, but in all honesty I had become hooked on her ministrations, all of them: I knew she wouldn't desert me if we married; I knew I'd be perfectly bored and would miss everything that was happening around us, but she'd take care of me, and one day I would admit, "That was my paper in Mr. Rosenberg's class," and she'd say, in her rocker across from mine on our farmhouse porch in Circleville, "Thought so, Mr. David," which she would have taken to calling me in what I imagined to be the quaint vernacular of the local folks, and I'd return to playing my harmonica.

None of this stopped her from leaving bright and early the next morning, five sharp, for a six-thirty flight. She might have publicly disparaged Circleville, but it was where she wanted to be in her heart, and she woke me that morning, standing in slacks and a pretty pink blouse and gold earrings and full-scale makeup, her long Mary Travers hair pinned up on top of her head in a coronet. She kissed me with her lipstick mouth and looked very much as if she were going home.

"I'll see you in six days," she said.

She felt my forehead one last time. My temperature was normal, I knew, but I made myself look deranged and wrung out.

"I'll call you as soon as I get in, okay?"

"Okay," I said, and as if to show her loyalty and bravery and love, she pushed her tongue in my mouth, which we'd avoided since I'd become sick, then whispered, "Feel better, David. I wish you were going with me."

Meanwhile, Ronnie had plans. He had organized a surprise outing, coincidentally when Becky had left town. The reason soon became apparent. Besides Calvin, whom I didn't recognize at first, he'd invited Myra, who had come down for her spring break from Wellesley. I had not seen her since she sat on the floor of her father's prosperous new shoe store lacing boots. She looked completely changed. She'd let her hair frizz out. She wore a red leotard top with a leather vest and colorful gold rope belt around a short jeans skirt. She had gone back to wearing glasses instead of contacts, small gold wire frames, and she had, if it was possible, grown a couple of inches, or maybe it was just the thick-heeled boots she was wearing. Her braces off, she had straight, polished teeth, a striking half-moon of white that no longer glistened with bumpy silver. She looked self-assured, full of moxie, someone from a women's college who liked eating at fine restaurants and saying things at the table like "No talking about men," and I was a little intimidated by her at first sight.

I also couldn't imagine why Ronnie had done this. I didn't think of it so much as a surprise as an ambush. I'd answered the door, unshaved after three days in bed with a fever, crusty with layers of sweat, my shirt off.

"How you doing?" said Calvin, grabbing my hand and giving it a power shake. Calvin was at a small experimental school in Washington, D.C., called the College of the Potomac. He'd gotten a scholarship, "for academics," he wanted us to know, though he couldn't help himself and had organized a school basketball team "among a group of pathetic brains." He had just been appointed next year's assistant editor of the student paper; he'd finally found a school that appreciated his energies, embraced his ideas. Ronnie had kept in touch with him.

"It's great to see you, Calvin. I've missed you," I said, glancing at Myra too. Calvin's hair was enormous. He had on a black turtleneck underneath a black leather jacket. Ronnie by comparison wore cuffed and creased slacks and one of the numerous hi-boy shirts I'd sold him wholesale from Maxie's.

"You ready?" asked Ronnie.

"Ready for what?"

Myra came and stood next to me. I recognized her smell that made me think of sugar and blueberries, the same taste I once liked in wine and how she tasted too, her mouth, her skin, her nipples. She kissed me on the cheek. I felt her slip her hand into mine, felt mine stay there and grab her fingers. I was David again. Instantly.

Everyone had mercifully, for their own good too, let me take a shower before we left. A limousine was waiting downstairs. "What's this?" I asked. The white limo stretched the entire length of the curb in front of the apartment building.

"After you," said Ronnie, holding the door for all of us. The driver, in a chauffeur's cap and vest, nodded at each of us in the mirror as we got in. A mahogany bar with silver decanters rested in the wide carpeted space between our facing seats. Calvin pulled out a joint once we were inside. "It's cool," he said. "Right, Ron?"

"We have the deluxe service," said Ronnie, and rolled up the back windows. They passed the joint to each other, then to Myra, who took a long hit—this was different—and gave it over to me. I hesitated. What would Becky think? She'd made it clear that flower headbands and long hair and bare navels were one thing, but marijuana was another. She didn't think she could ever smoke grass or take acid. She didn't have the brain cells to spare, she'd joked, and anyway, she was petrified of going to jail. It had been an academic discussion because though I'd gotten stoned with Ronnie a few times, I didn't like to smoke either.

I said no.

"Why not, David?" said Myra. "Don't you smoke?"

"Hey," said Calvin. "Leave the man alone."

Ronnie lowered the armrest of the limo, smiled. "*It's my party, I'll cry if I want to*," he sang in a high, squealing voice.

"You're getting married," said Calvin. "That's the news."

I looked at Myra to see if this came as news to her too. She looked interested, not overly surprised. Ronnie had briefed her.

"I guess so."

"You guess so? Aren't you sure?" asked Calvin.

"I am sure. It's just a big step."

"No kidding," he said.

"When's the date?" asked Myra, pleasantly neutral.

"It was going to be in June, but we've decided to wait now until August." Five months away. I'd been thinking of it, I realized, as years off.

"All the way until August," said Myra, and burst out laughing. So did Ronnie.

"What's so funny?" I asked.

"This," said Calvin, and handed me the joint. This time I took it.

The chauffeur dropped us off at a bowling alley in North Philly. "See you in a few," he said.

"I can't believe we're here," I said.

"What's not to believe?" said Ronnie.

"Bowling?"

"You got something against the great American sport of bowling? What could be more red-blooded fun than getting dropped off in a limo at a North Philadelphia bowling alley?"

We went inside, rented shoes. It was all black people. League night yet, except for a single lane, which Ronnie had, I speculated, managed to reserve with his connections. Myra tested out balls from the racks. Calvin said hello to all the brothers, gave them power shakes. Ronnie lit up a cigar and entered our names on the score sheet. I was feeling lost. The grass had only heightened my normal self-consciousness to extraordinary proportions. I felt like two large eyes on stalks that kept turning around the room. I had no idea how I'd gotten here exactly although I would remember every once in a while it was by limousine, and this was supposed to be spontaneous and fun, and I was being treated to a good time. Somewhere I'd sprung loose from David the track star, son of happy-go-lucky parents, soon to be married to Miss Becky of Circleville. It felt as if string after string of lies and confusions and pinings for sanity and ordinariness were being pulled out of me and tossed down the alley along with the first ball Ronnie rolled. I felt too as if I'd been sitting on the molded plastic orange seat for hours. Suddenly Myra was next to me, her hand on my leg. "How are you doing?" she said.

"Okay," but she must have seen my eyes as wide and black as

eclipses because she said, "David, do you just want to go home and talk?"

"Yes," I said.

———

"It seemed like a good idea at the time," said Myra. We were sitting in my apartment. Ronnie and Calvin had gone out to see one of Ronnie's bands play; he managed three now. Myra had convinced them it would be better if we were alone.

"I like bowling usually."

"Never mind," said Myra. "I feel as if I blew it. The bowling was my idea. Ronnie just wanted to take you in a limousine to a nice dinner. We were going to do that part afterward."

"I'm the party pooper," I said. I'd come down from the grass. Myra sat on the couch at one end, and I sat at the other. She had her hands folded in her lap. I wanted to offer her some iced tea or soda or coffee, but we had nothing in the house. Becky kept me on a regular routine of shopping and clothes washing, all of which went slack when she left.

"How's your father's shoe business?" I said.

"Great. He's going to open two more stores soon, one in Paoli and one in Broomall."

"He's spreading out, a tycoon."

"He expects me to come work for him this summer."

"Will you?"

"I'm going to do summer stock."

"Really?"

"Don't get excited. It's just a small community theater out in Bucks County. I shouldn't dignify it by calling it summer stock. It's not off-Broadway; it's not even the Hedgerow."

"Still—"

"I'm going to take any roles I'm offered."

"You're doing theater at Wellesley then?"

"I'm trying. David, are you really getting married?"

I pulled my feet up on the couch, looked at the toes I'd wiggled out of my sneakers. "Yes," I said.

"What's she like?"

"Becky?"

"Is that her name?"

"Yes. She's very sweet," I said, and hoped Myra would let this go by. But she didn't.

"Sweet? Like cupcake sweet or like Florence Nightingale sweet?"

"Well, funny you should say that, about Florence. She, Becky, wants to be a nurse."

"I see," said Myra with great dramatic pronouncement: *I see.* She had developed some techniques obviously. "What if you're making the mistake of your life and everything you ever wanted to do is about to be dropped off the side of a freighter into a hole in the sea?"

"Well, since you put it that way. I just think I want to do this."

"Just think I wanna."

"Don't start repeating my phrases," I said. "You used to do that all the time, and it drove me crazy." I couldn't say this with any real heat or threat, though, because in fact, everything suddenly felt familiar and enjoyable, unsettling too, but that was part of it.

"David . . ."

"What?"

"Can I come over there and sit by you?"

"I think so."

"I'm not going to touch you or anything."

"I know that," I said, and I did.

"I just want to sit closer to you. Could we do that?"

"Sure," and as soon as she did, I kissed her.

It turned out I wasn't the only one who was committed. Myra had a relationship back in Wellesley. Her drama professor. He was twice her age but divorced. It wasn't an affair, she wanted me to know, the sordid teacher-student kind. They were being very open about it, and so far the rest of the faculty and the students had accepted it.

I found this hard to believe, but I didn't want to discourage her from telling me more about him. He had directed several plays off-Broadway and had had some success with one, winning an Obie. Sometimes, though, she felt, much as she loved him, mismatched. She longed to let down her guard.

"What do you mean?" I asked. We'd been lying on top of the covers with the lights off and our clothes on, talking into the darkness. Myra would say something, and it would settle above me and I'd think about it awhile, and then I'd answer. The conversation had the same kind of considered spaces the talk had at Pendle Hill. I couldn't remember ever having had a conversation like this with Becky. Nothing had that substance where it lay thoughtfully on top of the air for a while, then dissipated and drifted down like silver dust or pretty confetti.

"I can't just say things to him off the top of my head. Or I think I can't. He wants me to, but I'm worried what he'll think."

"Don't you think that's normal, considering how much older he is than you?"

"It may be normal, but it's unpleasant. And when does it not become normal? When do I finally relax around him and become myself?"

"I don't know," I said. "That's always been an impossible question for me personally."

"David, you're so silly. You are normal around me."

I sat up on one elbow and looked down at Myra. Her face looked beautiful, so rounded and clear, her forehead sloping smartly and gently, her eyes shaded violet in the shadows from the streetlamps.

"Are you going to kiss me again?" she asked.

Her lips were supple when I did. She'd learned to kiss a little better, or maybe I had, or maybe we both were showing off a little: See what I learned while you were gone? See what *my* lover taught me? I kept envisioning Becky sitting beside my bed, her bright smile when I would wake up from my feverish sleep.

Myra sat up. She turned her wrist toward the streetlight and looked at her watch. "God, it's three in the morning. My parents are going to be frantic."

"Where did you tell them you were?" I asked.

"At a concert."

"Why didn't you tell them you were going to see me?"

"I know what you think, but that's not the reason."

"What do I think?" I said.

"It's all because of that stupid shoebox. It's not, David. It's because they saw how heartbroken I was about us and they don't want me to go through that again. I was unprepared to explain that it was just a visit."

I sat up next to her. Maybe it was the lingering effects of the grass, but I couldn't get over how lovely and desirable she looked. I could see staring at her face for the rest of my life, come what wrinkles and ravages to the body may. "Is this just a visit then?"

"I've got to go, David. Don't make me talk about this now."

I called Myra as soon as I got up the next morning, which was at eight, my very first thought of her jolting me awake.

"Who's calling?" asked Mrs. Berman.

"David," I said. "David Nachman."

"Oh," said Mrs. Berman, and there was a long pause, during which I realized Myra had successfully withheld from them her whereabouts and that my phone call came as a complete surprise. "Myra is still sleeping, David." Mrs. Berman waited for me to take this in, then said, "How are your father and mother?"

"Fine," I said. "How's Mr. Berman?"

"Pardon?" I'd never asked about Mr. Berman, but I had some wild hope that Myra would overhear her mother talking to me, grab the phone from her hand, and cry, *David, I'm here . . . come for me.*

"Would you tell Myra to call me?" I gave her my number, repeating it.

"I'll give her the message, David," said Mrs. Berman, promising a degree less than what I wanted. "Tell your parents hello."

"I will," I said, and called back in an hour.

"She's still sleeping, David. I haven't forgotten."

The next time I called, Mr. Berman answered.

"I'm calling for Myra," I said, not identifying myself.

"Who is this?"

"David Nachman."

"She's not here, David," he said, and out of character, he sounded almost apologetic. I must have realized then that she wasn't going to speak to me. Though I tried all weekend, I could not reach her, and on Monday morning, when I called, I knew it was true when Mrs. Berman said she had returned to college to finish her freshman year.

S E V E N T E E N

Becky came back full of excitement and plans. Her brother had con-
sented to marry us. It would be his first officiation. We needed to
register our gifts somewhere because tons of friends and relatives had
asked where they could buy something for us or order it and what
did we need anyway? "Everything! I told them," said Becky.

She returned in a peach-colored dress and small gold loop earrings. She'd plucked her eyebrows into slender, arched shapes. She'd
cut her hair; it curled in under her lightly rouged cheeks. She looked
as if she'd sprung from the navel of the Midwest, and I realized this
was a permanent regression and she would not be experimenting anymore. She would dress tastefully, with class, as she looked now, like
a grown-up with a husband and responsibilities, ready for luncheon
at the Crystal Tea Room or to attend someone's confirmation.

"Everybody's so excited about meeting you, David. We have to
take a trip back as soon as school is out. I told them all about you.
There's just one thing," said Becky, and took both my hands in hers
as I had taken Myra's in mine before she walked out the door, and

begged her to spend the night with me, not for sex, but just because I wanted her near me. She'd gently pulled her hands from mine.

But I didn't pull my hands away from Becky. I left them there because it was comforting to have her hold them, to have my unexplained self in one place. "A ring," said Becky. "Everybody asked where my engagement ring was."

So I borrowed some money from my father and went to find Becky her ring, a diamond, as she wanted.

Two weeks earlier I'd written a letter to both my parents telling them I was getting married. Adrian had called immediately, doing their dirty work. "Why are you getting married?" he'd said. "I'm not even getting married, and Naomi and I have been together much longer than you and . . ."

"Becky," I'd said, and realized that this perhaps had something to do with it: Adrian *wasn't* doing it. I'd beaten him to something for once. His phone call had been followed by my mother's and then my father's. He warned me of the practical considerations of interrupting my education, of a young lady—in the abstract, since he had never met Becky—wanting a family before I was ready. The more he lobbied against it, the more I was sure I wanted to do it.

When school ended, we went out almost immediately to meet Becky's parents. The same occasion with my parents had taken place at D'Ignazio's Towne House. I'd been apprehensive that Crow would still be working there, but he turned out to be long gone. I asked Mr. D'Ignazio, who had come over to greet my father. "To tell you the truth," said Mr. D'Ignazio in his thick Italian accent that had not budged one bit in the forty-two years he'd been in the country, as if it were good for business, "I think he's in Vietnam." I nodded and wondered if Mr. D'Ignazio's long, thoughtful look at me meant he felt pity for Crow or believed I should be over there too.

I tried not to think about Crow during dinner, or anything to do

with myself, while my father and mother made charming conversation with Becky about the two stop lights in Circleville and Becky
showed off her ring and complimented my mother on the lace shawl
she'd worn. I couldn't tell if my parents liked her or truly wondered
if they would ever understand their child's decisions or were just
relieved nobody was visibly pregnant.

The dinner ended sweetly, as I knew it would with Becky around.
She kissed each of them on the cheek, grasped my mother's hands in
hers, and said how much she was looking forward to being their
daughter-in-law. At this point Uncle Stonny and Aunt Rose, with
their lame pick of the litter in Cousin Eddie, would have been weeping for joy at the prospect of such a match. My parents showed more
restraint, and my mother simply said, "We are too, Becky."

Mr. and Mrs. Larkin met us at the Columbus airport. They were
big people, which surprised me because Becky was thin, if on the
taller side. But her parents were big, as in large-boned and thick-
wristed and square-ankled, and I felt like a delicate figurine next to
them. Mr. Larkin shook my hand warmly. He wore a short-sleeved
sport shirt and blue polyester pants with a patent leather white belt.
Becky had told me her father worked in livestock processing. I'd
pictured him slaving away at a slaughterhouse, dodging huge half-ton
carcasses of beef as they swung toward him on savage-looking hooks,
his rubber apron splattered with blood.

It turned out that her family was far from the struggling meat-
packers I'd imagined them to be. My pitying image had been something along the lines of the desperate family in *The Southerner*,
Renoir's subsistence farmers clinging together against nature's adversity. Maybe I had some idea that I'd save Becky from this dirt-poor
life, bring her out of generations of poverty, and redeem all the lies
I'd told her about myself. Her aunt, after all, had lived in only a
modest house in Conshohocken, and hadn't her uncle been working

the night shift as a bread truck driver? But that aunt turned out to be one of eight siblings on her mother's side. Becky's father's side was a different story. They were, if such a recognition were to be given, Circleville's leading family. Her great-great-grandparents had settled here and opened a general store a hundred and twenty years ago, and from there they'd gone on to real estate, farming, and—her father's domain—meat processing. He owned a whole packing plant.

Becky's house was situated on sixty acres, including the woods and lake. It had eight bedrooms, a sitting room, a music room, a game room, an enormous country kitchen, and a veranda that ran around three quarters of the house, with two porch swings. The dark oak balustrade that curved up three flights of stairs had over a hundred fifty pickets and seventeen newel-posts, I'd been told. An upstairs suite, where I stayed, had a ball-and-claw foot oversize bathtub, long green velvet drapes, the largest hook rug I'd ever seen, and a brass fireplace. My view was of the lake and woods. So much for saving anyone.

Everything was robust and sturdy in the house except for Becky. "Other boys have been intimidated by all this." Becky swept her hand out at the spread and beyond, half of Circleville evidently. "I was hoping since you were from a doctor's family, it wouldn't be such a big deal, so overwhelming. Is it?"

"No, it isn't," I said. If anything, I was a little gleeful: I could have all this? Even if it didn't really interest me.

Becky came over and sat on my lap. She had on jeans and a white shirt tied in a knot at her bare midriff. Becky's mother, from whom Becky had gotten her deep eyes—except on Mrs. Larkin the effect against her wide face made her eyeballs look like tiny olives lost in a martini—had brought me up a sweating pitcher of lemonade and a large stoneware bowl of fresh fruit.

Becky's bedroom was on the first floor, but she'd assured me we could "fool around" and nobody would hear. Her parents, by the way, had found nothing unusual in our wanting to marry. As Becky said, everyone in Circleville married early. By twenty-five you were considered an old maid.

"So it's really okay that I didn't tell you," Becky said, "about all this?" she made another sweeping gesture to indicate the Larkin estate.

"It's fine," I assured her.

"I was just afraid you might get scared away if you knew too early," she said. "I didn't want it to complicate things between us."

She looked sexy and healthy and raring to go out here in a way she never did in Philadelphia. Her complexion had color. Her eyes shone. She even moved her arms and legs with a swaggering confidence. I could see her as a child screaming with delight, playing kick the can and hide the flag, chasing her cousins in tag around the veranda.

I stroked and patted her back and told her I loved her—I did care for her—and then we pulled off our shirts and pants, and she showed an eager hunger I'd never seen before.

Becky's brother arrived later that evening, and we all dressed for dinner. He was Becky's only sibling, five years older than she. "He's really straightened himself out," she told me. "He used to be incredibly wild in high school, cars and drinking and fighting and girls." I tried not to swallow at each mention of delinquency. "He got somebody pregnant in ninth grade. She was in ninth; he was a senior. He got so mad at another kid one time that he made him drink his pee, or that was the story. My dad was constantly having to bail him out of situations."

"What happened to the girl?"

"She put the baby up for adoption."

"No abortion?"

"David, this is Circleville. Are you kidding?"

Becky had been shouting all this news to me on our way to pick up Mike at the airport. We drove along in her convertible, something else I hadn't known about. She'd left the sky blue Camaro home, preferring to drive her aunt's old Ford in Philadelphia. It was true, she'd truly tried to become someone else while there.

Mike patted his sister's shoulder when she hugged him. He shook my hand, not making eye contact. "I've heard a lot about you," I said. He nodded. His blond hair hung in his eyes. He was definitely a product of his parents' larger genes: about six-three, with a square, handsome face and bright blue eyes, tawny eyebrows, and broad shoulders that his solemn gray suit couldn't humble. He'd gotten the better share of raw attractiveness in the family, and I could see by the way Becky beamed at him that she'd always idolized him.

We drove home, Becky and Mike catching up on people I didn't even know. Except I noticed quickly that Mike said very little. He slumped a bit in his seat, while Becky chatted on. When she asked him a direct question—Was he still liking California? How was the seminary? Was he afraid of earthquakes?—he provided one-word answers: fine, no, maybe, okay. Becky didn't seem to mind, or maybe she was just used to her brother's terse replies.

She reached her hand behind her and grabbed for mine, which I dutifully gave to her, and we drove like that for thirty minutes until we arrived home at the pride of Circleville.

"He might act a little strange," Becky warned me about her grandfather.

"What do you mean, strange?"

"Oh, sometimes he just tells inappropriate jokes."

"What kinds of jokes?"

"Nothing," said Becky, dismissing what she'd brought up. We were about to go to dinner in Circleville at the Gaslight Inn. Becky's grandfather, who owned much of the town evidently and still went into his one-room office on First Street, would be joining us.

Twenty minutes later we sat at a round table with high-backed red leather chairs in a private room of the Gaslight Inn. It had fake gaslights on the wall and an 1890s motif, with a huge crystal chandelier in the main dining room. A waitress came to our table in a bustle and satin gown off the shoulders. Mrs. Larkin moved the conversation along pleasantly, from talk of Suzy Wilkens, who had graduated Phi Beta Kappa from Miami of Ohio, to a few remarks about how early the heat had come around this year.

"Becky tells me you're going into medicine," said Mr. Larkin, her father.

"Hospital administration," I said.

"Hospital work is a growing industry," said Mr. Larkin.

"I think it is," I said.

"Your father's a doctor?"

"In Chester."

"That's on the Delaware, isn't it?"

I nodded.

"Scott Paper is there, right?"

I nodded again.

"I was through there during the war. Used to be a Ford Motor plant there too, I recall." I thought about my parents, about Chester, about Adrian; it seemed like another world I'd perhaps never rejoin.

"We're going to be building a new hospital out here," said Mr. Larkin. "I'm sure they'll be looking to hire energetic young people."

"Oh, hush now," said Mrs. Larkin. "I know where you're going with this one." She had a pleased smile on her face anyway.

"Well, it's going to be a big project. Lord knows we're doing our part for it."

Mr. Larkin senior, the grandfather, who had not said a word the whole evening, the patriarch of the family, asked, "What's your last name?"

"Nachman," I said.

He stared at me a moment, his face a compact ball of yarn, and then went back to sipping his soup.

Mike was quiet, as usual, his hair falling in his eyes. We'd been alone for a few minutes in the hallway of the family home while we'd been waiting for everybody to finish getting dressed to go out for dinner. "Becky will want a family," he'd said in a monotone. I paused a moment. "She'll make a wonderful mother," I replied, and we shared a moment of silence in respect to how devoted and loving a mother Becky would be.

"Anyhoo," said Mrs. Larkin, "we're looking forward to meeting your lovely family. Your brother is a doctor also?"

"He's starting med school next fall. He completed his undergraduate degree a year early," I said, finding it easy to brag about Adrian.

I was about to dip way back and boast about his national merit scholarship when Mr. Larkin, the grandfather, spoke up hoarsely, "What's a Jewish golfer yell instead of fore?"

"Grandpa!" said Becky. "Don't you dare!"

But it was too late. "Three ninety-nine!" said the old man, cackling loudly. He sang, "Roses are red, violets are blueish, if it wasn't for Christmas, you too would be Jewish!" He was on a roll.

There was a moment of horrified silence, and then Mike jumped up and said, "Time to go home, Granddaddy," and escorted him away.

Two months later I stood on the expansive front lawn of the Larkins' home and prepared to be married. A large white reception tent, strung with Chinese lanterns, had been set up in back of us. Caterers rushed around putting on the final touches: floral centerpieces for the tables and engraved wineglasses that said *David and Becky, August 3, 1970*. Lavender napkins (the color of the wedding and all the bridesmaids' dresses) floated in the shape of swans in the center of the polished pooled surface of the crystal service plates.

A dance floor had been set up, and the musicians sat in back of it on risers playing classical arrangements. Little girls ran around with wrist corsages. A buffet table had five different kinds of meat, although we'd been spared a pig. I had on a tux. Becky had on a splendid white gown with lacy cuffs. She wore a veil that her grandmother, dead two years now, had worn when she married her grandfather—the jokester, who was helped to a seat in front by two ushers and had no clear recollection of seeing me two months ago.

I waited with Adrian beside me, my best man, holding the ring. In the first row were my parents, who had gotten used to the idea of a priest marrying us. I had told them in stages: first that it was to be at the Larkins' lovely country home, then that it would be Becky's brother who would marry us, which they'd found interesting, then that he was actually an Episcopalian priest, which they'd become upset about and for the first time said directly—my mother said, that is, with my father standing alongside—"Excuse me, David, but I find this very disturbing." A long argument had ensued. I'd told them it was my marriage, Becky's and my right to choose whom we wanted to marry us.

I called and apologized the next day, and they said they were sorry too and I should proceed with whomever I wished to marry us. For my part, I promised I would try to get Mike—Father Mike now that he'd been ordained since I saw him last in June—to leave out any mentions of Jesus Christ. If I was going to subject my parents to a Christian wedding, it had to be all but Jesus Christ, in deference to them—and myself.

Mike agreed reluctantly. He resisted until I threatened to back out completely, the only time I had used this weapon and something that shocked Becky and made her cry, which required numerous apologies on my part that I was kidding about backing out and shouldn't have made such a rash statement.

Uncle Stonny and Aunt Rose had managed to come out, and Ronnie, who had flown here, along with Calvin (at Ronnie's expense). I'd made them both ushers and tried to keep Becky's grandfather away from Calvin.

Ronnie had taken me aside and said, "So you're sure?"

"Of course I am." I had laughed. Everything was great. My history stretched out behind me, just knots on a kite's colorful tail, unseen at such a height but for a wavy line cutting letters in the sky.

"This is the time if you're not," persisted Ronnie.

"I'm not calling it off," I said.

"It's just my duty to check," said Ronnie, who was a businessman at heart and objected to a bad deal, as he saw it. His puzzled looks all seemed to indicate the same question: What about Myra?

I had gone to see her a month before. She'd been doing summer stock, as she'd planned, in Bucks County. I'd driven out one night while Becky was baby-sitting for her aunt. Myra was in Chekhov's *The Cherry Orchard* and was playing a governess, a woman quite a bit older than she. But she'd done a remarkable job, receiving a burst of applause when she'd walked onto the stage at the end. She had it. She had talent, and I watched amazed at how she threw herself into the role, calling out with perfect Russian pitch, "How dreadfully these people sing—Phooey! Like jackals." I was in love with her and had never been out of love and could imagine her being a sixty-year-old woman like her character and my still loving her then.

I went backstage after the performance, bringing her flowers. She was sitting with the other actors in a large room, one side for the women to get dressed, separated from the men by a blanket on a clothesline. True, it wasn't the Shubert, but I could hear the laughing and camaraderie even before I got down the hallway to the doorway, the excitement of being part of a production that could make people leap to their feet in appreciation.

"David!" Myra had said, and rushed over to me. She hugged me so hard that for a moment I thought everything was going to be all right. She took me over to her fellow actors and introduced me, holding my hand the whole time, half her makeup still on, the gray wig off, however, and just a hair net underneath. She seemed not at all self-conscious to be seen in transition like this, with her face rub-berized in wrinkles. "How did you find me out here?" she said.

Her mother had told me, after I'd asked her to keep it a secret. A surprise.

But the surprise was ultimately on me because in a few minutes a man came into the room, a gray-haired man himself, who looked not far from the age of Charlotta, the governess Myra had just played, although he of course was. I'd wanted him to be older, aging, some crazy father complex Myra had, which it may have very well been but didn't matter, because he took both her hands and kissed her full on the lips and didn't seem to know or ever have known about me. Even when Myra introduced us, he registered only a vague recog-nition, although that could have been jealousy on his part, I don't know. Myra suggested we all go out for something to eat—she was keeping the hours of actors, getting up at noon, eating at midnight— but I declined, claiming I had to go back.

She walked me to the parking lot, leaving her teacher-lover be-hind for a moment and delaying with me and then said, "So you're still getting married, I hear."

I opened my hands, nodded yes.

"I guess I won't be seeing you for a while then."

"Do you want to?"

Myra wrinkled her brow, her rubbery sixty-year-old brow. "What are you saying, David?"

"I tried to get in touch with you after last time," I said. "You ran away."

She sighed, not theatrically as she'd done in the production, just as Myra. "I missed Lawrence too much," she said. "I guess it's more serious than I had thought. And you were getting married, David. Remember?"

"Which came first—the chicken or the egghead?"

"That's a really bad joke, David."

257

I shrugged. I thought of Grandpa Larkin saying, "Three ninety-nine!" What was I doing?

"You're different than I thought," said Myra.

"So are you," I said, but I meant that she was much more than I had thought.

"I guess I'd better go back. *Mazel tov,*" she said in that convincing way that actors can make things sound sincere.

———

"Dearly beloved: We have come together in the presence of God to witness and bless the joining together of this man and this woman in holy matrimony," Mike started. There had been a delay, not because Becky wasn't ready but because of her brother. Mike had locked himself in the upstairs bathroom for quite some time. An hour. Finally, Mr. Larkin had coaxed him out.

He had stage fright. He apologized to all those gathered. His first wedding. The crowd had reassured him with their smiles that they understood.

While we'd been waiting, Adrian had whispered to me, "I've never heard of this happening before, the *minister* getting cold feet."

Uncle Stonny had run up from his aisle seat, the tons of change he always kept in his pockets jangling, and said, "Where the hell is this guy? What's going on?"

Meanwhile, my parents, during the delay, had sat courteously greeting people when members of Becky's family were brought up to them and introduced. Nearly two hundred guests had come, 95 percent of them Becky's friends and family.

"The union of husband and wife in heart, body, and mind is intended by God for their mutual joy; for the help and comfort given one another in prosperity and adversity; and, when it is God's will, for the procreation of children and their nurture in the knowledge and love of the Lord. Therefore marriage is not to be entered into unadvisedly or lightly, but reverently, deliberately, and in accordance with the purposes for which it was instituted by God."

I stood to the left of Becky. So far so good, I thought. I hadn't fainted; I hadn't objected to my own marriage. I hadn't come to my senses or lost them, just swayed somewhere in a pleasant hammock in between.

Mike closed his Bible and folded his hands on top of it against his chest, readying himself for his blessing to us, which we hadn't re-hearsed. He had coiffed his hair; it was perfectly still in the wind. He wore a black cassock, a white surplice underneath and a stole around his neck and looked godly. I imagined him dressing and redressing himself in the bathroom.

"It is truly a new beginning for David and Rebecca. But with every new start comes an awareness of ourselves as beings in an im-perfect world."

He stopped looking at our faces and gazed out over the crowd of two hundred and appeared instantly to lose his bearings. He spoke faster. "Beginnings can lead to glorious experiences along the road to life, but as creatures of God we must realize all such beginnings are lined with the mile markers of death." A slight murmur came from the crowd.

"In the grand scheme of things we feel ourselves to be small beings, minuscule grains of sand in a vast, indifferent cosmos that rains its blessings as well as its terrors down on us. Are we put here to enjoy God's rich, bountiful harvest? Are we to partake of His bumper crop? Or are we to turn our faces from the glory of His being and smother ourselves in the ashes of mortal doubt?" People stirred, whispered. I felt Becky's hand creep toward mine, her fingers hook themselves around my own.

"What is it in essence that a young marriage like David and Re-becca's offers? Hope, yes, but more than hope, love. But I do not mean any ordinary love. I mean divine love. But not just divine love.

I mean a love so swift that it carries us away. Unmoors us. Floods us. Storms our hearts. Cracks the jib and pulverizes the quarry stone. Splits open the coconut of our passion. Yes, passion. Reckless. Sacred. The abandonment of two young people. Sex—"

Mr. Larkin rose, and as he did, Mike, a frightened expression on his face, jumped back on track, discarding his personal message.

"Rebecca, will you have this man to be your husband, to live together in the covenant of marriage? Will you love him, comfort him, honor and keep him, in sickness and in health, and, forsaking all others, be faithful to him so long as you both shall live?"

"I will," said Becky.

"David, will you have this woman to be your wife, to live together in the covenant of marriage? Will you love her, comfort her, honor and keep her, in sickness and in health, and, forsaking all others, be faithful to her so long as you both shall live?"

My mouth opened. I had some preposterous fantasy that Myra would gallop up on horseback or some other heroic conveyance and, in a beautifully executed gender reversal of *The Graduate,* bar the door behind us with a large wooden cross and speed me away with her, forever.

"I will," I said.

Becky took my hand and placed a ring on my finger. Adrian handed me a ring; I slipped it on her hand.

"With the joining of hands and the giving and receiving of a ring, I pronounce that they are husband and wife, in the name of Jesus—" Mike caught himself, coughed. "Those whom God has joined together, let no one put asunder."

I kissed Becky, and everyone applauded. It was the beginning.

5

E I G H T E E N

I'm a few minutes late. Lilly sees me and waves me over to her baggage that she's been sitting on.

"I'm so glad you're here, Dad," she says.

"Sorry. I got caught in traffic."

"There's someone creepy who's been bugging me."

"Where?"

Lilly moves her head backward, but I see no one. She looks around. "He's gone, I guess."

"What was he doing?"

"He kept asking me if I needed a ride anywhere."

"Let's go," I say, and grab all three of her bags.

"I'll carry one, Dad," and Lilly pulls a bag off my shoulder. She has her mother's blond hair and my curls, which she wears long and down her shoulders. When she was younger, she used to wear it piled high on her head in ringlets, and along with her cowboy boots and tortoiseshell sunglasses, she'd stand in front of the bathroom mirror and sing country-western songs into a can of deodorant.

Now she's more subdued, just another college student, in jeans and a T-shirt. She's a curious mixture of boldness and reserve, and we've never known, her mother and I, from year to year, day to day, what we might get.

She's come home from the University of Colorado during her spring break for the unveiling of her grandfather's gravestone.

"There!" says Lilly. She points in the direction of a man coming toward us at a fast clip, though limping slightly, his hair long and stringy over his collar, about my age. I realize with shock I know him.

"Dave," he says, thick, hairy arm extended. "Remember me?"

"Hi, Crow," I say.

Lilly stands alongside me. I can smell Crow's breath, a little too sweet, covering beer, something. He has a yellow nylon jacket on, the sleeves torn, the cuffs frayed. His face is bloated, and if it weren't for the raven hair, the still-fierce dark eyes, I wouldn't recognize him.

Or maybe I would. Anywhere. Linked to him as I am.

"This one is yours?" he says, smiling at Lilly, and I see just how bad his teeth are, the ones not missing stained with smoke, how he keeps rolling his tongue around dryly in his mouth, how his belly drops over his belt and the jacket is zipped to try to minimize the bulge. His blue pants are too short, his black shoes—they could have been a thirty-year-old pair of rat stabbers, except loafers now—worn down at the soles, the leather cracked.

"This is my daughter, Lilly," I say. "Mr. Randazzo."

She of course knows the story, or the bits and pieces I've told her over the years. She has always been more willing to hear it than our son, Josh, made nervous by considering his father as anything other than a stable, successful provider, a pal to play basketball with on Sunday mornings, somebody who still on occasion, when he's allowed, kisses his fourteen-year-old son.

"You around town?" says Crow.

"Haverford," I tell him.

"Yeah," says Crow, more to himself than us, "I think I heard that. The hospital out there, right?"

"Yes," I say. "Director of communications," and I try not to make this sound important, condescending toward his position. "How about you?"

He lowers his voice. "I'm trying to offer a little cheaper transportation, see? These cabs will rip you off. That's what I was doing for your kid. Wouldn't talk to me, though. Smart girl. No hard feelings?" Crow says to Lilly.

She shakes her head, smiles prettily, which I know means get-me-out-of-here.

"They've laid everybody off at Scott," says Crow, by way of explanation for his illegal moonlighting at the Philadelphia airport. "You can't get on anywhere at my age." He coughs, hits his chest with his fist, calls me over to the side. "You wouldn't be able to spare a few bucks, would you?"

I take out my wallet, hand him a fifty. It's what he expects, though his eyes get wide. We might as well be playing poker in Chuckie Halbert's basement. It's our unspoken arrangement. I have a strange bond with this man that I will never fully understand.

We've run out of things to say. I wave goodbye and walk away from him. He shouts after me, "God bless you, Dave."

Lilly says, "That's *the* Crow?"

"Yes," I say, watching him limp away. "That's him."

It took Becky and me a year to get divorced. We struggled that long under the illusion we were meant to be together. I had to tell her everything about me, the least I'd owed her for all my lies. Telling her didn't change her feelings for me. If anything, it strengthened them, and even after we had decided to divorce, we went through many more phone calls and meetings in Philadelphia full of crying and pleas and sex until we both finally had had enough.

One afternoon, months after Becky and I had gotten our divorce, I went to a Quaker meeting on Pendle Hill, just because I hadn't been for a while. A girl was there whom I couldn't place at first, and then I remembered: Helen. She had been the student from Swarthmore College, the sojourner who had spoken up so smartly about John Woolman's dream and had touched my hand mysteriously at dinner that first night. She confessed to me she had no idea why she did it. Looking back, she said it was as if she were just moved to do so, like speaking out in a meeting. She had graduated from Swarthmore and, like me, was restless. I had one more year of school to complete at Temple, and after a little discussion and some wine one evening, we decided to travel across country. Everybody else was dropping out, why not us?

We drove over miles of freeway and back roads: by sandhills and cornfields in Nebraska; up fourteen-thousand-foot passes in Colorado, the radiator running hot, both of us holding our breaths until we crested and coasted down, the engine cooling; through deserts of yucca in New Mexico and saguaro in Arizona; past retirement villages in Las Vegas; by oil rigs outside Bakersfield. We'd stop for a day or two or a week in a new town, and I'd find work as a dishwasher and Helen as a maid, and we'd get a motel room for six dollars by the railroad tracks, a room that always seemed to have the same threadbare chenille bedspread.

Helen, whose father had died when she was thirteen, had grown up in Syracuse, the daughter of a Catholic mother who had become a Quaker. "A Quaklic," Helen said. "They're the worst. They still love all the pomp and circumstance of the mass, but they're suddenly thrust into this simple, egalitarian environment, and they go completely crazy for a while trying to pretend they don't care about ritual and ceremony and hierarchy. Meanwhile, they keep track of everything: every word said at service, every consensus at business meetings, every dime spent on the maintenance of the meetinghouse. They just can't abandon that structure," Helen said.

We settled in Santa Fe, but Helen's mother became sick. One of
her kidneys had to be removed, so we went back to Syracuse for the
operation and stayed there. The draft board had been knocking since
I'd dropped out of school, and then it suddenly wasn't bothering me
anymore. I'd learned that my father had sent in the medical records
of my suicide attempt when I was sixteen. I was furious at first, that
he'd done this without my permission. It wasn't that I wanted to go;
it was that he'd gone behind my back and made the decision himself
to get me out. "I knew you would never give me permission," he
said, "and I didn't want to lose you." I couldn't hate him for it,
although I did write him a long letter that I never wanted to exploit—
that was the word—what had happened to me for personal gain. He
wrote back that by taking no action, by leaving school and running
around the country, I was making a decision, and if that was my
decision, I could appeal my status of 1Y—to be called up only in a
national emergency—and he would understand. But God help me,
I'd better know what I was doing this time. It would break his and
my mother's heart if something happened to me for a principle I
didn't truly believe in. Hadn't I gotten that idea out of my system
already? Hadn't I sacrificed enough?

Two years later Helen and I married. We had a quiet civil ceremony in Syracuse, nothing like the burlesque I'd experienced with
Becky. Adrian and my parents. Helen's mother, who was doing fine
with one kidney. Her sister, then a freshman at Syracuse.

One year into our marriage—I'd gone back to school and gotten
my degree—we separated for a period of six months. I don't know
why this was exactly, except that we both, at the same moment,
seemed to become frightened of all that was ahead of us together, on
the verge of having children. Perhaps too there was my withdrawing
from her. Whatever the reason, I couldn't attribute it this time to
Sarah Vale. I had told Helen about that, and she had listened quietly

and held me while I spoke, asking questions carefully and crying finally when I explained about my suicide attempt.

It was not possible to re-create for her all that had happened, or for anybody. The closest I would get was telling about it plainly, without adornment or self-blame or justification, and I would have to settle for her steady understanding, her quiet intelligence. I realized she would not leave me or turn away, that if I stumbled again, it was not a last chance. I could not be annihilated in her heart.

But we did separate for six months early in our marriage. Adrian had gotten married, not to Naomi, who had left him for a man she met on a kibbutz in Israel, but to a woman named Cheryl, who was the daughter of a dentist from Philadelphia and Adrian's match in brains, a Smith graduate who, like him, was going to medical school at Columbia. My mother was quietly working at her pottery, my father steadfastly devoted to his patients in Chester. I had the sense, as I often did, of everyone being more fixed in orbit than I, more tied to each other, and when Helen and I decided to separate, I thought I would go back to live in Santa Fe, where I'd been happy and unknown, even to myself, lost in the thin atmosphere, the crisp coldness of seven thousand feet.

Instead I looked up Myra. She had left her old teacher, Lawrence, and was about to finish graduate school in Boston. We spent the evening together, made love, and in the morning we both looked at each other and laughed. It wasn't meanspirited, just a shock, as if discovering the paleness of our bodies by daylight. There was something lumpy about our sudden union, like a wobbly tire that you try to ignore or believe you'll get used to. "David, you don't love me," said Myra. "We're such queer old friends." I was surprised how right she was. When I'd taken off her clothes and she mine, I felt a misstep akin to mild trespass, as if walking on land that bore no fence and had no forbidding signs but whose house in the distance with its warm glow in its windows and a private life inside shamed you into staying back. "Can we stop for good now?" Myra said, and pushed me play-fully away. We ate breakfast, Myra in her robe and myself in jeans. Myra drove me to North Station and ran alongside the train, waving when it pulled out, just like in the movies, and I knew she wasn't acting and I would never see her again as a lover.

One morning fourteen years ago I went on a job interview to Bryn Mawr Hospital. The marketing VP and the head of personnel were giving me a tour, showing me the hospital's new emergency wing. I'd been working in Philadelphia at the time for another hos-pital, but we'd just had Josh, and with two kids and Helen deciding to stay home, I needed to find a better position.

I looked up, and there was Russell Vale, in surgical scrubs. He waved to me, surprised, just a flash of his palm hello, then put his hand down quickly and went on, unnerved, as I was.

Later that day he called. He'd gotten my number through per-sonnel. It's odd how you can talk to someone as if you have no past, and that's pretty much what Russell—Dr. Vale, he was beginning his ob-gyn residency—and I did for more than a year before we brought up his sister.

We managed to have lunch together occasionally, even play ten-nis several times, without the subject ever once coming up. After a year Helen said to me, "I can't stand this. I completely forget some-times what happened between you."

Finally we did talk, through the night. I knew his father had died, but I didn't know that the family had split apart years earlier: Paul, Russell, and Mrs. Vale going to Arizona to live with the grandparents, Mr. Vale taking off to California. He worked at a series of odd jobs as a day laborer and a cook, and then he came back to live with them in Phoenix, but things were never the same. He got fired from several jobs his father-in-law found him, and then he gave up trying all together. One evening he woke up with chest pains and was rushed to the hospital. Three hours later he was dead of a coronary. "All this might have happened anyway," said Russell.

We'd been sitting in his study in Haverford, and the sun had suddenly begun streaming orange through the blinds. His wife, Patricia, had knocked lightly on the door to ask if we wanted any breakfast. We asked for coffee. Russell ran his hand through his sandy-colored hair. "I have something else to tell you." He looked at me in a way I knew meant it wasn't going to be pleasant. "Your visit to us, my dad and me, coincided with my going through puberty. Once the hormones hit, I was out of control, causing everybody, my mother especially, immense heartache. I lost every peaceful bone I had in my body for a while." He looked down at his hands, his slender fingers. "I wrote you a few letters, David. Death threats actually. I wanted to kill you. Fortunately I had a scrap of good sense not to mail them or come after you. I had this idea that if you were dead, we'd be united again as a family."

Russell opened the blinds, the bright sun. We both squinted. He sipped the coffee Trish had brought us. "It's impossible to say how much any one person contributes to a family falling apart," he said.

And then we talked about Paul too. He'd stayed in Arizona with his mother. Paul, who I would have thought would wind up in medicine also, raising a family, went a very different direction. He didn't have children; he didn't marry. He became interested in computers and then started a company, the ILOX corporation, named after a bumper sticker he'd glimpsed on a trip to Boulder, Colorado: I ♡ LOX AT THE NEW YORK DELI.

Paul once said, after Russell finally admitted to him that he and I had become friends, "Well, that was then, this is then too," which, Russell explained, wasn't spoken with as much bitterness as it sounded—just Paul's stuckness, his isolation. He and Russell still talked, "but not really," Russell said. "It's not as if we would be close anyway," he told me when I asked if our friendship got in the way of his relationship with his brother. I chose to believe that it didn't. I know that neither brother told their mother, who still lives five minutes from Paul in Scottsdale, about my friendship with Russell, about our houses being three blocks away. It was clear such healing could only go so far.

In a small circle we stand around my father's grave for the unveiling. My mother leans on my arm for support. She lives in Swarthmore, where she moved with my father ten years ago from our house in Garden City. Last year he died, at seventy-seven. His funeral had been mobbed by his patients, black faces filling the seats. At several points the rabbi, an aged man himself, had demanded quiet when people had called out "Amen" and "Praise his name," referring not to God but my father. People reached into the aisle to touch his coffin as it was wheeled down the sanctuary and into the hearse. Ronnie, balding and paunchier, still running the drugstore in Chester but also a prosperous lawyer, had put his arm around me and later suggested we get our families together, though both our children were nearly grown now, something we'd been promising to do for years. Calvin, he told me, was a successful correspondent for the Baltimore *Sun*. He had four children himself, and they, Ronnie and he, still went to basketball games when Calvin was in Philadelphia. Myra was single, to my surprise, running a children's theater in the Northwest. She sent her best to me through Ronnie, who kept in touch with her, as he did everyone.

But now, a year later, there is only the immediate family at the unveiling, including Bezalel, a Korean baby Adrian and Cheryl adopted. They had, I thought, decided against children, yet four months ago they insisted Helen and I come over to their home in Rose Valley. They had someone they wanted us to meet. It was Bez, our new nephew.

"It is not easy to say a final goodbye to the dead," Adrian says, standing in front of my father's gravestone, which is covered with a clean white cloth. It is a ceremony, Adrian tells us, to bring closure to a year of mourning and for us to gather one last time as a family at my father's grave.

Adrian, in addition to becoming a father at forty-eight, has decided to leave the anesthesiology practice that he shares with Cheryl and become a rabbi. He is two years into rabbinical studies, and this is his first service. "Especially when the person is your father and has given so much to me personally and to many people who are not here. I barely know how to honor his memory except to remember that he lived a good life on behalf of others. It's not a life I imagine many people could duplicate, nor would want to, but it's one that is of the highest calling and I love him dearly for his generosity. I know it's been hard for us to live in the wake of his dedication at times, but I would ask everyone here to bless him for that and speed his spirit on to its new place—at the least a nice doctor's office in the suburbs."

There is laughter, my mother smiling.

"Does anyone have something they'd like to say?" asks Adrian.

"He used to let me wear his stethoscope around the office and help him," says Josh, then shrugs embarrassed. He is shy, nervous, and smart. His remark reminds me of how I once followed my father around the office too.

Bez suddenly spits up, and Adrian says, "A blessing in its own way," and there is laughter, cutting through the tension. It has been surprisingly hard on us all to have my father gone. For never being around, he was always here.

Adrian bends down to unstake the white muslin cloth that covers my father's gravestone. I am taken aback by how polished the granite is, how it glistens. Rather than a somber marker of the dead, the effect of seeing Adrian peel away the white cloth and reveal its covered prize is that of coming upon a solid, clean sculpture, dramatic in its plainness. It's a simple stone, much the way I remember Sarah Vale's.

"Let us chant the Kaddish," says Adrian, and we speak it together as a family.

———

We go back to my mother's house in Swarthmore for lunch. Lilly and Josh have gone out to find their friends. It pains me to realize we will see so little of Lilly now that she goes to college. I had a harder time with her, our firstborn and a girl, than with Josh, who is good at science and clearly on his way to becoming a doctor like his grandfather and uncle. With Lilly I hovered over her and worried that she would be taken from us, in return for what I had done: a child for a child. It was a crazy, irrational, superstitious fear, but at her three-year-old party I was beside myself and had to take a sedative, so afraid was I of that critical age.

For years I relaxed about her and then, right when I relaxed too much, when she turned fourteen, she became involved with her generation's version of Crow—Cran b., a troubled character, seventeen years old, who had her under his spell. He had a chain that ran through his eyebrow and nose and connected to his upper lip. Lilly went from being a confident, cheerful child who played soccer and could kick a wicked cross pass and had numerous sleepovers with her girlfriends to a DIB: a dressed-in-black sullen teenager completely under his power, who saw no one else, did nothing else but what he wanted her to do. More than once I dragged her away from skipping school and smoking cigarettes behind the 7-Eleven or from playing Mortal Kombat—that is, leaning on Cran b.'s leg while he played. It might have all been passed off to a harmless and even necessary adolescent rebellion if she hadn't gotten pregnant at fifteen. I wanted to murder him and had in fact set out to find him when Helen tracked me down in her car and demanded I come home. I was filled with a kind of fury I'd never known before. As we sat up with Lilly and she changed pad after pad soaked with blood and asked in tears if the bleeding would ever stop and we made several phone calls to my father, who said it would, I thought if I ever could kill someone, it would be Cran b., and I had a moment of knowing that what I'd done long ago hadn't been intentional, and I could forgive myself, finally understanding, feeling, the difference between inexplicable and unconscionable sin.

As for Josh, my worry with him is that he's too good, too afraid to make a mistake, perhaps in the shadow of the one his father made. But I have learned not to crowd either of them with my fears. That is the hardest thing of all, just to stand in the middle and watch and wait for them to ask for help.

Everybody sits around and talks about Bez, whom Helen holds asleep in her arms, how he naps and eats, how he has started smiling, how he always poops just as Adrian and Cheryl are about to go out the door. "It never fails," says Adrian. "We get him all bundled up in his snowsuit and then—" Adrian makes a raspberry in Bez's face, rubbing noses with him.

"That used to happen to me," Helen says.

"Poop?" says Adrian.

"No, silly. I'd get Lilly and Josh all bundled up and then I'd be looking for their mittens and they'd go. I'd have to undress them, boots, pants, hat everything. These snow outfits today are spiffy, high-tech stuff compared to the fireman suits we had back then. The good old days, it seems like already."

"The good old days are healthy and well," Cheryl says. "You know, I got invited to join an 'older moms' group."

"How old is older?" I ask.

"I'm the mean age—forty-seven," Cheryl says. "Our first discussion—not so jokingly—was what to do when salespeople say, 'Oh, your granddaughter is so cute!' "

"What do you do?" asks Helen.

I'm sitting on the arm of the sofa next to my mother, holding her hand. She has Parkinson's disease and trembles frequently.

"You say, 'This is my son, thank you, and I hope your remark can be made up to me with a nice discount.' Or something negotiable like that."

"No kidding," Adrian says. "Does that work for false-positive grandpas too?"

"Patriarchs," Cheryl says, "have four-hundred-year-old Abraham to console them. They don't need a support group to come up with witticisms."

Cheryl's beeper goes off. She unclips it and looks at the number. "Sorry," she says. "Got to make this call." She manages Dad's practice, with Helen's help, organizing a group of doctors to rotate into the office throughout the week.

My mother and I are left alone in the room. Cheryl and Adrian (I hear them talking on the back porch after Cheryl's phone call), two doctors in every way, are off consulting on changing Bez's diaper, and Helen has gone into the kitchen to clean up.

"Can we walk, Mom?" I ask. Her doctor has advised, even if it is hard for her, that she get out for a walk every day, to help her spirits as much as anything.

She stands up with me, and I call to unseen people that we're going for a walk.

We slowly go down Park Avenue in Swarthmore, not far from where my mother had her studio, which she had to close up several years ago because she could no longer work. She has aged fast since then, her body more stooped each time I see her.

We walk in silence past the library, past the ballet school, past the royal blue canopy of the Ingleneuk Tea House, which has been here for eighty years, outlasting almost any other business I know of in the area, and my mother leans into me. The students are gone for spring break, the town restored to its permanent residents, its well-kept Victorian homes and tree-lined streets named after Ivy League schools, this old Quaker town preserved from the development of other suburbs, unravaged by the ills of a gasping economy like Chester's, where

275

my father's office, his wine-brick building, stands in the middle of rubble. I'll remain here, I realize.

"Why did you stay with Dad all those years?" I ask my mother, and the question is more to myself than her. I don't expect her to answer. We go on in silence for another block, and she stops, breathing fast, and for a moment I am worried I have pushed her too hard; it is too much for her, all the events of the day, the unveiling.

But she puts a hand on her heart and very slowly, in short breaths tells me, "I admired your father. In my time that was enough, David."

I nod, and we turn around to head back.